TRADING UP

Max Tag dropped his jaw and stared at the sleek, low-slung tank beside the shop hangar. Its black, granular finish armor was coated with high-speed polymer, like Stealth planes, making it radar-invisible.

It was a dead ringer for the damaged XM-F3, except for the turret. The low dome of an independently rotating cupola was armed with Phalanx electronics and radar attached to a 37mm Gatling gun. Firing twenty-four hundred rounds per minute, it could bore through a Soviet T-80 tank in 3.5 seconds.

TANKWAR II:

FIREBALL

Berkley Books by Larry Steelbaugh

TANKWAR
TANKWAR II: FIREBALL

TANKWAR II: FIREBALL

LARRY STEELBAUGH

BERKLEY BOOKS, NEW YORK

TANKWAR II: FIREBALL

A Berkley Book / published by arrangement with
the author

PRINTING HISTORY
Berkley edition / December 1990

ISBN: 0-425-12090-2

A BERKLEY BOOK ® TM 757,375
Berkley Books are published by The Berkley Publishing Group,
200 Madison Avenue, New York, New York 10016.
The name ''Berkley'' and the ''B'' logo
are trademarks belonging to Berkley Publishing Corporation.

PRINTED IN THE UNITED STATES OF AMERICA
10 9 8 7 6 5 4 3 2 1

This book is dedicated to JAMES MORRIS,
whose friendship and editorial hand
have made it all possible.

1

General Ross Kettle stood behind his desk and returned Tag's salute.

"Sit down, Captain," the Supreme Allied Commander in Europe said, nodding toward a pair of leather wingback chairs that faced the desk in his private quarters at NATO Headquarters in Brussels. Unlike the war room or Kettle's impersonal operations office, this was his study—furnished with the stolid masculinity of a men's club, book-lined, smelling of oiled oak and sweet pipe tobacco, its sole concession to decorative art a bronze Hindu statue of a fierce-visaged, many-handed god that stood alone on a small table by the door.

Tag took one of the wingback chairs and sat erect on the front one-third, hands resting lightly on the creases of his class-A trousers. *So*, he thought, *this is Ross Kettle, SACEUR, gadfly of tank strategy, and all the reasons why I'm sitting here*.

Tag did not even try to keep from staring at the general, who remained standing, bending forward to leaf through the Service Record Book and thick manila folder open on the desk in front of him. A plummy British brigadier Tag had known in Oman once called it right when he said of Kettle, "Looks pure aborigine, you know, except for that hair and eyes, both the color of moonlight, what." Only now that hair was faded and cut so short it looked more white than not. When Kettle did look up, Tag found himself staring into the only pair of yellow eyes he had ever seen in a human— deep, smoky yellow, like a cat's eyes or dark topaz.

1

It took Tag only a moment to register the rest of what he saw: a wiry man in his fifties, a little short of middle height, with the wide, bony shoulders and long legs of a bronc rider. When Ross Kettle smiled, the only wrinkles on his face were a pair of creases that ran down either side of his mouth like marks left by a hatchet.

"Please, sit at ease, Captain," said the general, his voice containing just a trace of that flat inflection common to the English spoken by many American Indians from the plains. He sat and rolled his chair forward until he could rest his forearms on the glass writing-surface of the desk.

"Colonel Menefee will be joining us soon," General Kettle said, referring to Tag's superior officer in the XM-F3 experimental tank evaluation team, "but I wanted to have a few minutes with you alone, Captain. Coffee?"

"Yes, sir," Tag croaked. "Thank you, sir." Thinking: *Good Lord, the man's locked in command of a freaking world war, and he's acting about as excited as if we were organizing a base track meet.*

The general pressed his intercom and called for coffee. Before he could speak again to Tag, a uniformed orderly came in with a wooden tray on which were a steel coffee bottle, a steel cream pitcher and sugar bowl, and three eggshell porcelain cups. The general poured himself a cup, black, and settled back in his chair. "Help yourself, Captain," he said.

Tag poured and sat and sipped and waited.

"You are not unknown to me, Captain Tag," the general said without preamble, tapping the SRB and folder in front of him. "You are a maverick, Captain: aggressive, impulsive, a rule-bender, and a borderline court-martial candidate. You've made a living leading Third World trainees and Army draftees against three communist invasions, and in the process you have trashed-out enough U.S. armor to keep Chrysler and GM in the black for a decade. You have disobeyed orders, recklessly risked compromising your mission in order to attack overwhelming enemy forces, and generally acted like some kind of horse's ass who thinks wars are kicked up just for his own personal delectation. Wouldn't you say that's about right?"

Tag swallowed the gulp of coffee he had been holding in his mouth. "No, sir," he protested in confusion. "I mean, yessir, but not . . ."

Kettle held up one hand, palm out. "Easy, Captain. That's the good news. One of the reasons I wanted to talk to you privately was to tell you how much I appreciate those qualities. It's largely thanks to you, Captain, that my approaches to tank warfare gained credibility with those five-sided blockheads in the Pentagon. Do you realize, Captain Tag, that the Army's so-called 'armor general' at the time of your Oman incident didn't even have a driver's license? That he needed a secretary to turn on his computer terminal? As far as he knew, Rommel had written the last word on tanks that was worth reading."

Ross Kettle paused and took a whiskey-sip from his cup.

"I remember," the general continued, "writing—or, at least, signing—a letter of congratulation to you afterward. I should have been more attentive to it, Captain, but your success in Oman had given me the high ground I needed to get the Army to act on my proposals for tank designs to match the tactics you had already shown to work. And believe me, Captain, there is no enemy more implacably against the U.S. Army's best interests than a bureaucrat, and no bureaucrat worse than an Army bureaucrat."

Ross Kettle made a sour face and sipped again from his coffee cup.

"On the other hand," he went on, letting his face fall stony, "that grandstand play of yours at Hood, resigning your commission and all that, caused me not a little embarrassment, Max. I had your jacket flagged for my staff—and not as some aide making his way up the staff ladder, but as *my* field officer. That was going to be yours, as soon as the XM-F3's evaluation was finished here. But where do you suppose that jacket was when I asked them to pull it for me, *Captain*? In the goddamn inactive reserve pile, that's where."

General Kettle dropped his voice and added, "If it's any consolation, I had already spoken to Colonel Menefee about the matter of your rank status when he brought the XM-F3 here. You don't have any problem with your commission now, do you, Captain?"

"No, sir," Tag said briskly.

"Good, because your new billet is going to require it."

"Sir," Tag said, "what billet is that?"

"We'll wait for Colonel Menefee before I go into that, Max. Right now, while we still have a few minutes, I want a complete rundown on what you saw and did during Firebreak and whatever you have to say about the performance of the XM-F3."

For the next fifteen minutes, Max Tag recounted the four days that he and his crew had spent behind the Soviet line of advance during the opening moves of World War Three, a series of events that Tag found hard to believe had ended less than thirty-six hours before.

The general listened in attentive silence as Tag told of the battle of Bamberg and their linking up with the Jagd Kommandos. He made notes during Tag's description of the Stealth attack-bomber strike against the Soviet armored column, and looked bemused at the tale of how they picked up the GI contingent from the supply depot and survived the MiGs that hit them on the bald ridge. By the time Tag had reached the part about breaking through under the cover of a predawn firefight between the GI/commando force and an armored recon company, then fighting the XM-F3 against Hinds while it was submerged in a flooded creek, General Kettle had put aside his mechanical pencil and was flipping pages in the manila folder on his desk, apparently following Tag's story on the typed sheets.

Tag paused, and General Kettle leveled his flat yellow gaze on him. "So this *is* all true," he said, almost as an aside. He regarded Tag a moment, then sat back.

"I take it," the general said, "that you have read my books, Max."

"Yes, sir," Tag said, "and articles, and the entry you wrote for the Encyclopedia Britannica."

Ross Kettle nodded in satisfaction. "Then you probably realize," he said, "that those theories and the 'hypothetical armor' I postulated were not created in a vacuum or on some wild hair that ignored the relations of armor to the rest of the order of battle. Neither did our existing bible on armor. But what was being ignored was the changing face of battle itself. Every damn thing we had to work with through the development of the Abrams was based on assumptions formed by George Patton's successes, more than a half century ago. No amount of intelligence, field exercises, technological breakthroughs, or think-tank voodoo could cut through that boneheaded certainty that, in some way, our next war in Europe would draw its pages from the last one."

The general drew a lump of briar pipe from his tunic and began to massage the bowl in one hand. "I'm not," he continued, "talking only about the changes on the battlefield, the kinds of things we can actually simulate and dissect at the War College, the terrain, the technology, and the disposition of forces—all of that."

He dismissed it with a wave of the pipe.

"No, the changes I'm talking about are more subtle and, frankly, less precise. When I talk about the 'face of battle,' Max, I'm talking about the people who actually fight it, the soldiers and the field commanders. And I am fully convinced that soldiers have changed, and this in turn has created a change in the relations of command, a fundamental change in the very nature of military command. Soldiers today are probably no smarter than any others, but they do know more and possess a keener sense of individuality. In failing to recognize that, in insisting on training and motivation that did not take the character of today's soldier into account, the Army was bucking the very forces of history."

General Kettle rapped the briar down on the wooden edge of the desk. "Damn it, Max," he said, "it would sound like sacrilege to most of that bunch in the House of Five Corners, but this war cannot be run like a corporation—a holding company, maybe, at best—because lines *will* form, the battle *will* seesaw, and unless someone panics and jumps nuclear, the war will bog down into exchanges of snipers and artillery duels, while the air forces blast away at each other in the sky. Conventional armor will be part of all that. But if we want to win this war, we have to drag down

Ivan from behind, hamstring him, cripple his logistics and terrorize his rear areas, make him fight twenty-four hours every day, front and back.

"But to do that we need more than partisan forces or Special Ops teams. We need mobility and firepower, and we need the new soldiers, Max. We need their initiative, the confidence that allows them to function in extremely uncertain situations. We need survivors, with just a slash of street meanness and country smarts." Ross Kettle tapped the folders in front of him with the stem of his pipe.

"What do you say, Captain?"

"Say?" Max replied, not quite comprehending Kettle's drift. "Well, sir, I, ah . . ."

"This isn't a drill, Captain," Ross Kettle said, glancing at his black-faced wristwatch. "Do you want the job or don't you?"

"Yes, sir," Tag said immediately, thinking: *Oh, shit. Signed on without reading the fine print again.*

There was a knock on the door behind him, and the uniformed orderly stepped in to announce Colonel Menefee.

"Send him in," the general said. Then, to Max: "Now we'll all get down to taking scalps, Captain."

Menefee had abandoned his yellow ascot in favor of regulation dress, and looking as uncomfortable as Tag had felt earlier, he sat stiffly in the other wingback, toes just touching the floor, while balancing an eggshell porcelain coffee cup on his knee. His overdeveloped shoulders bunched beneath his tunic like burrowing moles.

Ross Kettle held a butane lighter to the bowl of his pipe and worked his flat cheeks like a bellows. "Gentlemen," he said, through a billow of smoke, looking in profile like an ancient Plains warrior making medicine, "what I am asking you to do—and I am *asking*—is not part of any existing operations plan, but I believe it may be critical to our success in the southern sector, especially in the Jura. I've already given each of you some idea of what I want to do to keep Ivan bogged down and out of the Black Forest. But intelligence is just as important. We're going to make it hell for Ivan in the south, gentlemen, and that scares the hell out of me. If the Soviets don't make the Rhine or the Black Forest in Stage Two, and they will not, that's where I'm afraid they may jump nuclear on us."

Kettle drew on the pipe, and the three men exchanged glances.

"Now," Kettle continued, "the way things are going in the north and in CENTAG, there's no way I could in good conscience pull any men or matériel out of there to form the teams I have in mind, teams with the mobility and the firepower and the intelligence-gathering capabilities to both keep Ivan at bay and give us some kind of warning if the Russians start bringing tactical nukes up to the front.

"What I have in mind is this: a team to be composed of one XM-F–series tank, two 'muscle' Bradleys, two ranger squads, and perhaps six scout vehicles equipped with anti-tank weapons.

"Does this sound familiar, Captain Tag?"

"Approximately familiar, sir," Tag said.

"Then perhaps you'll be pleased to know that we've been in contact with the Jagd Kommandos and the American unit you fought with during Firebreak. Since I really have no other units to commit, and since they are already in place, they will form the infantry and scout contingents of your team. You will be in command, and Colonel Menefee will coordinate with my staff from headquarters in Stuttgart. I've also located two Sheridan tanks equipped with slick-skin armor sheaths on loan to the SAS in Hereford, and I'm hoping the Brits will agree to donate some troops. If they do, we have other Jagd Kommando units behind the lines that they can work with. But none of that is certain. If it firms up, Colonel, you'll be in charge of all three teams.

"Questions?"

"Sir," Tag said, "begging your pardon, but at my last count, we had an XM-F3 that looked like a four-car collision, one dinked-up Bradley, and not a single ranger among us. I mean, those kids in the ordnance detail were stand-up, did everything they were asked to do—and more, in some cases—but they're no rangers."

The hatchet creases on Kettle's face deepened on either side of his smile. "Then, please, Captain," he said, "allow me to use 'ranger' in the broadest sense. As for the rest, following the firefight in which you and your crew broke free, the others also managed to disengage and lose themselves. At last report—this morning, wasn't it, Colonel?"—Menefee nodded—"they had picked up another stray Bradley and its crew and were moving south, parallel to the Soviet line."

Thank God, Tag thought. "I am very happy to hear that, sir," he said. "But what does that leave us for a tank?"

Kettle glanced at his watch. "I'm afraid I'll have to leave that to Colonel Menefee, Captain. Afterward, you'll all be briefed by Colonel Barlow; he'll be your liaison with my staff. Anything else, gentlemen?"

Kettle held the irregular lump of briar in both hands and drew deeply on the stem, as though in preparation to pass the pipe.

"Sir," Tag said, "in Oman, I worked with a Brigadier McBrien, and I promised that if I ever met the general, I'd convey the brigadier's regards."

General Kettle threw his head back in a hard, chopping laugh, spewing volleys of smoke. "McBrien!" he said. "McBrien! Captain, that bigoted, bloodthirsty poof used to tell people that I dyed my hair! Lord, God—his regards!"

Kettle chuckled silently and waved his smoldering pipe over the desk. "You're dismissed, gentlemen," he said. "And good luck."

Tag and Menefee rose and saluted and turned to leave. As he closed the door behind him, Tag could hear the Supreme Allied Commander Europe gathering the papers from his desk and mimicking the British brigadier's fruity accent, "Sends me his regards . . . eh, what?"

Tag stood away from the door and shook out his beret, wondering whether the general's eccentricities were chronic or just came with the job.

Once outside the building, walking toward Menefee's waiting jeep and driver, Tag said to the colonel, "So fill me in on the bad news about our tank, sir."

"The bad news, Max," said Menefee, "is that we don't

have a shop on this side of the goddamn Channel that can work on monopolar armor; same goes for the turbine—no parts. We're going to have to 'Dunkirk' the No Slack, Max."

"So," Tag said, resignation creeping into his voice, "what do we do, sir? Wait for one of the refitted Sheridans?"

Menefee stopped beside the jeep to let Tag into the back. "No," he said, "that's the good news. Your people are at the tank park by now; let's get over there and I'll show you."

Tag slipped on his sunglasses and made no attempt at conversation with Colonel Menefee in the open jeep as they drove from the headquarters area, crossed the base, and turned south on the paved farm road that led to the tank park six kilometers away. To him, things seemed to be moving even faster than they had during those four sphincter-puckering days of Firebreak. Maybe, he thought, it was because he had more to handle now—a bigger map and a more specific mission—but also because the whole magnitude of the situation—his situation—had finally come home to him. One part of him, he found, was consumed with the true ardor for his mission that a professional soldier ought to feel, while another was drawn irresistibly to thoughts of the people he would soon be rejoining.

The general hadn't said whether the Allied detachment got away from the firefight cleanly, how many casualties they might have taken, but Tag held a self-confessed illogical faith that Holz and Giesla and, yes, Prentice and Weintaub and the rest of those ordnance clerks had all, somehow, made it through. Still, tough as the German commandos were, their scripted role in the war's scenario would soon be done, and what he was bringing them was something new to them all. It meant a whole different way of thinking about their moves and their consequences. No longer would they be just a bunch of maniac freelancers, operating like pirates behind the lines, no longer was their single goal to stay alive. They had objectives to reach and targets to destroy; work to be done and throats to be cut. Armor playing cavalry in the nuclear age. And after a million considerations, there were still the handful of GIs to turn into "rangers" and the thoughts that kept coming back and back again about Giesla, poignant as thoughts of home.

The guard at the gate to the tank park saluted them through without stopping. Menefee's driver took them past the offices and the empty, packed-earth compounds that had days before been full of Abrams and Sheridan tanks, past rows of concrete munitions igloos, to the shops the size of aircraft hangars, where damaged tanks sat in various stages of dismemberment and repair. Beyond the third shop hangar, next to a crane and a house-size pile of warped and shattered turrets—an image that made Tag shudder with insight into the scope of the war around him—the driver stopped the jeep, and Colonel Menefee sprang to the ground.

"Come along, Tag, and have a look," he said.

"What's the deal, Colonel," Tag said, "we gettin' them in kit-form now?" He jacked the front seat forward and unfolded himself out of the back.

He followed Menefee to the front of the jeep and, standing just a fraction over six feet, towered above the colonel, who whistled through his teeth and spun the hand-and-arm signal for assembly.

Tag looked at Menefee impatiently. "Sir . . ." he began, when the groan and screech of shifting metal made him flinch, and the pile of turrets began to tumble. Tag stared in amazement as one of the turrets moved from under the mass and bulled its way forward on the dull-lustered body of an XM-F–series tank.

Tag dropped his jaw and stared as the sleek, low-slung tank clawed from the pile of scrap like a badger from a winter den, shook itself in a rapid series of jinks to clear odd pieces of junk from its decks, and wheeled smartly into the wedge of morning shadow cast by the shop hangar, where it stopped at idle.

It was a dead ringer for the damaged XM-F3, No Slack, except for the turret. On it, in place of the often-balky 75mm coaxial rapid-fire cannon, there was the low dome of an independently rotating cupola with the cluster barrel of a large-caliber chain gun protruding from its mantle, and a smaller chain gun mounted where the .50 had been, beside the main turret hatch. The black-tipped noses of War Club antiaircraft missiles poked from scalloped sheaths on either side of the turret. Across the glacis, in low-contrast OD paint, were the words *No Slack Too*.

As Tag looked on, wagging his head in amazement, the driver's hatch slammed back and Wheels Latta pushed his grinning, freckled face through. "Larry!" the driver shouted.

The turret hatch flew open and up popped Fruits Tutti, the loader and electronics whiz, who piped, "Moe!"

"And Cur-ley Joe," Ham Jefferson, the gunner, concluded, his long, black viz springing from the commander's hatch like a jack-in-the-box.

Tag had to check himself from giving Menefee a hug.

Instead, he said, "Where the hell did this come from? Sir. And what the hell exactly is it? Sir."

"Let's get out of the light here, Tag," said Menefee, taking his arm. "There really are eyes in the sky."

"Ah," Tag said, "that explains the grand-opera entrance."

Colonel Menefee grunted.

Wheels, Ham, and Fruits had dismounted and were assembling in front of the No Slack Too as Tag and Menefee passed from sunlight into shadow and approached the idling tank. Since Tag had seen them at breakfast, just before dawn, his crew had come up with new boots, fresh camouflage jumpsuits, even rank insignias for their collars. But the effect was compromised by the mangy assortment of personal sidearms: Latta's Ruger in a cowboy rig, Jefferson's Colt 9mm in its tooled-leather gangster harness, and Tutti's goddamn .30-caliber Luger and flap holster that ought to be in a museum.

Tag was curling his lips to snarl at them, when Wheels Latta threw out his broad chest and bellowed, "Ten-HUT!" and three sets of heels locked together in a single crack. Wheels wound up an elaborate swirling salute—like a sea-duty Marine's—and barked, "Sir, XM-F4 ready for your inspection, sir."

Tag allowed himself a grudging grin and returned Latta's salute. As he dropped his hand and began to say, "At ease," he stopped and goggled at his crew's rank insignias—

Staff Sergeant Latta, and *Sergeants* Jefferson and Tutti.

"Assholes," Tag hissed, stepping closer, away from Colonel Menefee. "Did you all decide to give yourselves a little promotion?"

"Nah," Fruits Tutti protested, in a whiny stage whisper. "It was Satin As . . ."

"I promoted them, Captain," Menefee said from behind Tag, "this morning."

"I'll be double-damned," said Tag. He turned and faced Menefee. "Do you suppose I'll ever be the first to know anything?" he asked.

"If you are, Max," Colonel Menefee said smugly, "I'll be sure to tell you. Now, would you like to have a look at your new toy?"

"Pretty please," said Tag. "Unless my driver is going to prep me."

"Good idea, Captain," Menefee said, as though indulging a fretful child. "Staff Sergeant Latta, you will do the honors, please," he said to Wheels. "I'm going to find the range officer, and he'll take you out for a shakedown. Meanwhile, you make friends with this beast here, Captain. Just be careful not to get bit."

"Yes, sir," Tag replied, offering a salute that the squat colonel did not return as he strode with muscle-bound stiffness out of sight around the side of the shop building.

Tag looked back at his smirking crew.

"Okay, people," he said, "let's get down to the nut-cuttin'. Wheels, talk to me."

Tag circled the tank, taking it all in, as his driver spoke: "You prob'ly recall, Cap'n, that one prototype turret we tested at Hood, with the coax-mounted chain gun—the one that shot the end off the main tube. Well, it seems that somebody liked the chain gun idea enough to keep tinkerin' with it, and then some genius remembered that the Navy already had the Phalanx system. What we got is basically Phalanx electronics and radar attached to a thirty-seven millimeter Gatling gun. Course, you can see they added a cupola for it, so it can swing from high noon to horizon ever-which-a-way."

Tag passed his hand along the track skirt, looking more

closely at the black, granular finish that was at the same time slippery beneath his touch.

"What's this?" he asked.

Ham Jefferson said, "That's our instant invisibility, boss."

"No shit," Fruits added. "Dey sprayed some kinda high-speed polymer all over it, Captain, like them Stealth planes got."

Tag looked at Wheels for confirmation.

"All Satin Ass told me, Cap'n, was that this stuff is supposed to break up about ninety percent of the radar waves hittin' it, dependin' on the angle and the strength of the signal."

"What's the rap on the new gun?" Tag said.

"Big story is the ammo, I reckon," Wheels replied. "We can use regular thirty-seven mike-mike, but they hot-loaded something special for us. Three out of every six rounds in our belts are mini-sabots, with depleted uranium cores. At twenty-four hundred rounds per minute, it takes about three and a half seconds to bore plumb through a T-80 turret. Course, Hinds are what it lives for, but it'll also track fixed-wing aircraft and just wither incoming missiles."

"You're sure about all that?" Tag said.

"I got Satin Ass's word," the driver replied in mock credulity.

"Ham," Tag said, turning to his gunner, "what's your read?"

"Can't tell anything worth knowing until we have us a shakedown, boss. This chassis only has twenty hours on it, and the turret wasn't fitted out until it got to Hereford."

"Fuckin' beautiful," Tag said. "But you've checked the systems, right?"

"We got continuity in ever'thing," Fruits Tutti said. "And doze Brits like redundant systems, too. So, we got two of just about ever'thing."

"Now see there, Toots," Wheels said, clapping the wiry loader on the shoulder, "if you'da been born a Brit you could've had two talleywhackers, one for each hand."

"You goddamn degenerate," Tutti said, shaking free.

Tag conned the area around the shops until he saw the

place where many sets of tracks had converged into a single route leading southeast from the park. He wondered how long Menefee would be.

"Hell," he said aloud, "let's take it for a spin around the block. Saddle up, sweethearts."

As the crew dropped through hatches and settled into their stations, Tag clambered into the commander's seat, tossed aside his beret, plugged in his CVC, and ran all his console screens through their preprogrammed tests.

"All systems up," he announced, and the console came alive with liquid-crystal images and digital data readouts. Tag pressed his face into the eyepieces of his periscope and ran it through both visible-light and infrared modes.

"Wheels," he said, "are the turbines strack?"

"I had 'em running at eighty percent for thirty minutes before you got here, Cap'n. They sound sweet to me."

"Fruits," Tag said to the loader, "what's your shell rep?"

"We got nothin' in the carousel for the main tube, Captain. You and Wheels got a full load for the seven-six-two coaxes, and there's a couple of thousand-round belts for the chain gun, and about the same for the mini-gun on the turret."

"Okay," Tag responded, "we have essentially a full combat load, then. Wheels, you see that tank track going off to the southeast?"

"Got it, Cap'n," the driver replied.

"Well, hit the sonofabitch, and let's see what the Too will do."

Wheels nailed the throttles, and the No Slack Too leapt on its tracks, peppering the aluminum wall of the shop with a hail of asphalt chips. The tank left the paved apron doing almost eighty kph and fishtailed down the rutted tank trail, gathering speed and absorbing the bumps effortlessly with its coil-spring and air-torsion suspension. At 110 kph, Wheels leveled off the throttles and let the No Slack Too cruise.

Tag punched in the radio scanner and locked on a frequency carrying a lot of local traffic—radio checks and reports from defense positions that Tag had no way to identify. He examined the Phalanx panel and spoke through his CVC to Fruits Tutti: "Hey, Fruits, you have a console for the chain gun?"

"Sure do, Captain; you can fire it from any seat in the house, but I got the manual controls too."

Tag grunted and turned his attention back to his periscope and the tree line that marked the staging area at the border of the tank range. He could see two vehicles—Bradleys, by their profiles—parked at the edge.

"Wheels," he said, "show us some fancy footwork off the road here, then let's go see who's on the range."

"A done deal, sir," the driver said, braking hard and slewing the No Slack Too off the roadbed, through a shallow ditch, and into a gully-rutted field of thornhedge and dry foxtail. Wheels turned and sped and braked and turned in a series of broken-field moves that threw rooster tails of weeds from the tracks and cut a jinking swath across the field, like a line of cursive Arabic.

The No Slack Too soared the ditch back onto the road and grabbed traction with both treads. The speed indicator was flashing 104 kph when the transmission at last shifted into high, and Tag felt the G-force release with a bump.

"Holy fuckin' moly," Tag heard his driver say. "Cap'n Max, I think we got us a keeper."

"Shut her down, Wheels," Tag said, feigning calm. "We don't want to go rushing up at attack speed."

Wheels dropped the turbines to a purr and pulled into the trees alongside the two Bradleys.

Tag came up through the commander's hatch just as a captain wearing a range officer's duty band came into view from behind the nearer Bradley.

"A little early, aren't you?" the duty officer said.

"Yeah, just waiting for the range officer and our colonel," Tag lied. "What are you all shooting?"

The range officer made a sour face and jerked his head over one shoulder. "Would you fucking believe it?" he said. "We got no working tanks here, so instead we got rangers fam-firing at drones with a new batch of Redtails, the Stinger replacements. You know."

"Yeah," Tag said slowly as a notion took root in his mind. "You know," he said, "I used to be an instructor at

Benning. You wouldn't mind if we kibbitzed on the shoot, would you? I might run into somebody I know."

"Knock yourself out," the duty officer said. "They're just beyond these trees, if you think you can squeeze through."

Standing in the hatch, Tag directed the No Slack Too through the strip of woods until it emerged at the rear of about a dozen men assembled around a first lieutenant, who was holding class on the missile launcher. He put down the tube he was using in his demonstration and approached the tank.

Seeing Tag's railroad tracks and ranger patch, the lieutenant stopped and saluted. "What may I do for you, sir?" he said.

"Carry on, Lieutenant," Tag said, returning the salute. "We're just killing time, waiting for our range officer. Don't mind if we watch, do you?"

"No, sir," the lieutenant said. "We'll try to give you an eyeful."

Tag and his crew watched from their hatches as two soldiers took up a position about fifty meters from the trees, one of them shouldering the Redtail launch tube, while the other ran a visual check on the shooter's stance and grip.

"Ham," Tag said to his gunner, who was sitting with his feet dangling through the main turret hatch, "put the Phalanx on auto tracking, and let's see what it does."

Ham Jefferson dropped through the turret without a word and reappeared less than a minute later, giving Tag a thumbs-up.

Well before they heard the whine of the subsonic drone, Tag and his crew were startled by the brief, powerful whir of hydraulics spinning the chain gun's cupola into tracking position. The six muzzles of the gun's barrels rotated once to arm themselves, dipped, rose, and steadied, as the cupola commenced an accelerating traverse to follow the incoming target.

The gun followed the dopplering sound and snapped across the apogee of its arc as the noise of the drone rose to a peak and at once began to fade down-range.

With a crack and a scream of propellant, the launch tube on the soldier's shoulder released its Redtail missile. The contrail squibbed to nothing behind the receding yellow tail of the rocket motor. At about the moment Tag's eye lost the Redtail against the open sky, the drone was erased by a black billow limned in flame. The shock and sound hit Tag's ears as metal fell like hail from the dark cloud in the Belgian sky.

A second crew brought down another drone, then a third and a fourth. On each pass, the tank's Phalanx system tracked flawlessly.

Tag walked over and spoke to the lieutenant in charge. The lieutenant nodded, and Tag walked back to the tank.

"Okay, you prima donnas, into your fighting chairs. The next one's ours."

Wheels Latta spun the turbines and dropped the transmission into gear. He looked across the crew compartment at Tag.

"Cap'n," he said, "we got a range officer comin' anytime now, you remember."

"Wheelman," Tag said, aware that he was feeling a little giddy with the new tank and the thoughts of their new mission, "this doesn't sound like you."

Wheels distorted his freckles with a grin. "Aw," he said, "you know how rank goes to some people's heads."

And the No Slack Too sprang past the wad of rangers.

The tank came to a halt with its full air defenses up, and in seconds the alarm klaxon sounded.

"Target," Tag barked.

"Confirmed," Ham Jefferson replied.

"Radar . . . locked." Tag threw a toggle on his console.

"Confirmed."

"At my command, Hambone."

"Nothin' but down-range, Cap'n Boss," the gunner said.

The drone passed into the air space of the range; the Phalanx cupola spun and slowed.

"Fire!" Tag commanded.

"Fart!" Ham Jefferson echoed, as the armor thrilled to the brief, deep, trip-hammer pulse of a 37mm chain gun, and Tag watched through his scope as the drone bisected along a fiery seam, its wings flying off like crippled boomerangs.

"Kiss my cowboy ass," Tag muttered, then said aloud, "Fruits, engagement report."

"Ah, right, Captain," the loader responded. "Looks like, call it a one-second engagement, forty rounds expended."

"Thank you, Mr. Tutti," Tag said. "I like that."

Colonel Menefee was less pleased. He was waiting with the range officer when the No Slack Too backed off the range, primed to unload on a commander and crew that he knew he could, in fact, do nothing to discipline. But an entire career spent polishing chairs and practicing the art of one-upsmanship stood Colonel Menefee in no stead against the harnessed recklessness that was overtaking the men of the No Slack Too: it took a hard look from Tag to keep Fruits from calling the colonel "Satin Ass" to his face.

Tag declared himself satisfied with the performance of the XM-F4, and reluctantly he turned it back over to the tank park mechanics for a final round of preventive maintenance before their scheduled departure the next morning.

Tag was already miles and days ahead of the black, balding, impossibly tall Colonel Barlow, who briefed them that afternoon. He knew they would find out more in an hour with Holz and the Jagd Kommandos than Barlow could possibly guess. He thought about a steak dinner at the O-club. He thought about the maps of the southern sector he had been studying, about the valley of the Neckar and the upper Danube and the spine of the Swabian Jura, that rugged highroad to the Black Forest and the borders of northeastern France.

That night, after steak and bourbon and a bull session with his crew, Tag thought of Giesla. But he would not think of her salt tongue or the clean sweep of her spine where it dipped into her buttocks or anything about their night together—or so he told himself.

2

Tag's view of the valley as dawn cast an aura like pollen on the haze was identical to the sand-table perspective that they had been briefed on at sector HQ in Stuttgart the day before, the same afternoon that he, his crew, and the No Slack Too had arrived from Brussels. From their fighting position on a wooded ridge southeast of the village in contention—a village that had become a choke-point of the Soviet advance, already lost and retaken twice—Tag could see the three smaller valleys that converged from the east and marked the only possible routes for Soviet armor. Dense woods protected the flanks of these routes from tank ambush, but they also provided cover and a means of escape for the two companies of rangers positioned in them and armed with Dragon antitank missiles. No one expected the rangers' ambush to halt the fifty to sixty tanks and perhaps one hundred BMPs full of infantry that intelligence had said to expect in the offensive. Their job was to act as a trip wire, providing accurate information on the actual disposition of Communist forces along the various routes, while also slowing the columns by taking out as many vehicles as possible, before withdrawing to secondary positions around the village.

Sharing the position with the No Slack Too were six Sheridan light tanks that represented the reserve reaction force, leaving forty-two Abrams main battle tanks to command the mouths of the valleys and the village itself. Using the immediate intelligence from the ranger contacts, the battle plan called for last-minute redeployment of the MBTs, according to Soviet strengths along the possible routes. Once in place, they would stage a classic armor ambush, shooting and scooting to secondary and tertiary positions, as they rolled back the Soviet assault. The Sheridans would be committed only if the Communist armor broke containment or threatened to overwhelm the infantry emplacements. The primary objective of the light tanks was to cover the No Slack Too's infiltration and, once behind the heavy armor, to destroy as many of the BMPs and their infantry cargo as possible. It galled Tag and his crew not a little that they had orders to avoid contact—to do the runnin' while the Sheridans did all the gunnin'.

Still, Tag knew as well as everyone else that anything could happen once the balls began to fly. He could feel a reservoir of adrenaline building inside him in anticipation of that moment. It came just as he could make out individual treetops on the hill beyond the village, five kilometers away.

A wave of distant staccato explosions rolled through the forest to the east, followed almost at once by the booming counterfire of 125mm guns from the Soviet T-80 tanks and the rapid chatter of machine guns rising and falling like death rattle. For more than five minutes, the sounds of battle swelled into a roar that obliterated all individual sound, then ebbed again as the rangers broke contact and began falling back.

Both of the radio frequencies that Tag was monitoring—the command network and the tactical frequency—came alive with reports from the infantry forces and orders to the tankers from command. From the reports, Tag put the rangers' hits at fifteen to eighteen tanks and a like number of BMPs, but with no way of guessing how many of those had been disabling hits or kills. The Communist tanks seemed to be about equally divided among the three approaches, with the bulk of the BMPs split behind the two outermost columns, one of which was expected to emerge into the main valley about fifteen hundred meters from the No Slack Too's position and directly into the converging fields of fire of a dozen Abrams tanks fighting from defiles in the valley's rolling floor and six more in dug positions on a wooded rise that stretched toward the shelled-out village.

At the apex of the Soviets' fan of dispersal into the valley, salvos from Multiple Launch Rocket Systems had laid down a carpet of antitank mines, which might or might not be neutralized by "floggers," Soviet tanks equipped with chain flails attached to long booms, designed to beat the earth and set off the mines at a harmless distance from the tank.

A wailing *freeesh* snapped Tag's attention back to the wooded rise opposite his position as Soviet ballistic rockets ripped into the trees. *Ivan*, Tag thought grimly, *guessed right on that one*. He prayed the flank could hold, even as he watched the rise blur under a pall of dust and smoke.

Standing in his hatch, Tag could just see over the root-wad of a toppled fir that had provided the No Slack Too with a fighting hole—from which he had been told not to fight. Tag didn't like the conventional, set-piece engagement—the kind that Ross Kettle saw as a dead end for tank strategy. It seemed insane to Tag—and, he supposed, to General Kettle, as well—to construct a strategy based solely on the notion of first-hit survivability. It made better sense, he thought, not to take *any* hits. He was antsy to be on the move, chilled by what he knew must be taking place beneath the rocket barrage. Other strings of rockets were ripping the fields and fence rows of the valley, but none with the lethal accuracy of those falling on the flank of the American ambush.

Tag lowered himself into his commander's chair and briefly scanned the screens and readouts on his console: all systems up. He readjusted the shoulder holster holding his Beretta 9mm, checked the cubby where his 8×40 day/night binoculars were stowed. He wiped his palms on his thighs.

"Hey, boss," Ham Jefferson said through the intercom, "I got heat signatures, three-two hundred meters at two o'clock, just a-blippin' through the trees."

"Confirmed," Tag rasped, reading from his own display. He dogged down the hatch above him and leaned into the eyepieces of his optical scope.

"Wheels," Tag said to his driver, "crank 'em up."

A pop on the TAC frequency alerted Tag to an incoming message from the commander of the Sheridans: "Butcher

Boy, this is Babysitter One. We have friendly fire coming in over us. Button up."

"Roger, Babysitter One," Tag replied. He pressed the mute button on the air-alarm klaxon. "Ham," he said, "see if you can lock on anything coming. . . ."

Tag let the order hang and stared in wonder as the finely tuned Phalanx radar system's screen displayed four groups of projectiles, six in each group, while flashing trajectory information and computing points of impact that were superimposed on the LandNav computer maps. Tag counted down the seconds to impact. The barrage nearest the No Slack Too fell two kilometers to the tank's right-front, sending shock waves through the earth that soughed like hard wind beneath the treads.

Rockets, Tag thought. The MLRS batteries that had scattered the antitank mines apparently had some HE sticks for their pipes as well. That hadn't been in the briefing; but, especially after the pounding that the far rise had taken from the Soviet rockets, Tag was satisfied to be surprised.

The headset in Tag's CVC popped again.

"Butcher Boy, this is Babysitter One. Full stand-to; it's going up."

"Roger, Babysitter One.

"Gentlemen," Tag said to his crew, "grab 'em and growl."

At once, each man's attention cold-riveted on his job: Wheels touched lightly at all his controls, like a choirmaster fingering the stops on an organ; Ham put his chin behind his left shoulder and ducked into the firing yoke; Fruits double-checked the rack of integral-propellant antitank sabots in the loading carousel, then swung his seat back to the chain gun's manual console.

Before he could see the enemy targets emerging from the forest, Tag saw the smoke and, in a moment, heard the reports from the Abrams tanks in the frontal positions in the valley below. A smattering of return rounds from the attackers fell harmlessly at random, as the American tanks shifted to their left, like a football team getting ready to cover an on-side kick.

Three rounds and scoot, Tag thought, wondering whether

the Communists were any less familiar with the drill.

From their secondary positions, the Abrams squadron presented a greater density of targets, but also a greater concentration of firepower. Tag watched as the last Abrams spun into place and a heartbeat later the twelve tanks fired as one.

The wedge of four floggers in the van of the Soviet formation lumbered into Tag's scope seconds before they were transformed into smoke-belching arks of death by the American gunners. He did not yet have visual contact with the body of the Communist column when its next volley engulfed the entire half-kilometer contour of rolling valley floor that concealed the American positions, smothering the line in dirt, debris and powder smoke.

Tracking his optical scope on the thermal signals, Tag began catching his first glimpses of the advancing T-80 column as it dispersed into a wheeling movement on the American positions, firing on the run. Tag glanced at his watch; the engagement was ten minutes old. Through his scope, he saw two of the Soviet tanks farthest from him shudder and halt, one of them with flames roaring from its exhaust grille. Tag prayed, *Let it be. Let it be the flank*. Scanning the twenty-five hundred meters of battlefront, Tag could count kills on eleven of the Soviet tanks, including the four floggers. Smoke and the lay of the land hid the American positions, but he knew not all had survived the Communist salvo. The numbers were about even now, he reckoned, but with the advantage of surprise lost and the momentum with the attackers. From here on, the battle would be decided by whose armor could take the greater pounding, like iron-clad knights banging away with their maces.

Tag silently damned the mentality that had led tank warfare to this sort of suicidal gallantry.

He keyed in the TAC net and broke radio silence: "Baby-sitter One, this is Butcher Boy. I think we have a situation here, One. It doesn't look like the good guys are getting the better of that deal."

"Negative, Butcher Boy," the Sheridan commander responded. "We are still under Command orders. I'm putting out our first two skirmishers right now; you be ready to scoot in three minutes."

"Roger, One," Tag said, and broke the connection. Through the intercom, he said, "Okay, outlaws, locked and loaded. Wheels, let's be ready to move. And remember, darlings, we're trying to sneak in—but if anybody so much as looks at you, blow the sonofabitch away. No prisoners and no witnesses."

Tag could see that the Communist sweep across the mouth of the valley was slowing, as the T-80s began zigging in evasive maneuvers, searching for the cover of high ground on the rolling fields. It was an eerie sensation to be insulated from the sounds of a battle he could see so clearly. Yet even that vision was skewed by the magnification of his scope, which gave the scene a depthless, telephoto field, like a painting without perspective. It occurred to Tag that this technological distancing was a part of that changing face of battle that General Kettle had discussed. Men felt and fought differently when war looked as distant and unreal as family-Bible illustrations of the Passion of Christ. They became at once more noble and more indifferent.

"Butcher Boy, this is Babysitter One. Proceed behind me to Point Alpha."

"Roger, One," Tag said. He looked across the crew compartment at his driver. "Okay, Wheels," he said, "let's start it like we planned it."

Wheels backed the No Slack Too from its position, pivoted on one track, and began a darting slalom through the trees, about twenty meters behind the command Sheridan, as they made their way perpendicular to the line of battle in their third of the field, edging down the slope as they worked relentlessly east in search of the rear of the Soviet column.

In ten minutes they had reached their first reference point, a bowl-shaped bite out of the side of the ridge, where the trees thinned and the slope broke more gently—gently enough for five turreted BMPs mounted with antitank missiles to attempt a flanking maneuver up it.

The officer in the command Sheridan must have seen them at almost the same moment as Tag, for his message popped over the TAC net immediately: "Butcher Boy, this is One. Buzz off. I say again, Buzz off. We have bogeys."

"Roger, One," Tag said, thinking: *What happened to the skirmishers?*

"Wheels," he ordered, "move us back beyond the crest and keep going up-wind."

Wheels reversed their tracks without responding, and the dark, low-slung tank slithered like the shadow of a cloud through the timber. As the No Slack Too dropped behind the protection of the crest and turned to climb along its axis, Tag saw the other two Sheridans wedged in brier thickets on the crown of the ridge, concealed but not covered from fire. Wheels passed behind them, then had to veer back toward the crest around a dense stand of birch, scattering loose stones, grinding down saplings and scrub.

Tag rotated his scope as the six Sheridans—the two skirmishers above, and the other four farther below— fired a coordinated salvo from their 105mm cannons, and the phalanx of Soviet armored vehicles was transformed into a chaos of mushrooming fireballs and the brief stricken screams of burning soldiers who fell and stumbled from the ruptured rear doors of two of the BMPs.

"Butcher Boy, this is Babysitter One. Do you have visual contact with our targets?"

"That's affirmative, One," Tag replied.

"Can you negotiate your way to their positions, Butcher Boy?"

"That's also affirm, One."

"Okay, Butcher Boy. Come on down and fall in behind us in their smoke; we'll follow their wake east. We should be behind all the heavy stuff now."

Tag responded and signed off, thinking about the gulf between *should* and *will be*. "Wheels," he said to his driver, "guide us in behind One's tank, down there in the smoke."

"Gotcha, Cap'n," Wheels said, and the No Slack Too snarled over the rise, tacking through the trees.

"Jeez," Fruits Tutti whined from the manual console of the chain gun. "We had 'em fuckin' dead. We coulda crunched 'em."

"Cheer up, Fruits," the gunner said to him. "They'll make more."

The burning hulks in the hollow of the wooded depression were pouring out oily, black fuel-smoke that wrapped itself to the trees in swirls thick as kudzu and hung in the still air like acrid, striated fog. The No Slack Too arrived ahead of the four Sheridans and stopped in the enveloping roil of smoke from one of the BMPs. Before the other tanks reached them, the No Slack Too's automatic chemical defense systems were triggered by the foul miasma, causing Tag to curse his driver for his—Tag's—stupidity.

"Goddamn it, Wheels," he said, "don't you ever let me do that again." It took him two stabs at the override button before Tag could reset the systems, and by then the Sheridans were in position.

"Butcher Boy, this is Babysitter One." Tag's CVC popped at the incoming message. "Proceed in diamond formation."

"Roger," Tag said, nodding to Wheels, who was patched into the conversation. And as the two skirmisher Sheridans swept past, the No Slack Too fell inside the escort of the other four, like the fifth pip on a French playing-card.

The seven tanks moved easily inside the sparse forest on the lower slope of the ridge, but being pushed farther and farther down by the denser woods, closer to the Soviet line of advance and the as-yet-unseen contingent of infantry in another thirty-five to forty BMPs. It was nearing nine o'clock, and the sporadic firing from the tank battle to the rear told Tag nothing as he stood in the commander's hatch and surveyed the landscape.

The ridge and the wooded rise opposite fell into a narrow valley that was cut by a wet-weather stream and a pair of roads flanking it, one of them gravel and the other lumpy macadam. According to the maps, the gravel road led only to a farmstead, while the pavement continued for several kilometers to another agricultural valley, where it connected with a highway. Tag did not need a three-dimensional projection to see from the map contours that the creek bed was not an option for tanks. The slope of the ridge did flatten somewhat a few klicks up the road, but until then they had no alternative except to hit the road hard and fast. If the BMPs were there, firepower and surprise would have to carry the day for the Americans.

"Butcher Boy," the Sheridan commander said over the radio, "this is Babysitter One. Hold your position behind Babysitter Three when we reach the road. We'll be moving in column for a few klicks."

"Roger, One."

As the tank formation came out of the trees, gathering speed, the two Sheridans on the flanks peeled off and fell in directly behind the No Slack Too. Tag pulled his head in long enough to scan the VDT maps again and to reset the air-alarm klaxon.

"Wheels," he said, "keep a fifty-meter interval. Ham, what have you got in the tube?"

"Sabot, boss," the gunner replied.

"Fruits," Tag said, "replace that with HE and stay on the manual controls for the chain gun. We may have some thin-skinned bogeys to deal with."

"Roger fuckin' wilco," the loader responded, spinning the loading carousel and exchanging rounds in the breech of the 120mm cannon.

The column of tanks hit the blacktop road at sixty kph and made their first contact two minutes later.

The tank commander in the lead Sheridan barked, "Targets," over the TAC net, and even insulated by the XM-F4 and their CVCs, Tag and his crew could hear the boom of the Sheridan's 105mm and the ratcheting clatter of machine guns. But all visual contact was blocked for them by the second and third Sheridans that veered to either side to shoot past the lead tank's turret, filling the narrow roadway between the stream and the slope of the ridge.

Without warning, an explosion on the left flank of the No Slack Too jolted the men inside, followed at once by a transmission from the Sheridan commander: "Bogeys at ten o'clock."

A jumble of green heat signatures lit the imaging screen of Tag's thermal sights. *The bastards*, he thought. *The sonsofbitches have split to either side of the creek.*

He sensed more than heard the explosions to their rear.

"Targets," he bellowed. "Main gun, chain gun, fire on opportunity."

Slowed but still traveling at forty kph, the No Slack Too fired on the run, shooting at an angle across the streambed into the trees at the head of the farm road, where a dozen BMPs were staged for their follow-up assault.

Fruits set the Phalanx's target acquisition device for twenty degrees of the main gun's axis, to keep it from locking on the Sheridans, and stuffed the 120mm with a succession of HE rounds, while the Phalanx kept up a flurry of bursts, moving with the stiff precision of its robotics.

With the fires and explosions from the BMPs rendering his thermal sight a blur, Tag ordered Ham and Fruits to switch to the radar/visual mode, and then spun his own periscope into position. As he leaned into the scope, Wheels braked the tank hard, throwing Tag against his seat harness. He grabbed the focusing yoke and instinctively twisted it to the front.

The number three Sheridan was down on its left track, its back end blown toward the center of the road, but still firing at the BMP that had hit it with an antitank rocket from across the gully of the creek.

"High side, Wheels," Tag said. "Keep us moving."

The ex-moonshiner gunned the turbines and juked the joystick, caroming off the rear of the crippled Sheridan as the No Slack Too ripped plugs of asphalt from the road and slewed crazily off the narrow roadbed, before finally shooting forward, now almost one hundred meters behind the two remaining Sheridans in the lead.

Smart motherfuckers, Tag thought. *Know they're over-matched, so they're trying to get down in our wheels.*

Caught up in the battle, Tag had tuned out the, to him, nonessential traffic over the TAC net, but now caught a scrotum-tightening transmission from the Sheridan riding drag: "One, One, we have heavy bogeys coming up on our six."

Shitfuckcrappiss, ran through Tag's consciousness. The Soviet attack had been rolled back, and now the survivors were tearing up the road in retreat, trapping the Sheridans and the No Slack Too between the Soviet tanks and the scrappy BMPs.

A second rocket whanged off the forward track skirt and exploded directly in Tag's field of vision, causing the No Slack Too to lurch drunkenly. The Phalanx responded with a heavy shudder that ran through the tank. As Tag screwed his scope to the left, he saw a sheet of flame slash through the trees where two BMPs had been.

"Nail it, Wheels," he said to his driver. "We got more bad guys coming up the rear."

For a moment he held a grim thought for the crew of the disabled Sheridan.

The creek and the road made a wide turn to the right that brought them back in sight of the lead Sheridans. The fire from small arms and machine guns was such a blizzard that Tag believed he could see the ricochets flying like sparks off the light tanks' armor, as they poured a continuous, running barrage from their 105s at the some two dozen Soviet armored vehicles arrayed in staggered columns along each shoulder of the road. He took no notice of the fusillade that greeted the XM-F4 as it came into the field of fire, except to wonder what was happening to the coating of "stealth" polymers on the skin of the No Slack Too.

"Cap'n," Wheels Latta said through the intercom, "look there, comin' up at our eleven o'clock."

Tag saw it: a narrow neck of the creek bed, with a high dirt bank on this side and rocky wash on the other. Just upstream was the sectional steel bridge that the Soviets had used to get their BMPs across and into the trees along the farm road. And even though it would never support the thirty tons of XM-F4 tank, Tag knew what his driver was thinking.

"I'm right with you, Wheels," Tag said. "Forget the bridge. Can you clear the creek off that bank?"

"Like a goddamn deer, Cap'n."

Wheels opened both throttles full and torqued the suspension controls to maximum stiffness; Fruits Tutti squealed, "Oh, fuck my dead fuckin' dog"; and the No Slack Too went airborne, sailing perfectly flat off the cutbank, its main gun slightly elevated, like the nose of a steeplechaser.

The *whoosh* of compressing air-torsion suspension didn't save the crew of the No Slack Too from a tremendous blow to their spines and diaphragms, as sixty thousand pounds of tank bottomed-out in the wash, crushing the men into their seat harnesses and killing one turbine.

"G . . . guh," Tag croaked with empty lungs.

Wheels could not respond, but he could jam the throttle on the live turbine and hit the restart button on the other.

Tag grimaced as he sieved searing air through his teeth; he felt as though he had only one lung, and it on fire. Half his systems' screens had been jolted into default modes, and he fingered his console awkwardly as he fought for breath. Phalanx, laser doppler, radar, thermal, LandNav—as the screens came up Tag gathered enough wind to command, "Targets . . . of . . . oppor . . ."

A rocket from one of the BMPs shied off the art-deco forward contour of the turret on the No Slack Too, exploding inches off the front and driving the XM-F4 back again on its suspension.

The Phalanx radar homed on the spoor of the rocket until it locked on the infantry weapons squads manning their crew-served launchers. Tag picked out the target visually and triggered the Phalanx from his own console, watching through his scope as a swarm of 37mm harrowed the armored infantry and their vehicles, sowing a row of flame.

Like a champion trapshooter snapping from high house to low, the Phalanx cupola responded to Tag's computer commands, adjusting its fire as Wheels got the stalled turbine to catch and accelerated through the wash, up the brier-choked bank, and over the small trees and saplings that grew at the edge of the woods on the slope.

Wheels topped a transverse hogback and had to heel the No Slack Too hard to the right to keep from tumbling into the deep V of an eroded hollow, leaving the tank astraddle of the narrow spine, nose down, facing back across the creek. Tag's scope snapped into focus, revealing a choking inferno where the columns of BMPs had sat. The surviving Soviet troop carriers were fighting a rearguard action to cover their retreat before the two Sheridans and the storm of chain-gun fire from the No Slack Too. Inside Tag's CVC, the voice of the Sheridan commander was nearly deafening.

"Butcher Boy, this is Babysitter One. Do you read me, Butcher Boy?"

Tag's voice was tight with pain: "This is Butcher Boy. Read you, One."

"We've lost you, Butcher Boy. Can you proceed?"

"Affirmative, One." Tag scanned the landscape rapidly.

"Buzz off, Butcher Boy. We have heavy bogeys on our six and a pair of cripples. Do you copy?"

"Copy, One. Good shooting." Tag signed off and swung his scope back along the road in the direction of the Sheridans riding drag. He could still see the tank with the shattered track that sat half blocking the road, and farther around the bend there was a twist of dark smoke rising above the trees.

The command Sheridan came around the bend at high speed, its gun to the rear, followed shortly by the other still in operation. The second tank ducked behind the cripple and brought its gun to bear on a target beyond the bend. Tag saw the smoke and the recoil of the Sheridan's shot, then the scene was a ball of spiny fire as a tube-fired missile from a Soviet T-80 penetrated the rear of the disabled tank and ignited its warhead just one thin thickness of armor from the second Sheridan's turret. The blast of missile, fuel, and ammunition collapsed the layered armor on the Sheridan, killing the commander and the driver at once. They were the lucky ones, for in the next few instants electrical shorts and hydraulic fluids came together in a cloud of gaseous flame.

If the No Slack Too stayed put, they couldn't hide; and if they ran, they couldn't fight. It seemed a simple decision to Max Tag.

"Sabot," Tag squawked from his raw lungs. As he heard the loading carousel hum, he said to Ham Jefferson, "Target coming up at two o'clock, Mr. Jefferson. Radar . . . mark."

"Confirmed," the gunner replied, taking a fix on the burning Sheridans in the bend.

The T-80 might have made it, if it hadn't had to slow to

negotiate around the destroyed American tanks. The Soviet main battle tank stopped, reversed, and went up on one track as it crawled along the face of the ridge.

"Shoot," Tag said.

"Shot," Ham responded, and the sabot peeled away from the penetrating core, which entered the T-80's turret inches from the hatch. The lumbering tank shuddered at the impact. Then, its magazine exploded with a force that ripped the turret from the body and flung it, warped and smoking, into the gap between the T-80 and the smoldering hulks of the two Sheridans.

"Butcher Boy, this is Babysitter Three. We have a visual on you now. How the hell did you get there?"

"Three, this is Butcher Boy," Tag replied. "Long story. We put a cork in the bottleneck. Can you cover us while we find a way back across?"

"You're covered, Butcher Boy. Buzz off."

"Thanks, Three."

"Cap'n," Wheels Latta cut in at the end of the transmission, his own voice breathy and thin, "I think I see a way over for us."

"Go for it," Tag said, and the XM-F4 lurched forward in a series of jerks as it cleared the hogback and skittered down into the creek bed.

Wheels clawed through piles of drift and deadfalls for about seventy-five meters, to a place where a cutbank had fallen to form a steep but negotiable slope out of the gully. He gunned the tank into the soft earth, the treads catching in fits, and gave his crewmates a stomach-fluttering moment as the No Slack Too teetered on the brink before falling forward on its tracks and regaining the road.

Fruits Tutti grunted through the intercom, "Fuck! Lemme off, an' I'll take the next train."

"I'm with you, Fruitman," Ham said, his voice in the upper register. "The cracker can let me off at the corner."

"Aw," Wheels drawled, "you city boys just don't know how to have fun."

"Can it," Tag told his crew as he keyed the TAC net.

"Babysitter Three, this is Butcher Boy. We are back on your side. What's the drill?"

"Butcher Boy, this is Three. We have blackbirds coming to cover our six. Proceed with Babysitter Five and Six to Point Charlie."

"Roger, Three. And a million thanks."

"Good hunting, Butcher Boy. Out."

As the No Slack Too accelerated over the rippled asphalt, Tag's breathing finally settled into an unconscious act, and he could swallow the knot of grief and gratitude he felt for the men in the three Sheridans that had died to get them this far. It was cold consolation that they had destroyed more than five times their number of the enemy—but it was consolation.

Within seconds Tag had sighted the Five and Six Sheridans and was back in radio contact with them. The few BMPs that had survived the flying wedge of American armor were now in full retreat, but only barely outdistancing the tanks. Tag calculated that traveling at or near the Sheridans' top speed of about sixty kph, they would reach Point Charlie—the No Slack Too's jumping-off place—in less than five minutes. Now that he believed they would make it, he grew excited and thought, briefly, with a mixture of bemusement and lust, of Giesla.

Tag ran a systems check and had Wheels stiffen and soften the suspension twice to make sure it had survived the leap across the creek. Fruits reported fewer than two hundred rounds expended by the Phalanx, and Ham didn't bother to mention that he had cracked a rib.

Point Charlie marked the crest of the gap, the head of the watercourse, where wide, leafy draws snaked back into the trees. Tag took a moment to memorize the display on the LandNav, then opened his hatch and scanned the road ahead. The two Sheridans had taken position rear-to-rear at the mouth of one of the draws.

"Wheels," Tag said, "take a right at the light." He keyed in the TAC net.

"Babysitter Five, this is Butcher Boy. Thanks, tanks. We are outta here."

"Roger, Butcher Boy. Shoot 'em dead. Five out."

The No Slack Too swung wide and into the leafy swale that wound deep into the Swabian forest.

3

In the wooded hills, Tag could smell the approach of autumn. It was the fusty odor of decay beneath the dust, the ripe scent of mulch. With the No Slack Too's turbines shut off, even the sounds of the forest seemed to Tag's ears to have the quality of fall, muted and anxious in preparation for winter, much like the mood that had descended on him and his crew since reaching their contact point and finding no Jagd Kommandos to meet them. For more than an hour now, holed up in the wreckage of an old hunting lodge large enough to accommodate the XM-F4, Tag had been trying to make radio contact, but to no avail. A thousand possibilities ran through his mind, none of them cheerful.

Wheels had shinnied up the shelled-out log frame of the lodge and taken up an observation post where the attic or sleeping loft used to be. Ham and Fruits were sprawled on the rear deck, eating PX cookies and drinking the last of the fresh coffee in their thermoses, while Tag sat with his legs dangling down through his hatch, his CVC on, and tried again to raise someone from the ad hoc raider unit.

"Meat Grinder One, this is Butcher Boy," he said softly into the mouthpiece, using the call sign he had adopted while working with the German commandos during the initial stages of Firebreak. "I say again, this is Butcher Boy. Are you out there?"

The radio answered with an indifferent hiss of static.

"Damn," Tag said, knocking his kevlar helmet smartly against the turret. As lately as 0500 that morning, the Jagd Kommandos had been in contact with Command, saying they were proceeding to the rendezvous. Now, a little more than five hours later, there was nothing.

"Cap'n," Wheels's voice said hollowly over the wireless intercom, "we got movement, something on foot, about two-five-zero mikes to the east."

"Stand by, Wheels," Tag responded. He stood and pulled himself on top of the turret.

"Ham, Fruits," he said to the men on the rear deck, "stand to. We've got movement at our three o'clock, foot troops. Could be recon or a lost farmer. Be ready."

As the gunner and loader took their positions, Tag eased around the turret on the track fender and spoke to his driver in the OP.

"What have we got, Wheels?" he asked.

"Can't tell, Cap'n," the driver responded. "I've lost 'em, but there can't be more'n three or four. Whoever it is ain't out there by accident, though. They're bein' too careful."

Tag thought for a moment. Quiet as the turbines were on his tank, they made a scream like rusty door hinges when they started up. But if the people in the woods were bad guys, they'd be sure to check out the lodge, anyway. If they were good guys—lost Americans or a Special Ops team—they might jump squirrely at the sight of a strange tank and open up on them. With Wheels in the loft, they weren't entirely blind, however, and the No Slack Too could fight all its systems on the batteries alone for a while.

"Wheels," Tag said, "what was your last fix on the movement?"

"Maybe two hundred mikes, at two o'clock. Wait. Something's happenin'. Come look at this, Cap'n. Holy shit."

Tag sprang straight up, grabbed a solid-looking roof joist, and hauled himself into the gutted loft. He ran the joist like a tightrope artist and crouched on it at the window frame next to Wheels Latta.

"There," Wheels said, pointing to a stand of thick, head-high brush that grew in the trace of the old road some 150 meters away.

Tag saw the commotion of the thicket, could hear the crash of limbs and leaves and a single, strangled cry. Then all fell still and silent, save for the scolding caw of a startled crow. He heard the hydraulic hum of the Phalanx cupola rotating into position beneath him.

"Ivan," Wheels said sharply, nudging Tag with the binoculars he held. "Look, he's slippin' out this side."

Tag took the glasses and focused on the stand of brush. A figure in a Soviet camouflage uniform was inching on its belly away from the scrub toward an overgrown ditch.

"Take him," Tag said.

Wheels extended the stock on his CAR-15 and brought it to his shoulder. He found the prone figure in his sights, relaxed, and squeezed off a three-round burst.

Through the binoculars, Tag saw an arm and a leg flail upward, then flop toward the ditch. "Nice shooting, for a country boy," he said. "Now, be still."

They waited in silence for as long as the smell of cordite lingered in the air. Tag continued to scan the area.

"Anything, Cap'n?" Wheels whispered from the shadow beside the window frame.

"Jack shit, Wheelman," Tag said absently, his eyes tight against the rubber cups of the field glasses. Even the crow had fallen silent or flown out of earshot; not a leaf or shadow moved.

"Come down from there!" a voice with a thick accent boomed from behind and below them, causing Tag to recoil, lose his balance and the binoculars, and fall gracelessly with both arms wrapped around the rough ceiling joist, hanging like a monkey by his heels, while Wheels gripped the window and swung his carbine in an arc that ended aiming at the barrel chest of Mathias Betcher, senior NCO of the Jagd Kommando group.

Betcher caught the binoculars in one hand and looked at Tag. "I am sorry, Max," he said, "but this old building, it is not for safe to climb. Jan"—Betcher spoke to one of the three commandos who had entered the lodge behind him—"get up and help."

As the young German mounted the fender and stood on the XM-F4's sloping forward deck, Tag let go his heels and swung down, then hung a moment before releasing his grip and letting Jan break his fall with his arms and hands. Tag stood just as Ham Jefferson's head appeared in the turret hatch, squinting down the sights of his 9mm Colt Commander.

"Peace, brother," Tag said quickly as he made Vs with his fingers and wagged them in Ham's face. "Just us chickens in here."

Ham lowered the gun, his face a mask of complete confusion, while from inside the turret came Fruits Tutti's adenoidal, "Whadda fuck's goin' on, Jefferson?"

Amusement, amazement, and anger crackled over Tag all at once. "Goddamn, Mathias," he said to Betcher, "I could have killed you."

The big commando nodded solemnly. *"Ja,"* he said, "you could have fallen on me."

As Jan gave Wheels a hand, Tag slipped down over the glacis of his tank and shook hands with Betcher.

"Think you can tell me what's going on here, Mathias?" Tag said. "I've been the last one told about every goddamn thing there is for two solid days, and it's gettin' kinda old, partner."

Betcher took Tag's arm in a hand like a slab of bacon and squeezed just hard enough to get Tag's attention. "Sure, sure," he said. "Just we don't stay long here. Okay?

"We picked up radio traffic," Betcher went on, releasing Tag's arm, "that tells us Ivan suspects there is maybe a tank loose behind his lines. Near this place, we hear something else, and Gies . . . Lieutenant Ruther, she thinks it means a patrol or an ambush here. So we"—he gestured at the other Jagd Kommandos—"come on foot and find the recon team moving in on this place. . . ."

"Spetznaz?" Tag interrupted.

Betcher shook his head. "Tank-killer recon," he said, then went on: "Well, we followed them. When they hear your radio signal and know you are here, they are going to call artillery. And that is when we hit them."

"With what?" Tag asked.

Betcher reached behind his hip and produced a long dagger with a tulip-shaped blade and deep blood grooves down the sides. "But you killed my prisoner," he said petulantly.

"Looked to me like your prisoner was escaping," Tag said.

"Nein," Betcher said, pulling an even longer face. "Not with the kidney I left him with; he wasn't going far."

Tag gave an involuntary shudder.

"Okay," he said, "let's move, then. How far to the others?"

To Giesla, he meant.

"Maybe twenty minutes," said Betcher. "You get this thing outside, and we will ride."

Betcher turned and motioned his men to follow. He stopped before ducking through the crushed doorjamb and looked back at Tag.

"A very dangerous place to climb, Max," he said.

Tag returned Betcher's grin and turned to his crew, assembled on the decks of the No Slack Too.

"Let's do it, my lovelies," he said, mounting the stirrup on the track skirt and swinging up into his hatch.

Wheels stirred the turbines to life, and as soon as the hatches were buttoned, he began to ease the No Slack Too back through the breached wall that they had entered. As he spun the tank around outside, Wheels brushed the log post that supported the lintel beam. With a groan and a keening of timbers, the entire end of the lodge came down in a cloud of chips and dust.

Tag came up through his hatch to survey the damage. Betcher and his men walked out of the cloud holding their noses and waving away dust with their hands.

"You see, Max," Betcher scolded as he and his men clambered onto the No Slack Too, "I told you it was not for safe."

Betcher sat next to Tag's hatch and directed them through the forest, his feet braced on the fog-lamp bracket on the glacis. They traveled for less than a kilometer along the overgrown road that ran past the lodge, then turned upslope through old stands of big timber—larch and fir and oak—until they came to an expanse of benchland. Five hundred meters through the vast trees brought them to a wasteland.

Tag ordered Wheels to stop at the edge of the trees, then stood in his hatch for a better look. A roughly wedge-shaped area of several hundred square meters lay like a moonscape of rocks, scree, and boulders that concluded near the base of a bald, steep rise that was pierced by a half-dozen timbered mine shafts. Near the mouth of the farthest shaft, the skeletal derricks of abandoned cranes lingered over mounds of rusty scrap and the picked carcasses of trucks. Looking more closely, Tag could see that the nearer mine shafts were fallen in, disused.

"You like this?" Betcher asked him. "See, no tracks, and even if we are caught outside, the pilots are now used to radar returns from the old equipment. Lots of ground clutter."

"Sure," Tag said, nodding slowly. "You have one of these tunnels working, right?"

"*Ja*, Sergeant N. Sain, he knew about this place and brought us here."

"Sergeant *In*-sane," Tag said, looking sharply at Betcher. "Who is this Sergeant *In*-sane?"

"In the other Bradley," Betcher said, "the one we found lost. *Ach*, I thought you would know."

"Right," Tag said. "Where to?"

"Just there, past the old machines."

Tag had Wheels move the XM-F4 out across the rocks at a crawl, taking them a full five minutes in the open to reach the abandoned equipment. Where the naked earth face turned to rejoin the slope, another tunnel appeared, this one newly refurbished with fitted timbers and large enough for two five-ton trucks, or one XM-F4 tank. Barely.

"From here we walk, Max," said Betcher as Wheels halted the No Slack Too and made ready to square it with the tunnel opening. "I will hold the light for you; it's not far."

The Jagd Kommandos slid off the tank and headed into the shaft, where Betcher stopped to turn on a flashlight and play it over the hewn-rock walls of the adit. Tag stood in his hatch and smelled the cool rock-dust breath of the mountain as they followed Betcher's torch. Fifty meters inside the shaft, the commandos parted the first of three sets of nylon blackout drapes. Beyond the third, the No Slack Too entered a domed chamber the size of a suburban lot. Against the far edge, the light from pressure lanterns illuminated two of the extended-body "muscle" Bradleys with turret-mounted 75mm guns flanking four of the Jagd Kommandos' gun buggies and the two remaining towed racks of antitank missiles. Ponchos and blankets hung from cord strung between the vehicles to form cubicles. Tag saw shadows moving against the wall of the cavern beyond them. Then the curtains parted between two of the gun buggies, and Heinrich Holz and Giesla stepped out into the light.

Tag was out of his hatch and moving in long strides across the gritty floor of the cavern almost before he realized it. And before he could speak, Holz had locked him in a Teutonic bear hug, was pounding his back and grunting a raspy laugh.

Holz stood back and held Tag by the arms. "So," he said, "did we save your ass again?"

The left side of Holz's forehead and his left temple were still slightly swollen and discolored from his near-fatal encounter with MiG machine guns, but his eyes were clear and intense, wolf-hungry.

"Yeah, sure, Rick," Tag said. "You assholes are just desperate for a leader." He turned to Giesla.

She stood at her brother's shoulder, sucking in one corner of a smile that she could not contain. Her hair was pulled back, knotted at the nape of her neck, showing off the fine bones of her face and giving her eyes a hint of Magyar slant. As Tag faced her, she stepped close to him and took one of his hands in both of hers.

"I am glad you are back, Max," she said.

"Just another happy accident," Tag replied, giving her hand a squeeze. "I'm glad to be here."

The other Jagd Kommandos and the American GIs were filtering out from behind the ponchos and blankets. Tag saw the amusement in Giesla's face and released her hands. Then he found himself and his crew surrounded by the troopers, shaking hands with Jagd Kommandos and the Americans, Lieutenant Prentice—his shoulders still wrapped but able to use his arms from the elbows down—First Sergeant Weintaub, Sergeant Dunn, the demolition man, and a dozen others.

These amenities completed—along with the required

razzing about Tag's commission: "Took an act of Congress to make a gentleman out of him, didn't it?"—Heinrich Holz stepped in.

"Max," he said, "I know you have things to tell us, and we have some information for you, as well. I think we should let Sergeant Betcher get your men settled, while we have an officers' meeting. *Ja?*"

"Right," Tag said. "And I want to meet this stray you picked up, this Sergeant In-sane."

Holz rolled his eyes. "*Ja, ja,* Max. But first, we talk."

Holz led Tag, Giesla, and Lt. Prentice into one of the curtained-off cubicles between two gun vehicles, where he had set up a crude situation table, fashioned out of weathered planks, maps, dirt, and rocks. Planks laid across ammo boxes made benches for them. Tag accepted a canteen cup of black coffee and got directly to his part of the briefing.

"For what it's worth," Tag began, "everything I'm about to tell you comes straight from the horse's mouth, directly from General Kettle himself. We are, in effect, working for him now.

"Basically, our orders are twofold," he went on. "First, we are to act as a reconnaissance unit, gathering intelligence on all the usual suspects: troop dispositions and strengths and movements, logistical estimates, and especially weapons. Right now, Command is especially worried that Ivan may try to bring up nukes here in the south, tactical nukes, that is. And if we do spot 'em, we've got carte blanche to stop 'em.

"That brings us to our other mission. Special Ops teams and partisan groups can do as well or better at the basic intelligence-gathering activities, and they are out there now, as I'm sure you know."

Giesla, Holz, and Prentice all nodded.

"But we are also an attack unit—guerrillas, raiders, call it what you will. In that role, it's our job to hit at any and all targets of opportunity we encounter, especially those in areas that Ivan thinks are secure. We're going to mess with his resupply, his logistics and support units, and particularly anything that has to do with troop morale—field kitchens, mail bags, traveling circuses, whatever we find that gives aid and comfort to the enemy. We're gonna make Ivan as nervous as a queer at a weenie roast.

"As for our own supply and support, Command has worked in a few new wrinkles. Now, we're expected to live off the land as much as we can, but we also have three methods of resupply by air. We can call for a conventional airdrop, and it might or might not be made. It's damned hard to hide a C-130, day or night. Our second option, for lighter loads, is a remote drop from a drone. This is a neat trick, because the drone can fly contours and stay below the radar horizon, then drop our gear and continue on to attack an actual target. Finally, in a best-case scenario, we can get choppers, but I haven't seen a best-case situation yet.

"The support elements are mostly in the form of intelligence coming to us from two sources. One is Command itself. We'll receive reports from Command that are put together from intel gathered by other groups in our general area, of course, as well as special orders, when necessary. But more important, I think, is our satellite link. There are three satellites that we can tap through our LandNav computers, including a LandSat bird that can map the lines on a parking lot. Until Ivan comes up with something to knock out our satellites, they are our ace in the hole.

"Any questions so far?"

Lt. Prentice bent one elbow and raised his hand stiffly to his chin. "Yeah," he said. "What's the big picture? How are we holding up, Sergea . . . uh, Captain Tag?"

"Max," Tag said. His misgivings about this young officer had been largely put to rest by Prentice's conduct during the opening stages of Firebreak. Now, with a week's worth of beard and constant combat, he had a lean, hard-eyed look and a manner that bespoke a confidence Tag liked.

Prentice dipped a comic salute. "Chuck Prentice," he said, then continued: "Are we holding them?"

The others looked anxiously at Tag.

"Yes, after a fashion," he said. "The north coast, Denmark, and Holland soon will all be controlled by Ivan, about as we expected at this point. After the initial breakthrough at Fulda, CENTAG has stiffened and even retaken some ground, but things are essentially in a stalemate there now.

It's here in the south that the situation is the diciest. As I understand it, we're playing at the ultimate brinksmanship, hoping that we can hurt Ivan enough here to draw off troops from the other sectors, but not make him jump nuclear on us."

"But we have nothing more specific than what you have said?" Holz asked.

"Not yet," Tag said, "and until we do, we call our own shots. Anybody have a suggestion?"

Holz nodded at his Valkyrie sister, "Giesla?"

Giesla, the Jagd Kommandos' intelligence officer, rose and stepped to the situation table, followed by the three men. She picked up a length of broken antenna lying on the table and tapped the maps pinned to one end.

"You may want to follow on the map," she said, "our table is very rough and not to scale, as you can see."

Pointing first on the maps and then to the ridge of dirt and stone heaped on the planks, she continued: "Here is our position. Beyond the crest of the mountains, in the valley of the Danube, and here in these hills to the north are the main lines of advance. We think that the Soviets would like to invest these mountains, but it would slow them too much. From the radio traffic we have monitored, we know that they do have small units operating in the Jura, primarily to deal with partisans and people like us. Unlike most Soviet units, these seem to have a high degree of autonomy, and that makes them more difficult to predict. The Jura represents the weak link in the Soviet line, and they know that."

Tag looked up. "A question," he said.

"Yes, Max," said Giesla.

"Where does the Soviet line run?"

"Ah, yes," she said, putting aside the pointer and collecting a handful of rocks from a corner of the table. She began making a trail with them perpendicular to the axis of the mountain range.

"Understand," Giesla said, placing the last rock and dusting off her hands, "that these are very approximate positions, especially to the south of the Danube. Still, we are now perhaps twelve or fifteen kilometers behind the front.

And if what you say is true, Max, I do not expect that to change very soon."

"How secure is this place, anyway?" Tag asked at large.

Prentice spoke up: "Well, it's not easy to get to and doesn't show up on at least some maps."

"Right, Chuck," Tag said, "but what about those ground units that are prowling around?"

"Come and gone, Max," Holz told him. "They were scouting it at the same time we did. This is our fourth day here now, and no more of them since."

"And how was it you got here in the first place?" Tag asked. "Betcher said something about some Sergeant *Insane*."

The three others looked at one another. Giesla stepped back and inclined her head toward Prentice. "I believe he is in your army, Lieutenant," she said.

"Yeah, well," Prentice stalled. "Sure. *He* just doesn't believe he's in it."

"You think someone could tell me a little about this?" Tag asked impatiently. "I get the feeling that there's something I ought to know before we start planning any operations."

Prentice cleared his throat and said, "We took a pretty heavy lick from that mech-infantry outfit, Max, the one we engaged just before you broke free in the other tank. We lost five men and one of the Dragons, but in the end we backed them up and managed to disengage, with my Bradley and all four of the commando vehicles intact.

"That day and night, we ran and hid and ran some more, until we ran out of woods and had several miles of open country to cross to get us to someplace where we could hide. We were also running low on fuel and really needed to let our wounded rest. We took a flyer on a small village where another Jagd Kommando unit had been stationed, hoping, at the worst, that it was unoccupied and that we could scrounge some gas. Well, we had some luck—if bad luck is better than none at all."

Tag saw the muscles in Holz's jaw tighten. *Blaming himself*, Tag thought.

Prentice continued: "The place looked deserted—not shelled-out or shot-up, just deserted, like a ghost town. I mean, there was laundry still on the lines, but not a sign of a person. We waited until sundown, and when no lights came on, we cruised into town like it was a Sunday drive."

Prentice looked down, clenched and unclenched his fists, then went on: "I was leading in the Bradley when the first mine went off, an AP, it turned out, so the Bradley was okay. But then it was like the whole world blew up around us. Remote detonators, I guess, but that was nothing compared to what came out of the town—machine guns, RPGs—and there we were with our tails hanging out, in the middle of a road, with nothing but open farm fields on either side.

"We scattered, returning fire as best we could and hoping we could find anything like fighting positions. I saw one of the commando vehicles cutting doughnuts in the field, with the driver dead at the wheel, and just said to hell with it; we'll stand and fight. I dumped my men in a shallow ditch and took what cover it allowed for the Bradley, and we started pouring it on. We drew enough fire that Rick and Betcher had time to get off their one-oh-sixes, but the situation was still in doubt, as they say. All of a sudden, there was this god-awful *scream* of electric rock 'n' roll music and all kinds of hell breaking loose inside the town—heavy cannon fire, machine guns, explosions—and all of a sudden, we weren't taking any more fire. There was still plenty of shooting going on, but just not at us.

My first thought was that we had misjudged the line of advance and had come up on the backside of some larger action, and maybe had a chance to hook up with some of our people. So, we charged the village, right into the positions where we had been catching the fire, but not a shot. I sent our two squads inside the buildings to secure them, and they came back with a report that there was nothing in there but dead Reds and missing walls on the other side. I heard the firing pick up again someplace else, toward the center of town, so we went for the sound of the guns—you know, as soon be shot for a wolf as a dog, and all that. Sergeant Dunn had first squad, and he was the one that found Sain's Bradley on the second deck of this little concrete soccer stadium, pumping white-phosphorous rounds into the biggest damned satellite dish you've ever seen, dead Rooskies scattered everywhere. And then here came Rick and his hot rods from hell, and things didn't last long after that."

Holz reached to clap Prentice on the shoulder but stopped himself in time, letting his hand hang in benediction as he said, "Max, I tell you, this man is modest. When we arrived, *ach*, there was nothing left to blast. He's like a Napoleon, but with two hands in his blouse."

"I'm ordnance," Prentice said haughtily, "Bonaparte was only artillery."

"You're by-God armor now, Chuckles," Tag said. "So let's move on with the story. I'm still waiting to hear about this Sain or In-sane or whoever he is."

"Right," Prentice said. "Well, it's easier to show than to tell, but when the shooting stopped, this other Bradley—Sain's Bradley—it kills the volume on 'Sympathy for the Devil' and highballs it out of town, won't even respond to the radio. So, on a hunch, I guess, we ran with him, for a couple of klicks, until we came to this factory of some sort—a cannery, I think—out by the railroad tracks, past all the houses.

"The warehouse doors are open, and we all follow Sain inside and see all the dead Ivans in there just about the same time a damned time-on-target comes down on the town. It's like a swarm of forty-five rpm hornets coming in on seventy-eight, and then there's this rolling explosion that's louder than sound and a shock wave hits and knocks the wind out of the air. The building we were in, steel beams and everything, I swear it moved a foot. Then stuff started hitting the roof. Bricks, chunks of metal, and some stuff that didn't come through. Then there's this crazy man jumping out of the Bradley—Sain, I mean—and he's doing some kind of jig through all this smoking metal and screaming stuff like, 'Holy effing shit! A whole mothereffing city!' and 'Eff everything but the circus.' Stuff like that."

"So? And?" Tag said impatiently, scrolling the air with his hand.

Prentice gulped visibly and continued: "So, we all got

out, but Sain just keeps leaping around saying, 'I knew it. I effing knew it. As soon as I saw that dish, I knew the deal was wired,' and telling us what wild people we are. . . ."

"Motherfuckers," Giesla corrected.

"Right," Prentice said, blushing, "what wild motherfuckers we are, and how we really know how to party, and how would we like to just catch us a train and blow this ef . . . fucking joint?"

Tag's newfound affection for Prentice was reaching its limit. "Please," he said, "just give me the drill on this character. I don't need the whole course."

Holz came to Prentice's rescue.

"Max," the Jagd Kommando leader said, "perhaps I should finish. The man says he is Sergeant M. N. Sain. He has two crewmen with him—he calls them his keepers—one of them named Mad Dog, and the other Rabies. They never speak to anyone except Sain. When I asked him what unit they had been with, he told me to love angels, because they have great strength and only barely disdain from destroying us. They play old, loud music through their intercom, and I think they smoke hashish. But there is more."

"You mean that's just the *good* stuff?" Tag asked dryly.

"No." Holz shook his bruised head. "I mean he is a fighter, Max. Crazed, mystic, *ja*, but a genius, I think. A guerrilla savant."

"But also, maybe, a mental case?" Tag said.

"More than maybe, Max," said Giesla.

Tag saw the concern and displeasure in her eyes.

He turned to Holz and said, "Can he be worked with, Rick, or is he just a loose gun? I don't need some hophead maniac covering my six, none of us does."

"He is a berserker, Max," Holz said, "but he is on our side."

"Whatever he is," Prentice said, "he *did* get us out of there on a train and got us to this place."

"Okay," Tag said, "tell me the rest of it, so we can get back to the operations table. I don't suppose Sergeant M. N. Sain will be going amok right away."

"Well," said Prentice, "there was this train—engine, two flatcars, two boxcars, and a caboose—on the siding by the factory, next to the loading dock. So when Sain had settled down a little bit, he went out and looted the caboose and pushed it off the track with his Bradley. He showed us a fuel pump, and we found cans for some extra. Then we put the Bradleys on the flatcars and the commando cars and the troops in the boxcars and backed away from town. Mad Dog, the black keeper, drove. We hid in a tunnel most of that night, with Sain and his keepers buttoned up in their Bradley. At about oh-four-hundred, ignoring questions, orders, everything, Sain starts up the train again and runs it past two road crossings. When we finally do stop, it's at a rural station with a high platform, where we can drive right off the cars. Sain says we're wild . . . motherfuckers again and that we ought to come along and help fix up a place he knows and, zip, he's rolling. So far, so good; so, we follow him, and here we are."

"Thank you for your brevity, Lieutenant," Tag said. "Giesla." He nodded toward the situation table.

"Yes," she said, and took up her pointer again. "Now, Max, we have only scouted physically enough for local security, since we learned you were coming back. We have nothing hard beyond two or three kilometers of this place, except for the way we all came. Still, I think there is one possibility we should investigate first, if we want psychological effects. It is here"—she waved the pointer over a row of matchbook covers meant to represent houses—"among the gentry homes above the Donau, the Danube, you say."

"On the far side of the Jura," Tag mused aloud. "Away from where we stay. Okay." He looked at Giesla. "But why? What's there, besides nice houses."

"In this area," Giesla went on, sweeping a section of the situation table, "from here on to the front, there is nowhere else to set up a decent field hospital or a retreat for the officers, nothing else but barns and peasant houses. No, if they are true Russians, they will not ignore the wine cellars and the hot baths, or the carpets and the family silver."

"How long to get there?" Tag asked.

Holz shrugged and said, "Moving at night, over un-familiar terrain, with no secure roads, five or six hours, perhaps more."

"That's it, then," Tag said. "We leave at dark, find a staging position, and send in foot recon. If we find any-thing, we'll play it by ear from there. Any questions or problems?"

"No problems," Holz replied. "We are ready."

"Do you intend to take the whole unit, Max?" Lt. Prentice asked.

"We'll leave any walking wounded for security, but all the vehicles, yeah," Tag said.

"Then," Giesla said, "there is the question of Sergeant N. Sain."

"Oh, yeah," Tag said. "And it's about time I met him."

4

Tag stepped out of the cubicle and walked across the short arc of vehicles, followed by the other three officers, up to the closed and silent Bradley at the end of the line. He pounded on the driver's hatch.

"Anybody home?" Tag said loudly.

There was no reply.

"Max," Prentice said, "they're probably running that weird damn music of theirs through the intercom. I doubt if they can hear you."

Tag looked around, picked up a brick-size rock from the floor of the cavern, and tattooed the hatch for a full thirty seconds before he stopped and shouted, "Sergeant Sain, open up."

As Tag raised the rock again, the turret hatch crashed open, and an impassive black face, its cheeks and jaw rough with several days' growth of curly beard, rose along with a scarf of smoke out of the opening, like a subterranean creature from a German opera. As the man looked at them all and the smoke floated toward the dome of the cavern, Tag caught a whiff of something heavy and sweet. *Incense?*

"I'm Max Tag," he said to the obsidian face, instinctively dropping his rank. "This is my outfit, and I need to talk to Sergeant Sain. Think you can tell him that, Mad Dog?"

The man's eyes widened a notch before he disappeared back inside the turret.

At the rear of the Bradley, the troop ramp opened with a rumble, and a man leapt into view from behind the vehicle. Bushy-headed, unshaven, and wearing a rumpled jumpsuit with no insignia, he was a solidly built six-footer whose walk was an exaggeration of an athlete's bouncy, slightly pigeon-toed gait, and whose mismatched eyes wore a sheen of fanatical intensity.

"O Captain, my Captain," the man declaimed, snapping to attention and swaying from his ankles like a gyro. He dropped his salute before Tag could return it and beamed a grin of pure innocence.

"Sergeant *N*. Sain," the man said, "United States Army Reserve, Arm of the Apocalypse, Scourge of the Antichrist, Instrument of Destiny." He leaned closer to Tag and stage-whispered, "But don't tell my keepers; they think I'm only crazy and, therefore, a guitarist. Have you been approached by angels, Captain Tag?"

The question caught Tag off guard. "Not," he said, "in this life."

Sain's eyes goggled and he sucked air through his teeth. "Roll on, wheel of karma, roll on," he said in a bluesy growl, then continued in a distracted, speculative tone, "Yeah, you could be the one, the avatar of the warrior, the fucking archetype. And the vision has its becoming in the hills." He brought his attention back to Tag. "Did they tell you we did a whole motherfucking town, man?"

"They told me a lot of things, Sergeant," Tag said, "but I've still got more questions than answers."

Sain bugged his eyes again and said cryptically, "There is no greater knowledge than that of ignorance."

"Sergeant Sain . . ." Tag began.

"*N*. Sain," N. Sain said. "You must think of me that way or else be driven mad. Sudden enlightenment can be fatal to those used to living in the cave."

"Sergeant," Tag said, barely controlling his rising irritation, "we have a military mission here. You were not part of our plans, but we can use you, use your help. But before we do, I need to know who I'm working with. Let's sit down, just the two of us, and put my mind at ease. Okay?"

N. Sain grinned his angelic grin. "I will ever follow wisdom," he said. "Yeah, let's rap."

Tag turned to Prentice. "Chuck," he said, "have Weintaub or one of your men get my crew up to speed, while I, uh,

brief the sergeant here. And, Giesla, can you work up
something more detailed for our order of march and give me
an estimate on what we're likely to find at our objectives?"

"I will handle the operations work, Max," Holz said.

"Whatever," Tag said. "See you all later."

"Well," he said to N. Sain, "join me in a cup of coffee,
Sergeant?"

"A little small for two, isn't it?" N. Sain deadpanned,
then added, "Unless infinite angels can dance on the head
of a pin."

With N. Sain bounding at his side, Tag walked across the
cavern through the edges of shadow to the field kitchen near
where the No Slack Too was parked. The two men tapped
some coffee from the urn and pulled up a pair of ammo boxes
for seats, N. Sain all the while giving off an intermittent
stream of obscure pronouncements. It was, Tag thought, like
a gunfight in a tank turret, with every idea initiating a dozen
ricochets.

It took Tag an hour to learn what he could from N. Sain,
and little of it was reassuring. Disentangled from the cosmic
swirlings of N. Sain's patter, the facts included that N. Sain
was, in fact, a reservist, but not one on active duty. He,
Mad Dog, and Rabies had been a retro-rock band called
"Brutally Frank," until MD and Rabies had some vague
legal problems with what N. Sain called "sacraments." As
a result, the two sidemen took their given option to join
the Army. When they were both posted to Germany, N.
Sain arranged to travel there with a USO group, which
is how he happened to be swilling beer with them in
Nuremberg when the balloon went up. In the confusion
of withdrawing under Soviet artillery bombardment, N.
Sain and his keepers commandeered the Bradley and, in
the words of the deranged sergeant, "declared a separate
war, a whirlwind of retribution, a oneness with the purging,
purifying flame of destruction."

"N. Sain," Tag said, "you are really out there, okay? You
are really everything you believe. And I believe you, too.
But I need you to harness your winds of war, turn them into,
uh, winds of madness, madness for our enemies."

Tag paused to wonder where he was going with this, and

saw a strange light dawn in N. Sain's eyes, as he began to roll his head in ecstasy.

"N. Sain," Tag said, as though to discipline a dog, "don't you fuckin' zone-out on me. I want you to help us create a nightmare for Ivan, let him know there's no place he is safe, have him jumping at shadows."

"PsyOps," N. Sain said dreamily. "Fear-fucking PsyOps. O the clear blue flame of madness, pierce my night. My keepers mistake it for harmless fun, and they will join in."

Suddenly N. Sain leapt from the ammo crate, his eyes bright, animated, and focused on Tag.

"Yes. Yes," he said emphatically. "All-fucking-right. We have contact; we have a mission. Whom the gods would destroy, they first make mad. You are a fucking seer, Captain, a wild motherfucker."

"Final briefing at eighteen hundred hours," Tag said.

"Dress or casual?" N. Sain asked.

"Casual," Tag said, "you'd look terrible in a dress."

N. Sain whooped and bounded across the semidarkness of the cavern toward his Bradley.

By 1800, Tag had accomplished a lot. Working first from Giesla's recollections of rallies in the Jura and the Rhine Valley, and then from twenty-four-hour-old satellite photos, he confirmed the locations of a half-dozen large homes in the wooded slopes above the river, as well as signs of recent, heavy activity around them. There were heat signatures dotted thick as measles around two adjacent home sites on the LandSat image, and the pattern of tracks leading in and out was clear as a highway.

The location of the two manors offered Tag and his raiders the best possible approach across the mountains, through stands of old forest, where the No Slack Too and the Bradleys had ample room to navigate and fight. Tag noted for reference the four odd, faint heat images that the LandSat picture registered in the forest, knowing full well that they could be glitches, or they could be bogeys, the buddies of those antitank commandos they had smoked back at the hunting lodge. None of the random blips fell in their line of march, but it would be another twelve hours before he could get a fresh satellite fix on them. Meanwhile, the Allied contingent would move out in an extended wedge, with the No Slack Too trailing a Bradley full of infantry off each quarter flank, a gun vehicle on either flank extended, another at point, and the fourth as an advanced scout, roaming as far as a kilometer in front of the unit. Once the scout had done its recon, they would all assemble at one of three possible areas, each about a mile from the proposed targets, and send out foot reconnaissance. Based on whatever intelligence the patrol uncovered, Tag would fine-tune their plans from there.

A brief inspection of Prentice's "infantry" left Tag encouraged. Of the twenty-two remaining men, all young clerks and motor-pool drivers, eighteen were fit for duty, and all, as Giesla might say, were sharp-set. A week of world-war combat had tempered them, burned away their youth, leaving lean-cheeked soldiers with a sense of what it took to get the job done. Their gear was so strack that, Tag thought, had he been a day later, they would have been Brassoing their bullets. The cache of weapons and ammo that they had pilfered from the supply depot before scuttling it still provided plenty of firepower. The two nine-man squads, under Sergeant Dunn, the demo man, and Sergeant White, the highest-ranking noncom under Weintaub, were armed like human weapons platforms. Each squad carried two .223 squad machine guns, in addition to seven M16s, a dozen LAW antitank rockets, an M79 grenade launcher, plus assorted hand grenades, and two of the compact PRC-M radios. They had six shoulder-fired Stinger antiaircraft missiles and three M60 machine guns in reserve, along with claymores and plastic explosives, and if needed, they could also field a Dragon antitank unit.

But the Dragon, as well as the Jagd Kommandos' towed missile stands, would be left behind with the wounded for this foray. Speed and mobility were important, but fuel was critical, and they had no assurance that there would be any to scrounge—or any chance to—once they made their objective. Each Bradley would carry an extra fifty-gallon drum, leaving just one hundred fifty gallons stored in the abandoned mine, after all the vehicles had topped their tanks.

"Any questions?" Tag asked as he concluded his briefing. He looked around him at the semicircle of faces: his own crew at his left; Prentice, Giesla, and Holz to his right; the arc of intent soldiers fanned around the situation table; N. Sain and his stoic keepers—the Rastafarian-looking Mad Dog and the pallid, bleach-blond Rabies—standing at the back, staring at the table and humming a monosyllabic chant.

"I got one, Cap'n," Wheels Latta said. "How are we supposed to navigate through them woods at night?"

"The tracked vehicles will have to travel close enough together to all work off our IR floodlamp, if we need it, Wheels," Tag said. "The four-wheelers will just have to play touchie-feelie, I guess. We have a half moon, but it won't be rising until a little before our rendezvous time. I think Rick and his bunch can handle it."

"Roger that," Wheels said.

Thirty minutes before dark, they were in the forest above the mine excavation and moving toward the crest of the Jura, toward the valley of the Danube, into the shadow of death.

Strange to have to think of death on a night like this, Tag said to himself. Even without a moon, this far from the city lights and beneath a clear sky, the stars pierced the forest canopy with a watery light that gave definition to the shadows. They had cleared the second-growth timber and passed into the big trees by the time full darkness fell, and now Tag could, as he had secretly hoped, negotiate the forest by available light alone, whispering through the light undergrowth at fifteen kph. By comparison, the much lighter Bradleys sounded like moose rutting in a thicket, all grunting motors and the clatter of tracks. Still, Tag knew most of it was adrenaline-amplified in his own ears and that these big trees made excellent baffles, soaking up sound in their thick bark like cork.

The No Slack Too climbed steadily through the beech and larch and oak, pausing only for hourly radio checks, until they topped the broad crest of the Swabian Jura a half hour before moonrise and stopped. Tag ordered a take-ten and got out himself to stretch. The sky seemed even brighter now that he had his night vision, the air fine and brittle as crystal. He stepped behind a tree to urinate and could hear the plash and relieved sighs of the men from the flanking Bradleys as they did the same. Someone farted, and Tag heard a voice say softly, "Hang in there, Lieutenant; we'll get you out."

Tag smiled as he zipped his fly. It was good that the men were loose, that nothing weirder than expected had happened with N. Sain, and that their fuel was holding better than expected. But he knew that every meter closer they came to their objective, the greater the risk. He wanted to enjoy this moment, for it might be the last he could for a while.

As Tag was preparing to move his column out, a message burp came through from the scout vehicle, confirming a rendezvous site. Tag scanned his LandNav maps and plotted a route for Point Bravo, marked on his maps as a church and a cluster of buildings, probably abandoned, situated just off an unnumbered, unpaved road that ran parallel to the valley, high up on the steep slope.

The gradient increased as they approached the rendezvous, leveling only across the narrow piece of benchland where the roadbed had been laid and the scattering of dilapidated buildings stood. From his position inside the woods, Tag could see that they were not houses, though one had a broken steeple, and could have been the church. The others were long, low structures, like the feeding barns in Montana, where they used to fatten cattle for spring sale. Tag boosted himself out of his hatch, slid down the glacis of the No Slack Too, and walked ahead to Holz's vehicle. Jan, driving the scout car, pulled in at the same time and killed his engine.

"What'd you find, Jan?" Tag asked.

"Is good," Jan replied. "Abandoned a long time, I think. Rotten roofs and floors."

"Tracks?" Holz asked.

"*Ja,*" Jan said. "Old tracks on the road, some footprints. Four or five days old."

"Okay," Tag said, "it doesn't look like this place is patrolled, anyway. Let's get a scrounging party organized, but I don't want the place looking like anybody's been there. We'll stay in the trees until we're ready to move out. Meanwhile, I'm gonna need three men to go with me and recon the objective."

"No," Holz said sharply. "I am sorry, Max, but no; you cannot do that. You are not some Sergeant N. Sain, not like before. You are in command now, Max. You don't have to do everything, you cannot. As a friend, I am telling you that this is not the decision of a wise commander, for you to go."

"I want one of our officers there," Tag said. "You've still got a mouse the size of Rhode Island on your skull, and Prentice can hardly scratch his own ass. So who's left?"

"I believe that leaves me," said Giesla from the driver's seat.

Tag glared at her, but she would not turn and catch his eye.

"She is right," Holz said. "Giesla is our intelligence officer, Max. She is the logical choice."

Tag took the better of his alternatives. "You're right," he said. "But I do want one of my men on the patrol, and take one of Prentice's squad leaders, and anybody else you want."

"Jan, I think, would like a walk—*ja*, Jan?" Giesla said.

Jan pulled a face of mock despair. "You are too kind, Lieutenant Ruther," he said.

"Max," Giesla said neutrally, "who from your crew?"

"Take your pick," Tag said. "They'll all do."

"Sergeant Jefferson, then."

"Fine," Tag said, disturbed by the notion that Giesla's choosing Ham was somehow linked to her getting over the ambush on the Pan-African Rally, when she was raped and her husband killed by Communist terrorists, black Africans led by Soviet advisers. He had to put it aside, however; this was no time for second-guessing each other.

Giesla told Jan to see Lt. Prentice for a man and to have their weapons ready, then she turned back to Tag.

"Max," she said coolly, once Jan was out of earshot, "a good commander knows how to use his best men. In chess, the queen can rampage the board, and she is called a 'man.' Like her, in battle I am a man."

"I would end this conversation right now," Tag said, "if it weren't for the fact that you're right. Enough?"

Giesla had a proud, happy look in her eyes as she said, "Yes, enough. Is there anything particular that you hope we might find down there?"

"The only exclusive we have is on tactical nukes," Tag replied. "Right now, we don't have any reason to think they're here, but keep your eyes peeled."

Giesla stepped out of the gun buggy. "I will have my men ready," she said, "in ten minutes."

In less than that, she had Ham, Jan, and Sergeant White from Prentice's platoon assembled around Holz's vehicle. They had taped the arms and legs of their loose jumpsuits and streaked their faces and hands with camouflage paint. Jan had armed them with the silenced, wire-stocked Walther submachine guns that Sergeant Betcher called his pets, and Giesla saw to it that each one also carried a knife and a garrote, no sidearms and no radio.

Giesla turned from the acetate-covered map she was studying beneath her red-filtered flashlight and faced Tag as he approached.

"Ready?" he asked.

"Yes, ready." She folded the map and slid it in the pocket beneath the dash of the gun buggy.

"We're putting out security," Tag said. "When you come in, the challenge will be 'candy,' and your response 'man.' Okay?"

Giesla almost smiled at him. "Yes," she said. "Man. Anything else."

"Yeah," Tag said, "please take care of my gunner." He turned toward Ham. "Don't you let her lead you into bad habits, Jefferson."

"Not a chance, bossman," Ham said. "I'll never change my sweet, lovable disposition." He jacked a round into the chamber of his Walther and threw the sling across his neck. "You rear-area wusses just have you a nice little nap while I'm gone."

Tag watched the four figures move out at Giesla's command, cross the road in the light of the rising moon, and disappear into the woods on the other side. There was nothing to do now but wait. Fruits Tutti had the cover off the Phalanx's closed-loop radar aiming system, memorizing the wiring, so he took first watch. Tag surprised himself by falling easily into a deep sleep on the warm rear deck of the No Slack Too.

He awoke to Wheels shaking him and realized at once that the sky was paling, the night nearly over.

"Cap'n," his driver was saying, "patrol's coming in, and it's your watch, anyhow. Want something like coffee?"

Tag sat up, unwrapped his sleeping bag, and took the canteen cup of bitter instant coffee that Wheels held out for him.

"What time's it?" Tag mumbled, still heavy with sleep and irritated by it.

"'Bout oh-five-thirty, Cap'n," Wheels said.

Tag drank, made a face, and drank some more. He looked at his watch. "Damn," he said. "They haven't been gone four hours, more like three and a half." He handed the cup back, stretched, and rubbed his face with the palms of his hands. "Well, hell," he said, rotating his head and listening to the stiffness pop out of his neck, "let's go see what the skinny is."

Tag found Holz awake, and together they met the patrol as it came into the woods. Tag could see that they were tired and muddy, but that was the worst. He turned to his driver.

"Wheels," he said, "round up some of that something like coffee for these people, will you."

"A done deal," Wheels said, and went back toward the tank.

Giesla and the others trudged up the slope to where Tag and Holz waited beside two of the gun buggies. As they drew nearer, Tag could see their faces were not grim, only impassive with fatigue. Again, he cautioned himself about second-guessing.

"Candy," Tag said lightly.

"Ass," Ham Jefferson snapped as he flopped to the ground and arched his back against the tire of the gun buggy. "Don't you ever let anybody tell you you can't go patrollin', Captain Max."

Giesla let out a short laugh and knelt on both knees beside

Ham. She kissed him on his paint-smeared cheek.

"Max," she said, "this man, he is a wonder. Look what he got for us."

She reached into the cargo pocket on the leg of her jumpsuit and took out a slim octavo volume bound in plain leather.

"This," she said, "is a code key—not the codes themselves, but the key to which codes will be used when. But there is more. In the back, on the flyleaf pages, there are notes on unit dispositions and resupply."

"Whose notes?" Tag asked at once.

"Oh, a certain supply colonel's," said Giesla coyly.

"A certain supply colonel who was so lovin' drunk," Ham added, "that he couldn't tell a goose from a gander."

"What the hell are you two talking about?" Tag said irritably.

"I fleeced him, boss," Ham said contritely. "I had to. He came stumbling drunk out in the woods to pee and fell right over me. He'd never have come where I was sober. And I mean, I had my blade in the mofo's uniform before I realized *he was feeling me up*. Yes he was. So I patted him down—that's when I lifted the book—and then started slapping him off and saying, '*Nyet, nyet*.'" Ham rubbed his back against the tire. "Worked too," he added.

"Yeah?" Tag said. "And what about when he wakes up this morning?"

"No worry, Max," Giesla said. "I saw the man; he was Russian drunk. He will be a blank. There are much more important things we have found."

Tag shrugged. "Okay," he said, "Wheels is getting some coffee. Let's get Prentice over here and get the show on the road."

Wheels came back with the coffee and Prentice, and everyone gathered around Giesla, who stood hunched over the gun buggy's possibles box, diagramming their objective with a grease pencil on a sheet of acetate.

"After Sergeant Jefferson's brief romance," she said as she drew, "we thought it best to leave quickly, but we had plenty of time to discover what we needed. These two houses and their grounds must have been a family compound. They are the only two in this part of the valley so close together, perhaps one hundred meters, with garden and orchard in between. They share this common drive down the valley to the highway. These are guest houses or servants quarters, these stables or garages, and here two rock barns. No walls or fences. The lower slope is steep and terraced for orchards. They have razor wire out, but their security is light, and we found no mines or listening devices, but there is no question that the compound is some sort of command center. We probably saw a half-dozen colonels, besides the one who wanted Sergeant Jefferson to be his friend. There are guards on the barns, and machine guns in the lofts. We counted two BMPs in antitank configuration, six BTR-70s, and three older models mounted with missile stands. The BMPs were in fighting positions looking out on the valley; I think the others were just visiting. Not counting the crews for the vehicles, there are probably no more than two hundred men securing the position."

"Whew," Tag whistled. "What is Ivan thinking about?"

"Not much, it seems to me," Prentice said. "He's twenty klicks behind the lines and thinks he's safe."

"That we can end," Holz said.

"Oh, yes," Tag said. "And we will.

"Giesla, I'll want the details, of course, and I'll need you to translate the notes in the code book, but first all of you need to eat and get some rack. We're not going anywhere before dark."

"I know an order when I hear one," Ham said, pushing himself away from the car.

The others from the patrol nodded their weary agreement and began drifting off. Tag turned to Holz.

"Rick," he said, "let's scatter these vehicles and have every one of them under a cammo net or some sort of concealment. Once we're done with that, there's to be absolutely minimum movement. No fires, no grabass, no sing-alongs."

"I'll pass it along to my people," Prentice said.

"Don't bother about the men in Sain's track," Tag told him. "I need to see N. Sain anyway; I'll tell 'em."

Tag mixed some cocoa powder with the bitter coffee in

his cup and walked through the long morning shadows of the trees to where N. Sain's battle-scarred Bradley was parked. The infantry onboard the Bradley had flaked out in the leaves and were just now, with the return of White, the squad leader, rousing themselves for breakfast and duty at the listening posts. The Bradley was silent and shut.

Tag had a word with White about the standing orders for the day, then walked to the rear of the Bradley and rapped on the closed troop ramp.

"Lazarus, come forth," he called.

Tag heard movement inside the fighting vehicle. A one-note drone hummed in the bowels of the armor for a full minute before the troop ramp clanked down and a tousled N. Sain padded out, his face still slack with sleep. Behind him, in the troop compartment, MD and Rabies sat cross-legged on the floor, their eyes shut and their faces raised.

"Captain Maximilian," N. Sain said cheerfully. "Have you brought raw meat for my keepers?"

"Better," Tag said, "I've brought you the promise of fresh Russian bear meat. Tonight, weird one. You want some coffee before we talk?"

"Pollution!" N. Sain exclaimed. "We'll fast on water till we fight, gain the keen edge that will fear-fuck their hearts. We are thunder, the voice of the god-king of destruction."

"Yes, you are," Tag agreed blandly. "Now, listen: get your vehicle concealed, and no unnecessary movement during daylight. We're going to cut a fat hog tonight, and I'll call a briefing sometime after noon to fill you in on details, as soon as the intelligence report is complete. Sergeant White was on the patrol, so you may want him to give you some scoop."

N. Sain was beginning to fidget, shifting his weight from foot to foot, his eyes flickering like dark mica.

"No," he said, drawing out the word. "We'll meditate on Iron Butterfly." He brushed the leaves away with his boot. "Draw me a picture of it here," N. Sain said. "By night, we will own the place, its image possessed by my soul."

Tag hunkered, took up a twig, and drew a picture in the dirt of the layout Giesla had described.

Tag finished and looked at N. Sain. "Does that give you enough to ponder?" he asked.

"Sad symmetry for the Great Satan," N. Sain said. "Two houses, two barns, two of everything, and two by two they go to their doom. Wheels within wheels, Juggernaut."

"Uh-huh," Tag said, rising. "You do that."

5

Tag found a cool, leafy niche in a thicket of saplings and vines near the No Slack Too and spread his poncho on the spongy ground beneath them, settling in with the logbook from the XM-F4 and the map sheets for their current area of operations, hoping that the mind-numbing routine of record keeping would help him pass the idle morning, now that the strategy for taking the manor houses was fixed in his mind. He found it hard to concentrate, however, and after several futile efforts to organize his thoughts into the telegraphic prose of an action report, he was more relieved than not when Chuck Prentice, slipping through the shadows of the trees, made his way to Tag's nest and dropped to hunker beside him.

"How's it going, Max?" the young lieutenant said.

Tag folded the maps and shut them between the pages of the logbook. "Well," he said, "this is the hard part, Chuck, the waiting."

"Yeah," Prentice replied, "I think I know exactly what you mean." He twisted a green twig off one of the saplings and clamped it between his molars. "I keep getting this damn silly grin on my face, and I don't even know it until my jaws start to ache. My mind is racing a thousand miles an hour, but I'm not thinking about anything, kinda like my clutch isn't engaged."

Prentice grinned, bobbing the twig.

Tag rearranged himself, stretching on the poncho. "Don't worry," he said, "it'll kick in when it's time. It's not like this is your first action, Chuck. You're a good soldier—you've shown that plenty of times already—and good soldiers all get scared, but they don't lose their nerve. Hell, ping-pong players get butterflies."

Prentice rotated the shoulder of his taped left arm, tongued the twig to the other side of his mouth, then realized he was grinning again and spat the stem on the ground.

"Yeah, I know, Max," he said, "but this is different. I mean, up till now we've been on the defensive, running when we could and only fighting when we had to. There was always something to do with the adrenaline. It seems like I'm getting the jitters *because* I know what we're going to do. All of a sudden, I'm wondering about my men, about how they'll fight if I'm this jumpy. You ever feel that way?"

Tag thought a moment and decided it would do them both good.

"Get comfortable," he said, flipping out the skirt of his poncho for Prentice to sit on, "and I'll tell you about it."

Prentice pulled the poncho under him and leaned back against a thick net of vines, half facing Tag, who stared at the toes of his boots and said:

"When I got to Honduras, my only combat had been in Oman, and that had been a lot like what we've already been through here. We were caught up in a situation that didn't leave us many options or much time to think about them. And the same thing happened again when the Pan American Marxists first hit us at the beginning of Golden Spike."

"The Pan Americans," said Prentice, "that was the combined Central American Communist Army, right?"

"Right," Tag replied. "Mostly the secret Nicaraguan divisions, but also plenty of Salvadorans, from the Stalinist faction of the Marti Liberation Front, some Indian irregulars, even a couple of Panamanian brigades, and the Cuban advisers, of course. They hit us hard, too. It took twenty-two days before we could organize a counterattack across the entire front. The three days we spent planning were the worst for me. I kept trying to hold the entire scenario in my mind, picture how every piece would fall into place, instead of focusing on what I had to do, what my role would be. I was fritzy as a goddamn road lizard. And like you, I'd been fighting with my crew for those three weeks, but I didn't feel like they really knew me, wasn't sure how they would react if I went strange on them."

"You! You never thought about going strange, Max."

Tag allowed himself a thin smile. "I thought about everything, Chuck," he said. "I thought about every way I could fuck up and every way I could get fucked up." He paused a moment, then asked, "Do you trust your men?"

"Like the U.S. Mint," Prentice said.

"Good. You won't let them down, if you really trust them. When we moved into position for our first set-piece battle of the counterattack, I was probably in worse shape than you think you are now, uncertain about everything. The Pan Ams had driven across from Nicaragua to El Salvador, cut off the Pacific ports, so they had moved us down from the hills to attack at a place called Pespire Something-or-other, right in the center of the Pan Am line.

"Our infantry was seventy percent Honduran and a hundred percent shaky. Even one of our U.S. battalions was a National Guard unit from Ohio. They had been there from the start, and I'd go back to war with them anytime, but they were still Guardsmen and not exactly what you'd call strack. On the other hand, we were armor-heavy, twenty-four Sheridans and forty Bradleys. I had already been kicked upstairs by the brass and given my railroad tracks, so I had twelve of the tanks under me and was assigned to lead the center. We bivouacked the night before the assault at a coffee plantation up in the high country, and if I slept, it was only because my nightmares weren't as bad as my imagination was when I was awake.

"The jets came in before dawn, while we were still miles away, and you could see this seam of fire open up all along the front, thousands and thousands of acres of corn in flame. So when we rolled down the mountains and came out of the banana groves at first light, fanning out in the fields with the sun at our back, the land breeze was still pulling the smoke back over the Pan Am positions. Couldn't see shit. For a minute, I locked up. I just couldn't think what to do with this new wrinkle.

"I remember Wheels Latta asking me if I wanted to slow or stop the assault, and I damn near said yes. Hell, I'd have said yes to almost anything that would move me off dead zero. Just a decision, any decision, sounded good.

"That was when I realized that Wheels wasn't suggesting; he was asking. I realized that they trusted me as much as I did them. They were soldiers, and damn good ones, and they were going to do anything I told them. But I did have to tell them something.

"Then it just all fell into place. All of a sudden, all the chatter in my head shut up, and I knew—just *knew*, without thinking about it—what to do. All the Pan Am dispositions that I'd memorized and everything my instincts told me to expect from the air strikes fell together. Time slowed down, and I was giving orders to the vanguard flanks. The infantry fell in behind us, and we were on the Pan Ams before they knew it, took fifteen or eighteen hundred prisoners, and only lost one Sheridan to enemy fire and two Bradleys that ran into each other in the smoke."

"I remember that," Prentice said. "We studied the problem in Basic School. And you were the guy on point, huh?"

"Guilty," Tag replied.

"Max," Prentice said, breaking the brief silence, "as long as I have you talking, there's something else I'm curious about."

"What's that?"

"Well, it's your crew. I mean, I don't really know them, but if I hadn't fought with them, I'd take them for the biggest bunch of spare parts I've ever seen. And you've all been together since Honduras, right?"

"Oh, yeah," Tag said, "and there's a book to be written about every one of them. Sometimes I call them my idiot savants. They are each and every one fuckups and shitbirds and some kind of goddamn genius. But they take soldiering seriously, and they're damn good at it."

"You don't seem to have any trouble with them."

"Didn't start that way, though," Tag said. "I was TDY from Hood when I went down for Golden Spike, supposed to be advising and observing with the HQ group. But there was a bad round of dysentery and a little outbreak of the carnal flu among some of the American units, so I volunteered to take a tank and got assigned with those three. God, they were slack-assed finger poppers. See, their deal was to coopt me, make me their buddy, figuring that if they did, then they could just keep sliding on along."

"So, what did you do?"

"Oh, I went along with them at first, for about twenty-four hours, then I pulled a detail on the Sheridan. It took 'em three times to get it right, about fifteen hours of work, scrubbing treads with a barrack's brush, the whole ball of wax."

Prentice grunted a laugh. "And I guess you're going to tell me that they loved you for it?"

"Um, better than that: it pissed them off. The next day, we took out five Honduran crews for a maneuvers-and-gunnery exercise, and my guys were primed. The tank range there had been bulldozed out of the jungle just a few weeks before, and it was a mess—mud, stumps, ditches, you name it. So, the first thing I do is have Wheels demonstrate the evasive-attack series. Lord, what a decision that was. I didn't know then that you can't ever tell what that hillbilly is thinking. He smiles that big ol' freckled smile, and you think he's all eager to please, when what he's really thinking is how he's going to fuck with you.

"Well, we hit the range, and my man Wheels was in rare form. The Sheridan's no hot rod, but he made it cut some chogies that raised my pucker factor to about nine-point greased toothpick. I swear to this day that he can put a Sheridan up on one tread and turn it at the same time.

"But you should have seen those Hondurans when they thought they were supposed to do it. There were goddamn Sheridans spilled all over the course, looked like a dirt-track destruction derby. We had a tank retriever out there all morning and a range officer all afternoon. But I didn't give a fuck, because I knew I had a driver. And I told him so, and that helped break the ice. Never chewed him out, just said, 'Okay, now let's show 'em something they can do.' It was the next day before we got around to gunnery and I saw what Mr. Jefferson could do."

"You know," said Prentice, "I can't help thinking that he looks familiar."

"You a fight fan?"

"Yeah, I watch a little."

"You remember 'Hand Grenade' Jefferson, middle-weight, about four years back?"

"Oh, hell," said Prentice in amazement. "Are you sure? I mean, jeez. . . . You're right, aren't you? What happened to him? I saw him once on the sports channel, I remember, against the ex-European champ, that Italian. Jeez, he was a buzz saw. Stopped the guy on cuts."

"That's the one," said Tag. "He had a hard enough bark that once he saw how really dirty the fight game can be, he got out. Some promoter who thought he owned Ham tried to get him to take a dive, threatened his family, all that. You really got to like Jefferson: he took the money and disappeared. He's quick as a snake, Chuck, hands and head. Best gunner I've ever seen, and maybe the best all-around tanker.

"Anyway, we went out on the gunnery range the next day, and most of the morning was pretty slow, showing the Hondurans how to use the Sheridan one-oh-fives for indirect fire, because in the conventional strategy for tanks down there, they were going to be used more like super-mobile artillery than like armor. But that afternoon, when we moved over to the assault-firing course, things got really interesting.

"This course, Chuck, was modeled on one we had come up with at Hood. There were six possible fighting positions facing six possible enemy tank positions across open, rolling country, about three or four hundred meters away. Behind two of the six enemy positions were full-front silhouettes of T-seventy-twos that moved on tracks between the positions. Each of them was equipped with a remote-control radar/laser setup to fire at the real tanks, kind of like a shooting gallery, except the targets shoot back.

"Each tank draws three fighting positions at random and is given six 'duster' rounds—you know, the plastic practice rounds filled with talc. The object is to maneuver into each of the three fighting positions, fire at least one round, and ultimately knock out both targets as they move between their positions, without getting tagged by their lasers. What makes it really hard is the dusters. They only use a pinch of powder, so you have to shoot a trajectory like a rainbow to carry three hundred meters.

"For the demonstration, the targets are already moving and firing as you bring your tank up to the fighting positions, and Ham called a mark on his first target before I had it in my scope. 'Shoot,' I say, and he powders it. Then, the turret's moving, and Tutti is working the breech, and that damn Jefferson marks the second one before I can see it, too. So, I think, 'Okay, wise ass,' because I know that the number two is programmed to juke to a new pattern if the number one is hit. 'Shoot,' I tell him. 'Check fire,' he says, just as I see the target duck back behind its cover. He asks for gunner's choice, and I say, 'Okay.' Then, here comes the target, coming back our way. It's supposed to move, on this particular stunt, too fast to be hit by a duster, and to reverse its course about two thirds of the way across. Guess I should have told Jefferson. He popped the sonofabitch just as it was making its move, damnedest shot I've ever seen.

"I was speechless, and he says, 'Want I should show 'em something they can do now?'

"Well, I still didn't have a crew, but, Lord, what makings. None of it really came together, though, until that first battle, and even after that it was a while before we all really knew each other, how we'd react when things got tight."

"What told you?" Prentice asked. "I mean, how did you know when you knew?"

Tag barked a short laugh at the lieutenant's syntax. "Different things, different ways, different times," he said. Tag picked up the logbook and maps, weighed them in his hand, and tossed them by his feet. "What the hell," he said. "You want stories? I'll tell you a couple of doozies.

"Let's start with Tutti. Now he is really one for the books, and I tell you, Chuck, it took me longer to dope him out than the others. I mean, he talks like one of the Bowery Boys and has a goddamn genius for always looking like he's slept in his uniform, but his brain is wired up like a Cray mainframe—you don't ever want to play poker, or especially blackjack, with him. He's a whiner and a bitcher, too, and it takes a while to realize that it's just habit with him. The way some guys whistle while they work, Tutti bitches. Between that and whatever language it is he speaks, a lot of people think he's some sort of congenital idiot or maybe a cook. And at first I didn't count on him to be anything but a good loader, just a warm body doing his job. Well, Chuck, his stock went way up with me the second night of Golden Spike.

"The Pan Ams had hit the day before, and my bunch and five Honduran crews, along with one of our officers from HQ, had been ordered to take up positions in a god-awful piece of jungle, absolutely the worst place for armor you can imagine, but we were short of ground troops in our sector and couldn't shift any, because the assault was on a half-dozen fronts and had all our units tied up. So, there we were. We had about a hundred meters of slash-and-burn fields in front of us and jungle everywhere else. Right at dusk, while we were all outside the tank, fixing chow and setting the watch, they hit us, all of us, all up and down the line, and from every side.

"We had two very thin companies of Honduran infantry with us, not even enough to really slow down the Pan Ams, but one platoon there near us had the sense to form a defensive line and try to fall back around us, but they were getting cut to pieces. And as for us getting back in the Sheridan and getting it in the fight—forget it. Our position was nothing except the first place we found with any sort of field of fire—no cover, no concealment. They had thrown a couple of RPGs at us, but they didn't need 'em to keep us out of action. They must have had a half-dozen shooters assigned to keep us out of the hatches. They were raking the decks of the Sheridan like it was drill, rounds everywhere. If they could do that for thirty minutes, just until dark, we were dog meat. They'd be all over us in the dark. We had our CAR-15s and a few strays from the infantry with us. The one platoon still hanging together was slowing them up on the front and right flank, but the rest of us were just slinging lead at the jungle to keep 'em honest. And that was when I noticed that Tutti was missing.

"I had moved my crew and the stray Hondurans to the left flank and rear and kept repositioning them so the Pan Ams couldn't get a fix on our positions or numbers. But when I came back around to Tutti's position, he wasn't there. The Honduran I'd left with him didn't speak any English—and he was an Indian, so his Spanish wasn't too good—but he kept pointing into the bush and making sounds like a grenade launcher—'broop, broop,' he said.

"Well, I didn't have time to try to sort it all out, because the Honduran boy and I were taking fire by then, and it was coming from real close, out of three directions, and then just two, and then it quit. I started moving to the next position, where Ham Jefferson was, when I heard the M-79 start coughing out in the jungle. Tutti must have put up ten rounds inside of a minute, and after that minute, we weren't pinned down anymore. We got inside the tank, Tutti got back, and we started breaking them down, freed up our other crews, and laid down cover for the infantry, and pulled a perimeter around some huts outside the trees. And that's all that got us through the night.

"What that bellyaching, ballsy little goon had done was low crawl right past the Pan Am line, dope out their positions, pick himself two or three places to fight from, where he could cover all their asses, then start running and shooting. He took out three with that ridiculous damn Luger of his before he even started with the blooper. They didn't know he was there, didn't know what was hitting them or from where. The Hondurans with us stiffened up and bought us time to get the Sheridan going, and that turned it around."

"What did you say to him?" Prentice asked.

"Oh, I asked him what the hell he thought he was doing, and he says, 'No muthafucker is gonna make me walk when dere's a pewfectly good Sher'din sittin' dere.' And, you know, at the time, I thought he meant it."

Prentice laughed softly, nervously. "Yeah, yeah," he said, as though he understood. "If you could figure out what he meant to say." The lieutenant was quiet for a moment before he went on, "And it's true that he's some kind of computer whiz?"

"Oh, hell yes," Tag said. "Computers, lasers, radar—anything electronic. Truth be told, he probably had as much to do with the XM-series electronic systems as any of the engineers or Ph.D. physicists, especially the software. He wrote this one program he called The Beast With Two Brains that really boggled the brass. What he did was design a 'brain' that integrated all the onboard programs for all the systems. But it also created complete backup programs within each of the systems. So, if you had even one system still up and enough memory somewhere, you could restore all the systems from it. It was some kind of bubble-chip voodoo, and it just blew their socks off. Nobody had any idea you could do it."

"And you've got that now?" Prentice said.

"Yeah. It's what allows me or the gunner to orient the tube from any one of our sights—or any combination of them—in an instant. The autolock will track off radar, laser, audio, or all of them at once. He's also the one who designed the VLD."

"The what?"

"The Very Large Display. We don't use it much, because we have to be stationary and not in any big hurry. It's a high-res liquid-crystal screen about two feet square and a half-inch thick that can display anything off any system, but it's best for satellite imaging, especially if you have overlays from different birds at different angles. Then, the brain compensates for the angles and gives you any shot you want on the VLD. Contour map, cross-section, even three-D."

"So, what's he doing a spec four?"

"That's a different sort of story," Tag replied, "but I'll give you one example and let you figure it out.

"First, you have to understand that Tutti may be a virgin—no, I mean it—*may* be. I don't know what it is, but he puts women on such a pedestal that I think hookers even scare him. So, he does have this little thing for pornography."

Prentice looked startled, but Tag ignored it and went on:

"Well, back at Hood we had this one real dickhead of a light colonel named Kincaid. Kincaid was the quintessential staff-hole officer: he'd had his eye on the Pentagon ever since he got his gold oak leaves. He was main toady to the R&D director and called a very close game on budgets and the like. Our own project officer, Colonel Menefee— that's *full* colonel—was—hell, is—a stickler himself, a sawed-off overmuscled button-counter, but his bark is a lot worse than his bite. We did it all by the book, his book, and listened to him crow, and he got us any fucking thing we needed for the XM project. Not a bad deal.

"Anyway, one of the civilian engineers working with us last summer was a woman named Lawson, Miss Lawson, and she was a show-stopper—about five-nine and slinky as a mink—but all business on the job. She never flirted or tried to come off sexy, but there wasn't a man among us who didn't have his tongue out over her, and that definitely included Kincaid and our own Satin Ass Menefee, not to mention Tutti, who locked up like a recruit every time she asked him something.

"It all started one day when we were testing the seventy-five millimeter in the F3 prototype turret. It was mounted on a skeleton in the shape of an XM-series tank that could record shock patterns from rapid-fire recoil. It was a new gizmo that Miss Lawson and her team had come up with, one the Army had put quite a few bucks into, so Kincaid was there for the demonstration, along with our project officers and the engineers.

"The skeleton was fitted out inside with seats and mock consoles for the commander and driver, as well as operable stations for the gunner and loader in the turret. So, Latta and I are sitting there in the open air while Miss Lawson is giving the Cook's tour to Kincaid and Menefee. They stop just behind my left shoulder, and Miss Lawson opens a big ring binder she's been carrying, to show the colonels some examples of what the machine is supposed to do. I lean back and can see them in the corner of my eye.

"First, Kincaid says, 'Here, let me help you with that, Miss Lawson,' and he all but takes it away from her, holding it between them like they were sharing a hymn book. I can see that Miss Lawson is a little put off by this, but Menefee is fit to croak. Even in his double-soled jump boots, Satin Ass doesn't stand five-five, and Kincaid has just squeezed him out like a kid brother—*Lieutenant*-Colonel Kincaid.

"But before Menefee can unpuff and say something, Kincaid turns and looks over his shoulder at him and says, 'Oh, here, Colonel,' and takes the binder from Miss Lawson and kneels, actually kneels down beside Menefee, holding the book open for him.

"Miss Lawson can hardly believe this. I mean, she saw what was happening, too, and I think she must have blushed.

Menefee damn sure turned red. But he got a grip on himself and managed to say, 'You can show it to me later, Kin,' which did get him a 'yessir' from Kincaid, but our man had to quit the field.

"When Wheels and I told Fruits and Ham about it, their first reaction was, naturally, that it was no better than Menefee deserved. He's not the kind of officer to inspire a lot of love. But that wasn't the end of it.

"We were several days, maybe two weeks, testing the turret on the frame, and every day Kincaid would be there, and every day he'd find some way to one-up Menefee in front of Miss Lawson. Everyone saw it, but all Tutti saw, I think, was how it affected the woman. She knew it was all, somehow, for her, that she was the object of a silent competition between Menefee and Kincaid, and she didn't like it. But Miss Lawson was young. Outside the practical matters of metal fatigue and frame ergonomics, she was just crippled with shy. When it comes to women, Tutti really is sensitive, and by the end of two or three days he had worked up a real hardon for Kincaid. And about the fourth or fifth day, I started to worry what he was thinking, because all of a sudden he quit bitching about Kincaid and quit hanging around the barracks and the base hobby shop at night, started putting on civvies and going into town.

"I hadn't known Fruits to go to town for anything except computer chips more than once a month, but he's a street-wise kid, and it didn't take him long to find the underbelly of even a Baptist bastion like Waco, Texas. On the Monday after he'd spent a full weekend off base, in the middle of testing the autoloader on the seventy-five, he says out of nowhere, 'You know, dat Colonel Kincaid is runnin' whoors in Waco.'

"After we got through Latta's going on about how to pronounce *whores* and Jefferson's thinking Fruits meant that Kincaid was a pimp, what we found out was that the good colonel had a standing date every two weeks with two professional ladies at a notorious hot-sheet motel west of Waco. I don't think any of us quite got the point, though, until Fruits said, 'An dere he is last night, comin' outta the officers' club with Miss Lawson. Just makes you sick.'

"This man was working himself into a fit of dangerously righteous indignation—the most dangerous state a man can be in, next to fear.

"Truth be told, by this time we had all had about enough of Colonel Kincaid. Hell, I was even feeling sorry for Menefee. It had just gone on too damn long, and Kincaid was liking it too much—gaffing Satin Ass about his size and acting like Miss Lawson belonged to him. But it took everybody by surprise when Tutti told us how he was going to snuff Kincaid.

"I don't mean kill him; Tutti is nastier than that. No, he was going to obliterate him as a man and as a soldier. We liked that, all right, and all we had to do was cough up five hundred dollars apiece. Fruits said he would match it out of his own pocket, but there were people that had to be paid—girls, a pimp, a motel manager—and could I get him just a few small items from the night-vision R&D people, only one or two of which were top secret? I mean, he had it wired, and he wanted it so much, we said, sure, why not? Things can get pretty dull in central Texas in the summer, and I think by then we really were a crew, and helping Tutti was just a part of that—that and a chance to blister a real asshole.

"Well, I got the hardware Fruits said he needed, and he greased whatever palms needed to be greased with our money, and here's what he did. In the motel room where Kincaid went to play, Fruits rigged a micro-aperture video camera and infrared miniflood in the ceiling molding and recorded an evening of the colonel's pastime. But he wouldn't tell us what he intended to do with the tape, said he had to edit it first. So we waited for the other shoe to drop, and waited so long it finally took us by surprise.

"When we got the turret back on the chassis, things got busier, more field evaluations, bivouacs, night testing. It was the final phase of that step of the development, and we had a little catching up to do before the final phase evaluation, a semiformal event conducted by Kincaid at the end of every cycle. Mostly it was for the brass and the civilians on the project, but we were invited—the crew and me—as well, since we were the only ones actually driving and shooting the XM-F3.

"The briefing room Kincaid used for these occasions was half video theater and half stage: three semicircular tiers of seats, about fifty altogether, around an equally large stage. Each seat had a TV monitor, and behind the podium was a rear-projection television almost as large as a shopping-mall movie screen. Kincaid's habit was to speak while whatever stills or videos he was using ran on the screens. Part of his show was that he never looked at a monitor himself, just delivered a smooth, rehearsed patter, then let the program officers try to follow his act. With him on the stage were Menefee and Miss Lawson. We, as usual, were back in the shadows of the top tier.

"Kincaid does a short spiel leading into his soliloquy, introduces Miss Lawson and Menefee, then looks out at us and presses the gadget to start the tape. At the same time I see Fruits monkeying with something in his sock. There's some snow on the monitors, then—*pow!*—there it is, Kincaid in the throes of lust, on every goddamn monitor *and* the screen behind him. Even Menefee and Miss Lawson don't see it, and Kincaid doesn't have a clue. He's completely wrapped up in some sort of joke he's trying to come in with, saying, 'As I have frequently thought . . .' and up on the screen, looking crazy in the red IR images, we see Kincaid about to be buggered by this woman with a dildo the size of a salami. And that's when the sound from the tape cut in, and we all heard Kincaid's voice in falsetto: 'Jasmine! Jasmine! I'll be your wife.'

"Well, the place just came apart. People were jumping up, cussing, screaming at Kincaid to shut off the tape. But all he could do was stand there half twisted around at the big screen behind him, watching, making Os with his mouth, and mashing the button on his remote control over and over. Menefee grabbed Miss Lawson and got her off the stage, and people from the front row poured onto the stage and started ripping at the cables on the VCR beneath the lectern. But the tape just kept rolling, the frame tightening to a close-up of Kincaid in ecstasy, bound and buggered.

"I finally cleared my throat and got Tutti's attention. He scratched his ankle, and the tape quit, and the briefing was canceled for that day. I don't think anyone ever saw Kincaid again, unless they looked at the tape in the backup VCR that had been patched into the briefing room's video system. And Tutti had been right: he was snuffed, a dead man as far as the Army was concerned.

"The CID were all over the thing, of course, not because of Kincaid, but because of the security implications. Somebody not only had gotten access to the briefing room but to some very sensitive hardware needed to make the tape. Fruits is good, though, I've got to give it to him. He didn't leave a footprint. But by the time the Criminal Investigation guys had gone over and around everything they could find out, they knew pretty well who'd done it, even if there wasn't anything they could prove. And after all the smoke cleared, I think Menefee must have realized, too, that the stunt had somehow involved him, been for him. He's not one to be beholden, but one day he did say, 'They ought to give a medal to whoever set that pervert Kincaid up—right before they execute him.'

"Now, Chuck, you still want to know why Tutti's a spec four and not in a Ph.D. program somewhere?"

"And no one ever knew for sure?" Prentice asked.

"You're the only one outside me and the crew."

"It's hard to believe that someone didn't talk, you know, just have to show off what he knows."

"Remember, Chuck, we had been through Golden Spike together by then. That's something I guess I'm trying to get you to understand. That—this—is what makes soldiers closer than family. You and your men have come through a lot already, and you're all probably closer than you know. You will not let each other down."

Prentice nodded. "Yeah," he said. "Yeah. Hey, thanks, Max. I think I'll go, now. See how they're doing."

"Sure," Tag said. "See you later." He picked up the logbook, sighed, and opened it in his lap.

6

Giesla slept until noon, then sat down with Tag to decipher the notes in the back of the code book and fill in details of the twin manor houses. Holz drew up an operations plan, and at 1530 Tag called the briefing, with Betcher, Weintaub, White, Dunn, and N. Sain present, along with the officers and the crew of the No Slack Too.

After reviewing the plan in detail and outlining the tactics and roles of each element, Tag summed up: "Once the backside perimeter has been compromised and we've moved the No Slack Too into its initial fighting position, the first two Kommando vehicles will move to cover the barns, but we won't make a move while you're sweeping the houses, unless somebody else starts it. If that happens—Dunn, White—get your people out of there; and, Chuck, you and N. Sain get your Bradleys up. Even if we don't get to pick our time to fight, we can still take these guys. But once we disengage, we'll scatter all the same, regroup here, refuel, and keep moving toward home base.

"It's going to be a long night; so, unless there are questions, I say we all get what sleep we can. We move out at twenty-three hundred."

When no one spoke, Tag said, "All right. We're through," and the meeting began to break up. He spent a few minutes with his crew before using an inspection of the perimeter as an excuse for a walk in the woods.

The morning had held the chill of autumn, but now at midafternoon the smell of summer dust permeated the trees. It was a magnificent forest, Tag thought. Here near the old road and the buildings of the abandoned religious retreat, there was some second growth, but most were old trees that had cleared broad spaces for themselves with their branches. Last year's leaves were already soft beneath his feet, melding into the mulched generations of leaves beneath them. He found where squirrels, deer, and boar had gleaned the leaves for acorns.

The men at each of the four listening posts were on the job, and Tag walked a way farther into the big trees to think about the night's strike. A flicker at the corner of his vision stopped him. He cut his eyes, tightened the muscles in the backs of his legs, and recognized Giesla standing less than five feet away.

Relaxing as he turned toward her, Tag said, "Goddamn, you're good. Were you following me, or had you laid an ambush?"

Giesla returned his smile. "I used one of N. Sain's magic powers. *I am the Silent Angel of Death*," she mimicked, lolling her head.

Tag laughed softly and took a step toward her; she took a step toward him; and they took each other tentatively in their arms. Then they both relaxed at once, and then they held each other hard and close.

"I've thought of you," Tag said.

Giesla took his head in her hands and leaned back to look at him. "No," she said reasonably. "You worried. As you worried last night. Max, it would sadden me more than I think you know if you were killed. But I will not let that influence my military decisions. Death is always at a soldier's side."

"Now you do sound like N. Sain," Tag said.

Giesla shook her head emphatically. "It is true," she said. "Think of me dead, ripped open by bullets; my breasts, my face, blown away."

"Stop it," Tag said, pulling her to him.

"No," she said, bracing her elbows against his chest, "you stop. That can happen—worse than that can happen. You cannot protect me; you can only endanger me by not thinking about your job."

The truth hit Tag like a slap. He dropped his hands and

stepped back. "I thought we had finished this conversation before," he said.

"That was only about what you do; I am talking about how you think. Max"—she smiled at him—"if you want to love me, don't love me to death."

"So it's love now?" Tag said archly.

She stepped to him and ran her hand up his arm. "Maybe that is—what?—a euphemism?"

There was nothing coy about Giesla, Tag knew, but her complexity kept him off balance. He felt abashed by his own stupidity, but, oddly, not by anything she had said. She was like his good conscience, and he could not resent her for that. *You goddamn fool*, he told himself, *all you have to do is do what's right and do it now*.

"Let's euphemism," he said.

Three quarters of an hour later, Tag rose from a bed of leaves and belly and breasts and thighs, of bites and muffled cries of pleasure, of mouth and cock and cunt and the rich scent of sex. And now it was done, and without a word between them, they had made their peace. Again.

They returned separately, arriving from different directions, and did not speak again until late that night, as the unit was preparing to move out.

"Remember," he told her, "if we go in hot, nothing gets down that common drive. Once we take out the BMPs, I'll move the No Slack Too inside the compound and won't be able to cover the road."

"I own it," she said. "Just take care of my friend Sergeant Jefferson."

The unit crossed the road in single file, then fanned into the forest and moved at a crawl for most of an hour, until they were within eight hundred meters of their objective, as close as the Bradleys could come without being heard. The infantry dismounted and followed the No Slack Too to its initial position, a shelf of jutting rock that looked down between the two stone manor houses and gave Tag a shot at each of the BMPs on the far side, overlooking the valley. The Jagd Kommandos, their mufflers baffled for quiet running, were already on the flanks, their 106s trained on the barns and the approach.

Tag ordered Wheels to shut down the turbines, and he watched the two infantry squads through his night-vision scope as they separated and broke up into pairs to take out the perimeter posts. From there, they were to move through the houses, room by room. If that went as planned, they would next hope to surprise the remaining troops quartered in the outbuildings. That done, the No Slack Too would hit the BMPs at the same time the Kommandos nailed the barns. The Bradleys would come in for the mop-up, and the fight would be over in ten minutes.

Fat chance, Tag thought. Parked in front of the villa to his right, he could see the two BTRs Giesla had reported, unmanned but their missile racks now armed. Three or four smaller 4×4s were sitting in the circle drive of the house to the left, and some sort of transport truck was now next to one of the barns. There were lights in a half-dozen windows, but Tag saw no movement outside.

"Ham," he said through the intercom, "mark our targets."

"Mark one."

"Confirmed."

"Mark two."

"Confirmed."

"Fruits," Tag said to the loader, "if we have to cover for the legs, you take out the upper windows with the Phalanx first, then the outbuildings."

"Roger," Tutti replied.

After a thirty-minute eternity, the first message blip came in—an electronically produced series of notes followed by three beeps to indicate the position.

"They just took number three, boys," Tag said.

Within minutes, the other blips confirmed that all six of the backside listening posts were neutralized.

Tag kept his eyes glued to his scope and wiped his palms on his knees.

"Ears up," Tag said, switching on the No Slack Too's audio-directional dish. He keyed the dish to his scope, strained against his own breathing to listen for any sound that might signal the Russians' alarm. As he panned left, he picked up the dampered noise of doors and what might have been a shout.

"Stand by main gun," he said softly. "Fruits, hold off on the Phalanx; we may have people upstairs by now."

Tag began to pan back to the right, when a burst of small-arms fire popped through the audio receiver.

"Shoot!" Tag ordered, and the No Slack Too rocked back under the recoil of its 120mm main gun.

"Shoot two," Tag said, watching as the first BMP was blown forward by the HE in a heap of fiery metal, and the machine-gun nests in the two barn lofts were blasted into charred maws by simultaneous hits from the Jagd Kommando recoilless rifles.

Trying to maneuver, the second BMP took Ham's round broadside, the blast ripping through the crew compartment and out the hatches in lashing knouts of flame.

Tag keyed the TAC net. "Bradleys up," he said. Then, to his driver: "Wheels, scoot it."

The No Slack Too backed from its fighting position and nosed down the steep grade, dodging trees, until it hit the estate gardens at sixty kph. Firing the Phalanx from his own seat, Tag reduced the two missile-equipped BTRs to burning hulks, then spun on the vehicles in front of the other villa, shattering motor blocks, wheels, and chassis with stuttering bursts from the 37mm chain gun.

Where a stone-and-wrought-iron fountain stood at the fork of the common drive, Tag told Wheels to halt the tank and wait for the Bradleys. He radioed all units to report: White's squad had surprised the dozen Soviet officers in one house before the shooting started and were now advancing on the outbuildings and barn to Tag's right; Dunn's squad was the one that had stirred things up, but they had shot their way clear, with prisoners, and were in position to cover the exits from the outbuildings on their side; the commando cars on the flanks were closing in; and Prentice's Bradley was in sight. There was no response from N. Sain.

Before Tag could call N. Sain again, the fountain in front of them disintegrated in a crushing explosion that drove the thirty-ton XM-F4 backward on its tracks.

"Target," Ham Jefferson shouted, even before Tag could focus his scope.

He saw a thermal image and responded, "Shoot."

The explosion in the mouth of the double doors of the barn to their left obliterated the target, but from behind it another tracked vehicle shot past and into the barnyard, firing from a turret cannon as it came. Tag engaged the Phalanx and watched as the small tank absorbed more than fifty of the depleted uranium penetrators before shuddering from internal explosions and lurching to a smoking halt.

Tag had a moment to register the fact that the small tank, while very like the Soviet airborne's 2S9 "toy tank," was not. Then, they took a hit.

A HEAT round fired from the 120mm smoothbore combination gun on another of the compact tanks in the other barn struck the No Slack Too on the right turret fin. The thin sheet of monopolar carbide puddled beneath the impact, and the high-explosive blast tore through to air behind the turret. Still, the force was great enough to rattle the men inside like so many peas in a dry pod.

"Target," Tag and Ham said at once. But a salvo of Jagd Kommando 106s turned the barn door into a curtain of flame before they could bring their guns to bear. Tag's thermal sight flared green at one edge, as a 75mm white-phosphorous round from Prentice's Bradley took out one of the outbuildings between the house and the barn.

Tag brought their gun to the left and watched two outbuildings on that side, one after the other, blow up in the rear and let their ridge beams collapse in a shower of rubble and dust. Half-dressed men came running from them with their hands in the air and stood huddled back-to-back on the wrecked lawn.

"Bradley One," Tag said into his radio, "move up with your prisoners. Bradley Two, cover first squad while they secure the Reds you flushed out; there may be shooters in the second story."

Tag silently prayed that N. Sain had heard him.

"I'm putting the top down," Tag said to his crew. "Wheels, Ham, Fruits—all of you stay sharp."

Tag swung up through the turret, popped the hatch, and reached through to charge and cock the naval-mounted minigun, before hauling himself clear of the lip. He gripped the handles of the gun and surveyed the moonlit scene. Four flashes from down the slope beyond the barn, followed by a sound like afterburners, told him Giesla had targets coming up the road.

"Wheels," he said through his CVC, "the barn to our right, hit it."

The compact tanks had been a surprise, and Tag wanted to know what else might be inside, as well as check out the transport semi parked outside.

Back to his left, prisoners were crossing from the house to the smoldering servants' quarters, with GIs walking backward beside them, their eyes on the upper story of the house. Tag saw movement there and vaporized two sets of French doors with the howling spray from the mini-gun.

Where the hell is N. Sain?

From behind the barn now directly to their left, another of the compact Soviet tanks darted forward and stopped, its muzzle tracking the turret of the No Slack Too.

"Bogey. Nine o'clock," he shouted, and opened up with the mini-gun, aiming for the bore of the cannon itself.

The wall of the barn exploded, sending an avalanche of rock down on the small tank, followed shortly by a second explosion from the tank itself, sending smoke and oily flames through the stones, like some volcanic display.

N. Sain, Tag thought, furious for the man's disobeying orders *and* saving his ass in the process.

"Go, Wheelman," he said. "The barn, remember?"

"Bradley One," Tag radioed, "this is Butcher Boy. Skim the cream off what you've got and be ready to disengage in five minutes. Same for you, Bradley Two. I think Meat Grinder Two has contact."

"Roger, Butcher Boy," Prentice replied.

N. Sain's radio was silent.

The tank was still burning in the double doors of the barn; Tag halted them outside.

"I'm going naked and see what's inside," he said through the intercom, "and, Fruits, I want you to come check out the truck. Let's go."

Tag came out of the turret and slid down over the fender, followed by the scrambling Tutti. He motioned the loader toward the transport, whipped the Beretta 9mm from his pistol harness, then sprinted across the packed earth of the barn lot. He held up one hand to protect his face from the flames, paused, then ran past the burning tank and into the barn.

Tag had to blink for several seconds before he believed what he saw: occupying most of the barn was an Mi-28 "Havoc" attack helicopter, the heavily armored, two hundred mph replacement for the Soviets' aging Hinds, its rotors stacked on the floor beside it. Tag hurried around the chopper, pistol at the ready, but the barn was dead. Looking more closely at the Havoc, he saw that the hard points on its stubby "wings," where weapon pods were usually attached, were missing. Even stranger, under the belly of the flying weapons platform, was a bomb or missile rack. From the rack's configuration, Tag estimated that the ordnance for it was a single two-foot tube more than fifteen feet long. Nothing he knew of Soviet helicopter arms registered with this setup.

The popping of small arms and another *whoosh*ing salvo of 106s reminded Tag that he had no time for woolgathering.

He turned back toward the burning tank, this time to memorize the features of it he didn't recognize. By the light of the blaze, Tag now saw that only its size and turret configuration really resembled the 2S9. This piece of armor was clearly wider and heavier than the airborne's toy tank, with skirts over its broad tracks and a much steeper glacis.

Tag ran back past the burning hulk and met Fruits Tutti coming from around the side of the barn.

"Christ on a creeping crutch," Tutti blurted. "They got freakin' cruise missiles in the truck."

"Saddle up, Fruits," Tag told him. "We got to shoot the cripples and move out."

As Tag followed Fruits through the turret hatch, he saw N. Sain's Bradley come careening out of the other barn, towing a large storage tank, and dig its way up the ruined lawn to where the crowd of prisoners were huddled.

The sonofabitch doesn't miss a trick, Tag thought grudgingly. He dropped through the turret and into his chair.

"Ham," he said to his gunner, "HE. There's a Havoc stashed in the barn. We'll take it now, then move back to

the house and let the others clear before we take the semi.
Fruits says it's got cruise missiles in it, but I don't know
if they're armed."

"Locked and loaded," Ham Jefferson said.

"Wheels," Tag said, "give us an angle."

The driver spun the No Slack Too to face the barn doors,
just left of center.

"Target," Ham said.

"Confirmed," Tag responded. "Shoot."

The force of the high-explosive round as it struck the
Mi-28 inside the barn filled the air with a plasma of fire that
roiled out through the doors and the maw of the shattered
loft.

"All units, break off. I say again, break off," Tag spoke
over the radio. Then, to Wheels, "Let's get it, Mr. Latta."

Wheels locked one track and spun the agile XM-F4 in
place, then shot across the barn lot, up the common drive to
the shattered fountain, and to the right toward the Bradleys
by the house.

Tag slammed back the commander's hatch and came up
shouting, "Move, you people. What the hell are you doing
here?"

But no one could hear him over the crashing chords
of Jefferson Airplane's "Volunteers" that wailed from the
loudspeaker on N. Sain's track, punctuated by N. Sain's
voice cutting in with promises to kill every third man
and castrate the rest. Prentice's ring of infantry guarding
the prisoners glanced nervously among themselves. There
was another volley of 106s just out of sight below the
barns, followed by two reports and a series of secondary
explosions that marked clean kills.

"Butcher Boy, this is Meat Grinder One," Holz's voice
popped over the TAC net. "Have heavy armor approaching.
Meat Grinder One and Two disengaging now."

Tag leapt out of his hatch and ran to N. Sain's Bradley,
unholstering his Beretta. He banged on the forward hatch,
got no response, thumbed back the hammer on his pistol,
and shot away the armored cable that fed the loudspeaker
on the nose of the track.

The silence was immediate, except for the idling motors

and the rattle of small arms and the diesel snarl of approaching armor. First Sergeant Weintaub appeared in the turret hatch of the other Bradley.

"Top," Tag shouted at him, "get the prisoners we're taking and get the hell out of here."

N. Sain's hatch fell open and the transcendant sergeant said to Tag, "Oh, fear-fucking PsyOps. Does it have to end so soon?"

"Have you got fuel in that tank?" Tag said, waving his pistol toward the rear of the Bradley.

"The lifeblood of war," N. Sain affirmed.

"Okay," Tag said, "we're putting the troops in through the top, so unbutton. I'll put the prisoners in the other track."

Tag dashed to the No Slack Too and told the crew to cover the approach from the valley, then sprinted to the gaggle of prisoners, where White and Dunn were trying to sort the ducks from the geese. In the darkness, some of the Soviet officers and NCOs had exchanged caps and tunics; most others were in various stages of undress; and there was no time to wait for Giesla to arrive and interrogate them.

Twenty men had sixty seconds to sort a hundred prisoners down to six or seven. In the dark. With Soviet armor already within cannon range.

"Look at their boots," Tag told the squad leaders. "Take anybody with a spit-shine or wearing low-quarters. Look for rings—not wedding bands, but class rings or signets."

He moved into the prisoners with the men, culling suspects behind them. He grabbed one likely looking Russian who was wearing a sergeant's shirt two sizes too large, ordered the rest of the Red soldiers into one of the surviving outbuildings, and gave the word to scatter. Both Bradleys, with men and prisoners aboard, had cleared the grounds when Tag hit his seat in the No Slack Too.

"Wheels," he said, pulling his CVC down over his ears, "back to our initial fighting position. Fruits, load sabot; we have heavy bogeys coming. I'll take the truck out with the Phalanx. Ham, you shoot anything that moves."

Wheels Latta, the tip of his tongue sticking out one corner

of a reckless grin, drove with his hatch open, hurtling the XM-F4 at one hundred kph through the gardens, following the route he had memorized coming in. Like any good whiskey-runner, he didn't *go* in without learning the way out. It was almost as though he could actually see his earlier tracks in the light of the new-risen moon. In the woods at the edge of the grounds, he slalomed deftly through the trees, losing no time in getting the No Slack Too into position.

As the tank heeled over the shoulder of the salient on the ridge above the manors, Tag scanned the scene below a final time with his day/night binoculars, before dogging down his own hatch and ordering Wheels to do the same.

"You want I should take the truck?" Fruits Tutti asked over the intercom.

"Negative, Fruits," Tag told him. "Stay with the main tube; you and Hambone have got some shooting to do. We're not giving our position away until we have some live targets."

As he spoke, the first of four Soviet T-64B battle tanks came into the XM-F4's thermal sight. The Russian tank ran hard up the road between the two gutted barns, then broke right at the fountain, presenting a three-quarter profile in Ham's reticle.

"Target," the gunner announced.

"I gotcha, Ham," Tag said. "Let's see what his buddies do."

The second Soviet tank broke left, and Tag could now distinguish others behind it.

"Shoot," Tag commanded, and the 120mm recoiled in its dampers and recovered as the rear of the first T-64B burst into flame amid an earsplitting explosion.

The second Soviet tank was shielded by the orchard, so Tag took the third still coming up the road. As the loading carousel whirred, he locked on and called to Ham, "Target."

"Confirmed," Ham said.

"Shoot."

"Shot."

The penetrator core of the sabot round struck the commander's hatch on the T-64B, killing the commander and driver instantly, but not stopping the machine, which slowed to a crawl but continued to grind up the road.

The second of the two Red tanks emerged from the cover of the orchard and fired on the move, striking the jutting elbow of rock beneath the No Slack Too. The thermal sensors of the XM-F4 locked on the heat signature of the muzzle blast, and Ham fired at a green smudge on his sights, one that swelled to fill the screen when his shot went home just behind the Communist tank's turret and found the magazine. The explosion ripped through the rear deck where it joined the turret, nearly tearing the tank in two.

Tag wanted to move them, but he knew he had to at least take out the missiles in the truck before he did. He heard the carousel cycle and the breech lock shut.

"Fruits," he said, "you go ahead and take the truck with the Phalanx on manual. Ham, target."

The fourth T-64B had been screened by its disabled mate still inching crazily up the road with a gaping hole in its upper glacis. When the healthy tank came up separately in the sights, Tag swung his turret and centered the image in his sight grid.

"Confirmed," Ham said.

Tag's order to shoot and Ham's reply were both smothered by the heavy stutter of the Phalanx's 37mm shredding the parked semitruck and its load of nuclear-capable missiles. The Phalanx ceased as the 120mm roared and the semi went up in a ball of fire almost simultaneously. The destruction of the last tank was curtained by the fire, smoke, and dust that billowed from the exploding trailer and the collapsing barn.

"Wheels, go," Tag ordered.

Wheels swung the No Slack Too in place and threw rooster tails of rock and forest mulch from the tracks as he accelerated into the cover of the woods. Woods were supposed to be a tanker's enemy, a place where infantry could get close enough to disable armor with hand grenades or gasoline bombs, but Tag and his crew knew that here, behind the lines, with only scattered ground units on the prowl, they had the edge in this forest.

Despite the others' head start, the No Slack Too arrived at the rendezvous area just as the last two gun buggies pulled into the woods above the abandoned chapel. While the raiders refueled from the two barrels of gas they had stashed there, Tag made a quick after-action inspection. From the various reports, he estimated that they had killed forty to sixty of the Soviet troops, not including the crews of the tanks and APCs. They had taken seven prisoners, and their own worst casualty was a cut that Sergeant Dunn had received from his own garrote. The roll cage of Betcher's vehicle was nicked and burred by small-arms fire, but otherwise undamaged.

They moved out in a staggered column, with Kommando vehicles at point and drag and on each flank. The Bradleys were no speed merchants, but in the moonlit forest they all made good time. False dawn had come and gone, and the sky was purple in the east, when Tag halted them a half klick from the mine and transmitted a coded squelch to the wounded who had been left there. He got the countersign and ordered the column forward.

The infantry dismounted at the entrance of the mine to scratch out any tracks the armor might leave, then trudged through the tunnel to the cavern. They were proud, happy men, but they were veterans now, and too tired to show it.

The No Slack Too was the last to enter the cavern, and Tag did not see the dozen armed men standing in the shadows until he was out of his hatch and walking toward the Bradleys. In the periphery of his vision, he registered a weapon and someone not in uniform. He had spun to one knee and had his Beretta in his hand when he heard Giesla shout, "No, Max." Then she appeared herself out of the shadows, saying something in German as she came.

The men she had been speaking to followed her into the light that had just increased by another gas lantern lit on the other side of the cavern. Tag saw at once that these must be partisans. The youngest of them was no less than fifty, and the oldest a stick-thin white beard. They were dressed in moleskins and Swabian hunting jackets and armed with a motley assortment of weapons that included bolt-action Mausers, a couple of H&K assault rifles, and one elegant, antique drilling—an 8mm rifle barrel beneath the bores of a 16- gauge double—that Tag knew was worth at least $5000 to a collector.

Giesla took Tag's arm and said, "Max, these men are from a village about fifteen kilometers from here; they used to work this mine. They came to see whether the Russians were using it, planning to destroy them. This is Johann, their leader."

A sturdy man with a thick, white mustache and carrying a semiautomatic sporting rifle stepped forward and shook Tag's hand. He greeted Tag in German, then spoke to Giesla.

"None of them speaks English," Giesla said, "but Johann wants you to know that they will work with us. I think we should talk to them now."

"I think you're right," Tag said. "Let's go jerk the chain on our prisoners and see if any of the dogs bark."

Then he told her about the modified Mi-28 and the trailer full of missiles and the compact tanks.

"So," she said as they walked across the cavern at the head of the group of partisans, "they were not 2S9s. I suppose it was not just a rumor, then."

"What was not?"

"About a month ago I received an intelligence circular that was sent to all Jagd Kommando units, updating estimates on Warsaw Pact armor. In it there was mention of a new light tank, similar to the 2S9, but designed for antitank recon units, to replace some of the BMPs and BRDMs."

The Bradleys and the commando cars were parked in a bunch. The men were still milling around, getting a good look at the seven prisoners squatted on the floor of the cavern.

"Men," Tag said to them, "you've done a hell of a job tonight. You engaged the enemy, and you hurt him. You'll all get the full rundown when you're rested enough for it to matter, but it looks like we took out about fifty of them, plus more than a dozen pieces of armor, not to mention our guests here."

The young troops responded with a ripple of "All rights" and "Yeah, we kicked some ass."

"Rick, Chuck, let your people stand down and get some chow and some rack. Ham," Tag called across the cavern to his gunner, "come on over here; we might need your expertise in winning hearts and minds."

He turned to Giesla. "You want to start questioning them."

She nodded without ever taking her bore-sight stare off the Russians. "Strip them," she said stonily, then repeated it in German.

Four of the partisans put aside their weapons and cut away the prisoners' clothes but not their bonds. Giesla stood staring down at the naked Russians. She flicked one's genitals with the toe of her boot and snorted in contempt.

"Stand them up," she said to the partisans, "until I've had some coffee." The vigorous old men jerked the prisoners to their feet and shoved their backs to the wall of the cavern.

Weintaub sent two men with a boiling bucket of instant coffee. The raider officers, Ham, and the partisans arranged ammo crates and sat in a semicircle facing the seven Soviet prisoners.

After a few minutes of silence, Giesla said, "Max, I want to question them one at a time, so the others cannot hear. We will need someone to guard the others in one of the Bradleys."

N. Sain, who had yet to emerge from his track, bounded off the troop ramp and whirled like a dervish in front of the agog prisoners and equally stunned partisans.

"O, Queen of Quietus," he intoned, dropping to one knee in front of Giesla, "honor me with that privilege. Let me instruct the heathen in the ways of fear."

Giesla looked at Tag. He played a hunch.

"N. Sain," Tag said sternly, "we've got seven walking, talking intelligence assets here, and I want all seven of them to stay that way. Right?"

"When I have shared the vision with them, they will sing," N. Sain said. "But I will need that coffee for the elixir."

"Okay," Tag said. "Which one you want first, Gies?"

"That one," she said, pointing out one particularly flabby specimen, "the one with the soft belly."

"Mad Dog, Rabies," N. Sain called. "Come. We have converts." He picked up the half-empty can of coffee and carried it to the rear of his track. He took a brown ball of something that looked like mud from the cargo pocket of his jumpsuit and began to crumble it into the bucket, while his two keepers, eyeing the prisoners like so much meat, herded them into the back of the Bradley.

"Oh, the horror, the horror," N. Sain said, stirring the bucket with his sheath knife. "Oh, the sacrifice." And he disappeared inside the track, closing the troop ramp behind him.

"What was that?" Prentice asked. "What did he put in there?"

"Right now, Chuck," said Tag, "frankly, I don't give a damn. Just think: how would you like to be tied up and naked with those three?"

Prentice and Holz both grinned.

Giesla said to Ham, "Mr. Jefferson, would you please bring our friend over here?"

"A pleasure," Ham said, showing all his teeth.

He stood behind the Russian while Giesla asked a few questions. Tag didn't understand what was said, but when the Russian gave the same answer twice, Giesla lowered her voice to a growl.

"Persuade him," she said to Ham.

The black gunner leaned over the Russian's shoulder and spoke the sweetest-sounding string of obscenities he could compose as he drew the point of his knife slowly up the back of the trembling man's leg. He let it slip into the crack of his ass and rotated the point a half turn around the puckered sphincter, let it rest, increased the pressure, then suddenly whipped it away. He grabbed the Soviet officer by the shoulder and spun him around. Ham stepped back a foot, twirled the blade in the man's face, and dropped it to his belly, shaving an inch of pubic hair and stopping at the base of his penis.

He looked at Giesla, who nodded.

"NYET," the Russian cried.

"Sorry, Ivan," Ham said, "I don't speak Russian." He increased the pressure on the knife, and a thin red line of blood began to seep from beneath its edge.

"Nyet, nyet," the Russian repeated, adding a rapid babble meant for Giesla, though he never took his eyes off Ham's ferocious smile.

"Ah," she said, "Ham, I think you have broken the ice. You have such a winning way."

There was thumping inside N. Sain's Bradley, muffled sounds of struggle, then the beat of rock 'n' roll encased in steel. The Russian under Ham's knife rolled his eyes in that direction and babbled some more.

"Untie him and let him sit," Giesla said, opening a notepad.

Ham cut the camouflage tape on the man's wrists and kicked an ammo box behind him. The Russian sat, rubbing his wrists, holding his knees together, and talking a torrent. He could not keep from stealing glances at Ham, who stood at his side, toying with his knife.

With Tag feeding an occasional question, Giesla grilled the man for forty-five minutes, getting ready replies. Even before the other six stumbled from N. Sain's Bradley, the pot-bellied Russian had confirmed that the manor houses had been the operations and logistics command center for the entire southern front, excluding occupied Austria. He claimed to be a major in the logistics group, but that two of the others were regimental commanders, full colonels, one in charge of a motor-rifle brigade, and the other of an armored regiment.

The troop ramp on N. Sain's track fell open. N. Sain, Mad Dog, and Rabies filed out with a weaving Russian on each arm. The one by Rabies's side was giggling uncontrollably. The others were red-eyed and stupefied, lurching drunkenly, muttering to themselves or imitating strident chords from N. Sain's retro-rock collection.

N. Sain piped up like a Las Vegas emcee: "Far-esh from the belly of the beast and a show-stopping tour of the kingdom of angels, let me present the Salvation Six, ready to rock and roll for the god-king of destruction."

The prisoners were soaked with sweat, and N. Sain and

his keepers, stripped to the waist, likewise shone with it. Mad Dog and Rabies were their impassive selves, and N. Sain had the smoky, unfocused look to his eyes that Tag had seen before. They dropped their prisoners in a heap, where the giggling of the one infected the others, until the pile was wracked with laughter.

Holz, his Teutonic sense of discipline offended, snapped at N. Sain, "What is the meaning of this?"

"It does not mean," N. Sain replied, "it *is*. Behold, the happy warriors, happy to sacrifice their knowledge to the Angel of Death. Coffee, anyone?"

"N. Sain," Tag said earnestly, "I am happy that your mission was successful, that you have made converts of these jackals and taught them to bark like the dogs they are. Now we will hear their confessions of sins against the light of war's consuming flame, of cowardice and conversion."

Prentice, Holz, and Giesla all looked at him as though he were speaking in tongues.

N. Sain bobbed his head in acknowledgment. "And not all their mewling and puking will cause the gods of war to relent; the infinite spaces will never be silenced until the Antichrist of rock and roll plays slide guitar."

"You've earned a warrior's rest," Tag said. "Take it."

"Death is a warrior's only rest," N. Sain said. "We will sleep now." And he and his keepers went back inside the Bradley and buttoned up.

Giesla looked at the pile of chortling Communist officers, sighed, and said to Tag, "I'm sorry, Max, but this may take a while."

The hour Giesla spent in tedious interrogation of the stoned Communists paid off. By the time the partisans had left and everyone else was ready for some rest, Tag had learned a staggering amount about men and matériel in the area, and had confirmed the presence of an antitank/recon battalion sent to suppress guerrilla activity and nibble at the flanks of the tenuous NATO positions. The giggling officer had consistently claimed that the cruise missiles and the modified Mi-28 were for deploying cluster bombs in support of infantry assaults, but Tag's mind was not at rest over it.

Better was their contact with the partisans. Before leaving, Johann had promised to make arrangements to take the prisoners off their hands and to return that evening for them, and to bring the men of the raider command fresh food from the village. By then, Tag would have had time to mull over what they had learned from the prisoners. Combining that with the local intelligence supplied by the partisans, he hoped to draw a clearer picture of the situation, compare it with the satellite images coming in in the next twenty-four hours, and make their plans accordingly.

First, however, he wrote a brief after-action report/ intelligence estimate for Fruits to encode and send out on a message burp. That done and the sentries set, he allowed himself to wind down into a shallow sleep for four hours.

Tag awoke with a fist of anxiety gripping his chest. The sounds of men moving about the cavern, low talk and occasional laughter, the hissing of the gas lanterns, all sounded ominously hollow to him, like whistling past a graveyard: where was their back door?

He threw back his sleeping bag and sat up. His skin tingled. His mouth was dry. He took several deep breaths, held the last one, and let it out slowly.

Okay, he told himself. *First, survey the position for defense and evacuation, then scout fall-back positions. Third, get the LandSat pictures and collate all the intelligence with Giesla.*

Tag laced on his boots, stowed his bedroll, got a pouch of freeze-dried chicken à la king and another of malted milk, and went to the makeshift mess area for some boiled water. Betcher, the bearlike Kommando NCO, was there, and Tag drafted him to give a Cook's tour of the mine complex.

The place had held a marginal lead deposit that had been mined off and on since World War Two, until it was finally abandoned four years ago. Each time the mine had been reopened, another horizontal shaft had been dug in the face of the bluff, to chase the thin seam of lead that ran parallel to it. The cavern where the raiders were assembled was the result of explorations made when the seam finally did run out. The Kommando vehicles and the Bradleys could manage the passages between the earlier shafts, but not the No Slack Too.

Betcher played the beam of his battle lantern off the walls and ceiling of one of the shafts and looked gloomier than usual.

"Not good," he said.

Tag saw what he meant. Some of the shafts had been shored with iron beams, but the earliest ones had been braced with timbers, timbers now hollow with dry rot and buckling under their own weight. But what had looked from the outside like a collapsed mouth of the shaft proved to be a heap of scrap timbers and rock. With Betcher's light off, they could see pinholes of light leaking in.

"Yeah," Tag said, "this one stinks, Mathias. We might be able to salvage some of that scrap and shore up part of it. We'll get a couple of work parties down here this afternoon to try to put all of them in shape."

The laconic commando grunted, and they moved cautiously out of the shaft and back down the passage to the cavern.

Most of the troops were up when Tag returned; many were eating, but others already servicing the Bradleys. He sent Wheels and Fruits outside to scout escape routes and fighting positions, then found Holz and Prentice at the situation table.

"*Ach*, Max," Holz greeted him. "Giesla has overlays already. Come."

Tag saw that Prentice had unslung his left arm.

"How's the wing, Chuck?" he asked.

Prentice rotated the shoulder gingerly. "This one's really not bad, but it'll be a while before I'm ready to arm wrestle."

Tag returned his grin and looked at Holz. "Whatta we got, Rick?"

Holz had made some improvements on the table, putting better definition and scale on the features and providing paper "flags" to identify the Soviet units by size, configuration, and name. An antitank/recon battalion was the only combat element marked this far behind the lines. Apparently the motor-rifle brigade and the tank regiment commanded by two of their prisoners were reserve units in positions farther up the Danube Valley, near the main battlefront. It had been the colonels' ill luck to be back at the villas for a hot bath when the raiders attacked.

The light security and weak resistance that Tag and his outfit had met made sense now. The southern sector was proving as difficult as Ross Kettle had predicted, and the Soviets were throwing everything they had on the line to try to punch through to the Black Forest and the French border on the Rhine. But there was an asymmetry to the Russian battlefield array that puzzled Tag. Although the ridge of the Swabian Jura, the natural high-ground approach to the Black Forest, was held by the Soviets for thirty kilometers below Ehingen on the Danube, the bulk of their forces seemed poised for a wheeling maneuver to the south, using neutral Switzerland to protect the Red Army's flank as it moved up the narrowing valley in the foothills of the Alps.

"That looks like bad country to maneuver in," Tag said, indicating the area northwest of Lake Constance on the Swiss frontier.

"It is, Max," Holz confirmed. "I don't understand it. They would be completely without their heavy artillery, and their tanks would be useless. If your army and the French corps can retake the Jura, the Soviets will have given up the high ground and have their backs to the Alps. It would be a slaughter."

Tag rubbed the stubble on his chin. "This deal stinks on ice. Ivan hasn't made a wrong move yet, and damn sure nothing that dumb."

Prentice cleared his throat. "Uh, what about Mao?" he said.

"Mao?" Holz looked at him quizzically.

"Mao Zedong," Prentice said. "What was it he said about making a noise in the west so he could attack in the east?"

"But attack with what, Chuck?" Tag asked.

Prentice shrugged. "Maybe that's what we need to find out." He made it sound like a question.

Holz questioned Tag with his eyes.

"Maybe," Tag said thoughtfully. "Let's get tonight's LandSat pictures, though, before we make any decision. We should be getting a transmission from Command tonight, too, and that might tell us something.

"Right now, I want some work details to get started on those old shafts. We can fight from them or run from them, but not in the shape they're in. When my men get back, I'll go see what they've found for us in the way of escape-and-evasion routes. I may even have to move the No Slack Too outside. I don't like just having one door."

"What about those freaks," Prentice said, meaning N. Sain and his crew. "Are they going to work or not?"

Tag thought a moment before replying. "So far, N. Sain and his boys have done everything I've asked of 'em, Chuck. I know they're weird and not much as soldiers, but the sonsofbitches can fight. For now, let's just leave it at that, unless you think some of your people are going to resent it, that it'll cause morale problems."

Prentice snorted. "I don't think any of my men will be

pissed because they didn't get to work with that bunch."

"Yeah," Tag agreed jovially, "I'd as soon play with a snake myself, but nobody asked me."

The meeting broke up, and Tag went back to his tank for a closer look at its after-action condition. The stealth polymer coating on the nose and the front of the turret had taken a terrific scouring from small arms and shell fragments; one of the hydraulically dampened arms on the mini-gun's mount was bent; and a long, shallow crease ran down one track skirt. But what caused him to whistle in respect of a near-miss was the hole burned in the turret fin and the raw blast mark on the back of the turret itself. The fins were designed to protect riflemen riding on the rear deck from small-arms fire, but they were solid monopolar carbide, though only a fraction the thickness of the XM-F4's main armor. Nevertheless, Tag had to shake off an involuntary chill that moved up between his shoulder blades.

When Wheels and Fruits returned, Tag was grateful for a chance to get outside the cavern, which felt even more confining to him now that he knew there was only one way out for the No Slack Too. He stood with them at the edge of shadow in the mouth of the tunnel, looking at maps and listening to their descriptions of the terrain immediately surrounding the mine.

Fruits Tutti cocked his head like a bird dog suddenly catching a scent and said sharply, "Freeze. Choppers."

Then Tag heard them too, heard the rush of the prop blasting engine sound down into the forest, not the sounds of the engines themselves.

"They're coming in low," Tag said. "Ease back and get down."

Tag stretched himself along one wall of the shaft, resting his elbows on the floor to steady his binoculars as he conned the rectangle of sky framed in the mouth of the mine, listened, and looked again.

"What do you make them to be, Wheels?" Tag said over his shoulder.

"Probably Hips," the gunner said, referring to the Soviet Mi-8 utility helicopter. "Doesn't sound like a Hind, and it's too big for a Hop."

"There they are," Fruits said, pointing.

Tag rolled back on his stomach and brought his glasses up, as two brown-and-green camouflaged helicopters hove slowly into view in the opening of the shaft, moving toward the northeast at about two hundred feet of altitude.

"Yeah," Tag drawled, "Hip gunships, all right. Any bets on what they're looking for?"

"Cap'n," Wheels said speculatively, "suppose they don't find what they're lookin' for from the air. Reckon they'll run another patrol by here to check the place out?"

"You're reading my mind, Wheelman," Tag said as the two helicopters passed out of sight. "Let's go see what you two have found for us."

Tag liked what he saw. Just inside the woods at the edge of the wasteland surrounding the mine area, Wheels and Fruits had found massive piles of stone tailings from the mine. After so many years, they had collected enough soil to support a scraggly growth of weeds and vines that nicely blurred their outlines, blending them with the wall of greenery that grew at the edge of the forest. The tailing piles offered a half-dozen good fighting positions, with easy movement and good cover between them. Up or down the slope of the ridge, all routes were about equal, but to the south, perpendicular to the slope, things got interesting.

Some geologic quirk had fissured much of the mountain to the south, allowing wind and water to cut wide, shallow crevasses that were well disguised beneath vine-covered tangles of rotten deadfalls. They were natural tank traps, but not impossible to navigate.

"You got this memorized yet?" Tag joked to his driver.

"Every inch," Wheels said. He was not joking.

Tag and his two crewmen walked an arc through the woods about one hundred meters inside them, then another even deeper, but there were no surprises among the game trails through the big trees.

N. Sain may be a fighting fool, Tag thought as they moved in the shadow of the abandoned crane toward the mine adit, *but he doesn't know squat about security or defenses.* He wondered why Holz or even Prentice hadn't put out listening posts. Still distracted by their wounds, maybe, or just numb from unrelieved combat. He was in no position to judge, and he didn't. Just taking care of it now would be enough.

Six of the aging partisans were back in the cavern when Tag arrived. In their shooting jackets, baggy trousers, and slouch hats, they looked more than ever like some nineteenth-century photo engraving.

"Oh, man," Fruits Tutti said, "are those guys for real?"

"I tell you what, Tutti Fruity," Wheels said, "I got this black-sheep uncle that's a po-lice, a deputy sheriff. Now, he's seventy-two, but about four years ago he got word that three ol' boys from around home had broke out of the state prison, so he just went off by hisself over to where their people lived, and, sure enough, they was there, holed up in an ol' trailer house up about Linville. Well, the shootin' started, and uncle, he called for backups. When they got there, them three boys in that trailer was all shot and bleedin', but they wasn't coming out till there was enough po-lice there to protect 'em from Uncle. See, he'd ast 'em to give up, and when they said no, he said he reckoned he'd just have to kill 'em all, don't you see. You don't wanna fuck with a mean *old* man, Fruits."

Tag sent his men back to the No Slack Too and then joined Holz, Giesla, Prentice, and the partisans. As he came up to them, he saw loaded packboards piled on the floor beside two large, basket-covered demijohns. The prisoners squatted nearby, their taped wrists joined by a single rope.

"Max," Holz said to him, his face drawn, "we have a complication."

"What's up?"

"Coming up here, these men"—Holz gestured to the villagers—"spotted two patrols, each with two missile-equipped BMPs and some sort of small tank."

"Show me where," Tag said, stepping past them to the situation table.

Holz motioned the men forward and questioned them, while comparing their descriptions to his map and the table. Giesla translated as they spoke.

"They say," she said to Tag and Prentice, "that the first patrol was moving into their village on the road as they were leaving; they saw it from the hills. The other was about here"—she pointed on the map—"working its way southwest through the forest."

"First the Hips and now this," Tag said.

"Hips?" Giesla asked.

"Yeah, Mi-8s. We saw 'em go over when we went out. We must have really pissed some people off." Tag grinned.

Giesla shook her head in response. "I am beginning not to like this place," she said.

Holz faced them. "Max," he said, "Johann and his people can get our prisoners out, they say, so I have agreed to turn them over."

"Okay, Rick. Let's stay light to fight. We may have a lot to do in the next couple of days, like giving those patrols something to think about a long way from here."

"What are you thinking?" Prentice asked.

"Those thin positions farther down the mountains, what we were talking about earlier. They need to be checked out, anyway."

"Tonight, you think?" Holz asked.

"Have to," Tag said, "patrols or no patrols. And we've got to get this place in shape to defend." He said it more sharply than he meant. "Once we get tonight's pictures, Rick, we'll take the No Slack Too and two of your cars for a look-see. That'll leave most of the men to work on this place."

They talked briefly about listening posts, communications, and defensive tactics; the partisans left with their string of gagged prisoners; and Tag, his stomach growling, personally inventoried what the villagers had brought. Besides the two jugs of fruity May wine, there were a dozen cold, roasted chickens, a cured ham, a bushel of rye bread, eight jars of kraut, one of mustard, and a bag each of apples and onions. For men who had been eating from plastic pouches, it looked like a feast.

Tag and Prentice took Top Sergeant Weintaub out to establish positions for the listening posts, two on the slope above the sheer face of the mining area and two in the woods below the wasteland of tailings. They left each two-man post with one of the PRC-M radios.

Weintaub pulled Dunn's squad off work detail and set them to camouflaging the positions, in preparation for taking the first watch. When the men from White's squad broke for chow, they took ham sandwiches and apples out to the posts, so they could be familiar with them before dark. Amid some grumbling, Tag nixed a wine ration.

"We'll save it," he said, "until we have something to celebrate. Right now, we still have work to do. Got to get our licks in before Kettle wins this war without us."

N. Sain came out of the back of his Bradley, with MD and Rabies in single file behind. Each carried his bayonet like a Roman short sword as they marched to the spread of provisions and speared half a chicken and a loaf of bread on each blade, then as silently marched back inside.

It was dark by the time everyone had eaten. Tag moved the No Slack Too out to the mouth of the tunnel, where he could get a fix on the passing LandSat satellite with his micro-dish receiver, as well as pick up the prearranged transmission from Command. He had them both in half an hour and was back at the situation table with Holz, Prentice, and Giesla. Giesla began examining the satellite images with a magnifying glass, while Tag scanned the decoded message before reading it aloud.

"It says here," he began, skipping over the list of approximate coordinates marking Soviet positions, "congratulations . . . desirable effects . . . excellent intelligence . . . blah-blah, oh, here we go. Command's wondering the same thing we are about Ivan's strength here in the Jura and wants us to probe from this side. Okay. Engage targets of opportunity consistent with mission . . . report any Red Star medical relief convoys—what the hell's that about? I wonder—and, here, they say we ought to get in touch with guerrilla groups in the area. What do you think?"

"Not as much help as this," Giesla said. "Come, look." She offered the magnifier to Tag.

He turned the computer-generated picture to get a better angle in the light from the lantern and moved the glass back and forth to focus on the areas Giesla had marked in pencil.

"What am I looking for, Gies?" he asked.

"Just tell me what you think you see here, in our sector of the front."

Tag studied the enlarged quadrant slowly. "It looks like," he said, "a solid goddamn rank of armor. Hell, it goes off the sheet."

"Then look at this one," Giesla said, handing him a second image.

"More of it," Tag said. "That means every piece of armor, every self-propelled gun, Ivan has in the southern sector is right there. Shit, must be a couple thousand tanks."

"Yes," Giesla said, "but look at this." She handed him another sheet, this one a wider shot rendered in thermal radar images.

"Where are we on the map now?" Tag said, taking up the magnifier again.

"The alpine hills south of the valley, where the army has to start moving in column. Look at the ridge tops."

Tag saw it then—pinpricks of color, heat signatures in the familiar pattern of Soviet tanks deployed for defense. Lots of them. He looked up at Holz and Giesla.

"Ivan's got too goddamn many tanks," he said flatly.

Prentice, who had been standing by anxiously throughout, spoke up. "What do you mean, Max?"

"According to what I see here," Tag said, "Ivan has about twice the armor he should."

"Well," Holz said, putting on his most wolfish grin, "tonight, then, we find out."

At their nearest point, the Soviet forces that spread across the Swabian Jura were less than thirty kilometers from the raiders' redoubt. From the sparse depth of the line as seen from the satellite, Tag felt confident that the No Slack Too and two gun buggies could approach to within one klick before they would have to dismount and recon on foot. Holz took one commando car, with a trooper named Horst to drive, and brought Jan and Karl in the other. The patrol moved out three hours before moonrise, quartering up the slope to avoid the tract of fissures, with the Jagd Kommandos at point and drag.

The moonless night and the canopy of leaves gave Tag the luxury of running the No Slack Too down the crest of the mountain ridge. He rode with his head through the open hatch, feeling the cool of night whisper past, constantly alert to the eerie cast of shadows in his night-vision goggles. Although not yet September, these hills held an autumn chill at night, one that both invigorated Tag and made his mind cast apprehensively forward to thoughts of winter fighting in the forest.

Two kilometers from their objective, Tag halted the patrol and put up the No Slack Too's audio directional scanner. There were scattered sounds of engines and troop movements, some perhaps as close as one thousand meters.

"Okay," Tag said, removing his CVC as he stood in his hatch, "this is as far as we take the vehicles. Ham, let's get it."

Painted in camouflage, armed with the silenced Walthers, and each carrying four sticks of plastic explosive with remote detonators, Tag, Ham, Holz, and Jan slipped through the woods on foot. There were no shadows but plenty of light from the stars for the four raiders to keep a ten-meter interval as they moved swiftly and silently through the night, pausing about every fifty meters to listen. After they had traveled for half an hour, Tag threw up his hand to halt the patrol and signaled them to take cover. Tag moved forward and after a minute crept back to Holz and spoke quietly in his ear: "Rick, we've got men and SP howitzers still in column formation. Let's backtrack and move around them to the left."

They crawled for a hundred meters, then passed like wraiths through the trees, parallel to the battery of 152mm self-propelled cannons, close enough to hear men fart and laugh, each of the raiders aware that the next step might take him in the path of a perimeter patrol or within earshot of a listening post on the column's flank. Tag counted the humped outlines of six of the guns, but calculated that there was no more than a company of motor infantry with them—enough for security, but no more.

Another five hundred meters brought Tag and his patrol within hearing of the Soviet line and the familiar sounds of diesels idling to charge their batteries and the metallic creak of hatches. Tag saw a pinpoint of light brighten and disappear:

a cigarette suddenly cupped behind a guilty hand. Tag waited until he saw it again and took a fix on the position. He waved the others in close.

"There's a perimeter post of some sort about two hundred meters at two o'clock. There's someone in it sneaking a smoke. Look."

In a moment, the half-hidden glow waxed again.

"Here's what we do," Tag said. "We'll move on that position and take it out. Then, I want to move inside their perimeter and get as close to the tanks, or whatever they are, as we can. Once we see what we can, we plant the charges and go out the way we came in. Any questions?"

"Any mines, you reckon?" Ham Jefferson said.

"Claymores, maybe. Photos don't show they've cut any fields of fire, so probably not any direct-detonation types. But let's be careful of trip wires," Tag added, "and there may be razor wire."

The low crawl across the forest floor was excruciating, slow and painful to elbows and hips, as each man's breath and pulse seemed to roar in his ears, and every brittle twig snapped with the crash of falling timber. Sweating in the cool midnight, Tag led them to within fifty meters of the outpost, where a single, loose coil of unanchored concertina wire had been hastily strung along the ground. Ham removed a half-dozen empty cans with pebbles inside that were hung on the concertina, then simply cut the section of wire and eased it back for the others to pass. Jan followed a harness of wire and found four claymore-type mines, which he turned to face the Communist positions.

Tag motioned his gunner forward, and they moved directly on the outpost, while Jan and Holz closed in from the flanks. Tag could smell the cigarette smoke from here, could hear the guard clear his throat and spit. He could see now that the OP was a shallow foxhole with a single course of sandbags along the top, probably meant for three men. A helmeted silhouette appeared over the parapet, then turned away at the sound of a diesel grinding to life somewhere in the darkness nearby. In the concealment of the sound, Tag and Ham scuttled forward and came up over the sandbags, firing as they rose.

Even without the revving diesel, the soft *phut-phut-phut* of the subsonic 9mm rounds would likely never have been heard by the OPs fifty meters to either side. Tag's first burst ripped into the upper chest and soft neck tissue of the smoking Russian, who fell dead with a grunt, the smoldering cigarette still in his fingers. Ham methodically shot the other two soldiers in the head as they slept. The two Americans dropped into the hole seconds before the two Jagd Kommandos joined them.

"Count ten, then follow me one at a time," Tag whispered. He slithered out the back of the foxhole and worked his way toward the sound of the clattering diesel, stopping once he had it in sight. He waited until the others silently joined him, then got his feet beneath him and moved out in a crouch.

The diesel was the engine of a self-propelled gun, which sat cheek-by-jowl with other vehicles facing out on a small natural clearing. Working from tree to tree in the space between the perimeter outposts and the clearing, Tag led the patrol past more than a dozen pieces of artillery and armor, before something told him things were not right. He halted the raiders and squinted through the darkness.

"You see any movement around those two tanks?" he said to Holz.

"Nothing," Holz replied. He looked at Tag inquiringly.

"Ham," Tag whispered, "check 'em out."

Ham gave the thumbs-up and disappeared as he sank to the forest floor and crabbed toward the tanks. After five minutes of breathless silence, he crawled back.

"Got no Ivan; got no tanks," he said to Tag. "Those are phonies, boss. Plywood and shit."

"Anything under them?"

"Missile stands."

"Multiple launchers?"

Ham shook his head. "Single tube. Big suckers."

"Okay. We've seen enough. Let's give these bastards the hotfoot and get out of here," Tag said.

There were real tanks among the phantoms, but they were T-72s, the export model seldom seen in first-line Soviet battle units, as well as another battery of self-propelled guns. Tag's raiders took the SPs first, creeping up on them and their sleeping crews to place C-4 charges in their treads, then laid their remaining charges on the T-72s, wedging the oblong blocks of plastic explosives in the tanks' exhaust grilles.

The work was nerve-wracking. Tag and his patrol were often just a few feet away from the bored Communist soldiers standing radio watch, and twice the duty officer passed within spitting distance of the raiders as he idly inspected the lax perimeter positions. The three-quarter moon had begun to rise in the east when they sneaked back to the neutralized foxhole.

Jan moved forward to check out the foxhole, while the others waited beneath the sparse cover of the brush. Jan disappeared over the parapet of the hole seconds before the wandering duty officer ambled out of the trees, heading for the position and speaking softly in Russian.

The Soviet lieutenant was alone, and Tag bunched the muscles in his thighs and calves, ready to take him from behind. But as the Russian reached the hole, his face was lit by two diffuse muzzle flashes, accompanied by the *phut-phut* of Jan's silenced Walther. The man fell into the hole with a tremendous racket of strangled yelps and crashing gear. A single *phut* put an end to it, but not before Tag and the others heard sotto-voce calls from the other OPs and the sound of boots squeaking on armor plate somewhere to their rear.

Tag rolled to one side and motioned Holz and Ham forward as he dug in a cargo pocket for the remote detonation device. The charges they had set were programmed separately, so Tag could trigger them individually at will. He pressed the number "1" on the keypad, then "armed," then "detonate."

One hundred fifty meters down the line, the one-kilo block of C-4 wedged in the treads of the first 152mm howitzer ripped through the drive carriage, slinging links of track like shrapnel and peeling the track fender from the body. Lubricants and hydraulic fluid ignited, engulfing the entire side of the self-propelled cannon.

Tag touched off charges "2" and "3," and two more

of the most distant guns roared into flame. And on one, the explosion reached the magazine. The initial blast was followed in milliseconds by blinding light and a deafening concussion. Hot metal screamed from the holocaust, scything the treetops and the stunned Soviet troops who hadn't the wits to find cover. Smoking steel was raining like hail as Tag crouched and sprinted past the foxhole. He was twenty meters into the kill zone between the OPs and the wire when the first rounds cracked around him and he heard the hollow pop of a flare being fired.

He dived into a shallow depression, burrowing in the leaves, and the flare burst overhead, swaying on its parachute and casting an eerie metallic light over the woods. With his head buried in his arms to protect his night vision from the glare, Tag let enough light leak in to know when the flare began to die.

Can't hold up the show, he thought. At the last guttering of the flare, Tag leapt up, spun, and ran. One of the OPs heard him, and realizing another flare would not illuminate the perimeter before the raider made the wire, the Communist soldiers opened up with their AKs. One of them cranked the hell-box detonator connected to the mines in the kill zone, and the rearranged claymores consumed the two nearest OPs with thousands of screaming BB pellets, shredding sandbags and flesh and leaving the survivors in hysterical agony. Confusion reigned for a half kilometer along the Soviet line.

Ham held the wire, with Holz and Jan covering, as Tag came through. There was no need to speak: each of them knew what to do. They put another fifty meters between themselves and the wire, then stopped at Tag's command and threw themselves into a hasty defensive perimeter. Tag worked the remote detonator rapidly, as howitzers and tanks went up like a string of fireworks, boiling fire into the night sky in balls of gaseous flame.

"Lord," Ham whispered wistfully, "I do love a good ambush."

With scrap from the last explosion still pelting through the canopy of leaves, the raiders loped away from the carnage, running swiftly and easily in the moonlight, taking an angle that would lead them farther around the column of howitzers and infantry than the route they had taken coming in. Still, they were close enough to hear motors starting and the scurry of frightened men roused from sleep by the string of explosions. It was a sound Tag liked, and it set him to thinking.

With Tag setting the pace, the raiders covered the remaining distance back to their vehicles in fifteen minutes. Holz was faltering by then, clearly still bothered by the aftereffect of his head injury, staggering and pressing one palm to his yet-discolored temple.

"How you making it, Rick?" Tag asked.

"Ja, ja," Holz said impatiently, "I will be fine."

"Would smoking some more of Ivan's artillery make you feel any better?"

Holz looked out from under the hand he was holding to his head. "Hit and run?" he said.

"Wham, bam, and thank you, Ma'am."

"We take the flanks, and you shoot column length," Holz said, dropping his hand.

"Let's do it," Tag said, "before they wake up."

In less than a minute, Tag had his crew briefed and was navigating the No Slack Too through the trees to a slight rise two hundred meters behind the artillery column, one offering just enough elevation for Ham to sight several of the SPs. Tag coached Wheels through a series of touch maneuvers to align the XM-F4 with a natural alley through the trees that looked down on most of the Soviet column.

"Load HE," he said to Fruits Tutti. "Ham, take the farthest one first, but wait for the one-oh-sixes."

"Roger, dodger," Ham said in grim glee. "It's Humpty Dumpty time."

The double flashes from muzzle and breech on the Jagd Kommandos' recoilless rifles lit the woods on either side of the column. Through his scope, Tag saw the rounds walking down the column, as one, two, then three of the heavy guns ruptured with internal explosions and Ham triggered the No Slack Too's 120mm gun, obliterating a fourth howitzer.

"Target," Tag barked, locking on the next howitzer.

As the loading carousel spun, Ham replied, "Confirmed."

"Shoot."

"Shot."

"Target."

"Confirmed."

"Shoot."

"Shot."

"Hit it, Wheels," Tag ordered, and Latta spun them in a bootlegger's turn, racing away from the carnage of blazing guns and men dead and dying from more than a dozen high-explosive rounds that the raiders had unleashed in less than fifteen seconds.

Tag came up through his hatch and smelled the crisp night air and heard the syncopated rattle of wild small-arms fire amid the tympani of secondary explosions still cooking off. He settled his elbows on the lip of the hatch and smiled. Whatever else might come to pass, he knew that this had been a night's work.

8

"Max," Giesla said as Wheels killed the turbines and Tag crawled from his hatch into the gas-lit cavern, "come quickly."

"What's up?" he said, shedding all thoughts of rest as he hurried to Giesla's side.

"A lot, Max," she said. They crossed the cavern toward the situation table. "Maybe you know something that will make it all make sense."

Holz and Prentice were waiting at the table, along with Johann and another of his geriatric guerrillas.

Holz, a wet rag held to his head, said, "I think we have a situation here, Max. Or, perhaps, we have two. True, Sister?"

Giesla gave a short nod and spoke to Tag. "Max, this evening the Russian antitank unit was back in the village. This time they were questioning people and searching for contraband. Johann says they seem to know what they are looking for. When they left, one of his people came in to report a convoy moving through the mountains, along the far side on the old road past the religious retreat. From what I can gather, it was a supply convoy, with just troops and BMPs for security. But he also said there are at least two more of the tank-killer reconnaissance patrols working between here and that road."

"A small world and getting smaller," Tag mused. He studied the situation table that Giesla had remarked to identify the convoy and the antitank units. "How large was the convoy?"

Giesla spoke in German to the two partisans. Johann's companion answered telegraphically, ticking off items on his fingers.

Giesla turned back to Tag. "Thirty-two covered trucks with Red Star medical insignias, five open trucks full of troops, and six BMPs."

"Okay," Tag said at last, "at first light, we're going to extend our listening perimeter. How's the work on the old shafts coming?"

"Not bad," Prentice said. "When we got the word from Johann, I put both Bradleys in position—well, actually N. Sain put himself in position, but he took that one really flaky shaft. The others are usable, but they still have too much trash at the entrances for the gun buggies to push past."

"Work on it, Chuck," said Tag. "We may need them sooner than we expected."

"I've got people on it now."

"What did you find, Max?" asked Giesla. "Does it make any of this make sense?"

Tag sketched out what they had seen and done along the disguised Soviet line, with Giesla translating for Johann and the other partisan.

"So," he said, "it's no mystery why the tank killers are sniffing around, only what they're doing here to begin with. I'm more curious about that so-called medical convoy and what it's carrying. I know it's got something to do with those phoney tanks and the missile stands, and I know it isn't good. But what?" He looked at the others and got no response.

A voice out of the darkness trilled, "Illusion, illusion; it's all *maya*," and N. Sain came bouncing, bare-chested and disheveled, from the shadows. "Nothing is as it seems or even *what* it seems. The Antichrist of rock and roll will look like Chuck Berry, and his incantation will stir the souls of even the righteous."

N. Sain stopped to peruse the two partisans, his eyes glinting and expectant, while they stared at him in dignified revulsion.

"N. Sain," Tag said patiently, "remember that they don't speak English."

"Oh, but I can see the mark of wisdom on them, Heideggerian authenticity." He popped his heels together and made a stiff, formal bow, then faced Tag again.

"Captain Maximilian," N. Sain intoned, "god-king of carnage and instrument of the ineffable, I got a scoop for you: the infidels are fucking with your head, playing a shell game, *stunt-fucking the beatific booty!*"

"Yes," Tag said solemnly, "but what's puzzling me is the nature of their game."

The allusion to antique music delighted N. Sain, who rolled his eyes and hopped on one foot.

"Ooooo," he crooned, "too fucking much. You are the max, Cap."

"So," Tag said as N. Sain settled down, "what's their scam, my man?"

N. Sain fixed his dancing eyes on Tag. "I have heard much by just listening," he said, "enough to know what I do not. I fear the convoy, because it is so easy, but fear more letting it go unnoticed. Do not pretend, especially to yourself, that you do not know what's meant by mobile missile stands and self-propelled artillery with no infantry to support. It is the fire, this time."

Holz, Giesla, and Prentice exchanged quizzical looks. The two aging partisans eyed N. Sain as though he were a biological specimen.

Fighting back a natural aversion, Tag clapped N. Sain on the shoulder. "You have shared a searing vision," he said matter-of-factly, while inside he computed frantically: time, distance, fuel, ammunition, the raiders' odds in a fight with the Soviet tank killers.

"And," Tag continued, "it is a righteous vision. But we will need other eyes to see it clearly." He turned to Giesla. "Can Johann and his people keep any kind of tabs on the antitank patrols?"

Giesla spoke to the partisan leader, listened to his brief reply, and turned back to Tag.

"He says they can put twenty men in the hills, but they have no radios."

"Okay, then," Tag said, "how many Prick-Ms can we spare, Chuck?"

"Four, if we keep just one to a squad," Prentice said.

"Make it three," Tag told him, "then let these guys go home. And, Rick, you could use some rest, too."

"Both of you," Giesla said. "We have the watches set, and there's nothing more you can do tonight."

Tag reluctantly agreed. He woke his crew and moved the No Slack Too outside between two of the piles of stone tailings at the border of the wasteland and the woods, giving the XM-F4 a clear field of fire across the entire expanse fronting the mine shafts. Tag activated the passive air-alarm radar and the electronic "ear," then cooled his crew's complaints by taking the first watch.

Tag used his time to write and rewrite the intelligence report he would be burping to Command just before dawn, trying to shape it so that its very brevity conveyed his broad suspicions about the Soviet gambit. N. Sain was right, of course. Ivan was playing a shell game, with nuclear weapons the pea. And if he didn't know where they were coming from, he would bet on where they were going: there was only one use for single-launch missile stands in a ground war like this one. Yet except for the unarmed cruise missile they had destroyed in the fight at the manor houses, Tag had found nothing to fill those empty racks. The idea of the convoy moving unopposed and lightly guarded toward the Communist line knotted his stomach. He could not concentrate well enough to encode the report he had drafted, but found the fatigue strangely relaxing. He sat for the next hour in blank reverie, until it was time for Fruits Tutti to relieve him.

Tag slept soundly for more than three hours and awoke feeling sharp-set and alert. Fruits had encoded the report during his watch, and Prentice, who was out early to reset the listening posts, had one of his men bring coffee and sandwiches out to the tank. Gnawing hungrily on the tough bread and salty ham, Tag keyed in his report, locked the mini-dish antenna on the communication satellite then over-head, and at exactly 0550 zapped his three-second message burp into outer space and back at the speed of light.

He finished his food, drew a second cup of coffee, and waited for Command's scheduled contact at 0610. At 0615, he was anxious; at 0620, Tag ran an autoanalysis of the computer-communication system. At 0625, the message started coming in and was more than thirty seconds in transmission, the equivalent of almost an hour in real-time broadcast. Tag was soon to see why: map after map scrolled across the video screen and off the printer platen, followed by page after page of weapons profiles. But his impatience turned to grimness when the written portion appeared.

Tag ripped the message from the printer, snatched up the sheaf of maps and drawings, vaulted out of the No Slack Too, and sprinted in the open across the wasteland to the mine shaft. Giesla was waiting for him at the situation table in the cavern, with Holz asleep on an air mattress nearby.

"Max," Giesla said, alarmed at his obvious urgency, "what is it?"

"Look at these," he said, shoving the maps and drawings at her, "and listen to this." He flipped back and forth between the two closely printed pages of the message, then began moving one finger down the type.

"It says here," Tag continued, "that G-2 believes basically what we do about Ivan's little game, but they don't know either just what it means. *But* they are convinced that the Russians are moving nukes into this sector, and they even think they know when and how." He paused and looked up. "But, Gies, I don't think they've included that convoy out there right now in the estimate." He returned to the printed pages: "It looks like, despite all that, there's going to be a counterattack here in the Jura."

"Look at this, Max." Giesla stood at his shoulder, pointing on the photo map she was holding. "Here, where the Red Army was staging for the swing south, look how they are bleeding back toward the Danube. And here"—she shuffled another map on top—"see how the column of trucks is splitting. From there they can easily be on the Jura line in four hours, maybe less."

Tag nodded. "Or turn back southwest," he said, and handed her the message pages. "Find the sheets with these convoy routes on them. Wake Rick up and fill him in. I'm going to get Prentice, and then we've got a convoy to stop."

"Can we reach it before it gets there?"

"Gotta try, babe," Tag said, amazed at his own use of the endearment.

In a half hour, the entire raider contingent was ready to roll. Tag had the cavern completely evacuated, leaving four of the recuperating wounded in a listening post with a PRC-M, and the now half-emptied fuel tank that N. Sain had scrounged buried in a mound of gravel tailings. At 0720, a partisan patrol radioed sighting a tank-killer unit on the south side of the mountains moving parallel to the valley.

Tag pushed his raiders through the forest as fast as the Bradleys would allow, too fast for safety, even with the Jagd Kommandos at the point and flanks. One gun buggie, with Jan and Karl aboard, had raced ahead alone to locate the convoy—or the ambush. Holz, in the point vehicle, found fire trails and old log-road traces with unerring knack, allowing the main body to be within thirty minutes of the advanced scouts when they reported sighting the convoy at 0905. At 0907, the partisans reported the Communist antitank unit moving on a course for the raiders' line of march.

Giesla pulled her vehicle in from the flank and halted the No Slack Too.

"Max," she said as Tag stuck his head out of his hatch, "I do not like being the hunted. I want to take Mathias and stop them. You won't need our guns to ruin the column."

Tag opened his mouth to object, shut it, then said, "I'll tell Rick. Do it."

The place that Jan directed them to over the radio was enough to satisfy even Ham Jefferson's high standards of ambush. Set well above the road and overlooking a curve, the creeper-covered ruins of log buildings gave the raiders both cover and concealment and murderously open fields of fire into the defilade. With the vehicles all in position, Tag and Holz lay amid the litter of rotting logs and their primeval musk of fungi, gazing through binoculars as the approaching column crawled along the pitted and washed-out roadbed.

"Duck soup, *ja*, Max?" Holz said.

"Maybe too ducky, Rick. Let's give them a good look."

The four BMPs leading the convoy were, along with the muscle Bradley, the bad boys of APCs, with turret-mounted 73mm cannons and racks of AT-4 Spigot antitank missiles. They were traveling with all hatches closed, not as casual as a naked convoy behind their own lines would suggest. Tag took note. He saw the tracked APCs claw through a section of potholes less than three hundred meters away and kept his attention there as three of the infantry trucks made their way through, followed by the first of the covered trucks that bounced and wallowed over the bumps. Then, the dime dropped.

"Rick!" he rasped. "Those goddamn trucks are empty."

Holz lowered his glasses and looked at Tag. "We must go," he said. "Now, Max."

Tag opened his mouth to reply, and that was when he heard the helicopters. He and Holz looked toward the sound as six Mi-28 Havocs, in two wedges of three, seemed to rise from the forested slope below them, noses slightly depressed in attack attitude, the hard-points on their stubby wings bulging with pods of Tree Frog missiles.

"Get your vehicles back in the woods," Tag shouted, adrenaline amplifying his voice. "Go, Rick."

Holz broke from their OP, running broken-field through the scattering of logs, as Tag bolted toward the eroded gully on the exposed face of the hill directly beneath the No Slack Too's position.

The first shots he heard were the distant, breathy drumroll of 106s. In later years, he would often recount, as though he had been there, the ambush Giesla staged against the antitank recon unit, how she laid her positions to take the toy tanks and BMPs from the rear, then sparred with the survivors among the trees, until the lone remaining tank panicked and ran headlong into the lethal sights of Mathias Betcher. But now, as he hit the erosion ditch, his back to the Havocs, and scrambled up six feet of naked earth, Tag's one thought of Giesla was bitter recrimination for letting her go.

He was just coming up off his hands and knees, ready to dash the few remaining yards to the No Slack Too, when the swarm of 30mm fire from a Havoc's nose turret shattered the silence and turned the air around him into a maelstrom of whining rocks, ricochets, and splintered wood.

Tag dived forward, rolled, and came up running beneath the covering fire of the Phalanx. As he dropped into his hatch, he saw one of the flying tanks wheel wildly, its tail engulfed in flame, and disappear beneath the hill, only to rise a moment later as a coil of inky smoke. He locked the hatch above him and threw himself against the eyepiece on his periscope.

A pair of Tree Frogs fired by a second Havoc detonated in the treetops, showering the XM-F4 in shrapnel. But even the robotic reflexes of the Phalanx were too slow to recover before the Mi-28 swelled like a cotton boll, only its nose and tail rotor visible in the white-phosphorous envelope that consumed it.

N. Sain.

"Wheels, Position Bravo," Tag said. Then, keying the TAC frequency, he ordered his command, "All units, fall back to the woods."

Moving upslope into the woods exposed the No Slack Too to fire from the road as well as from the air. Tag had no sense of the battle raging around him, as machine-gun fire and futile 73mm rounds peppered the nose and turret of the XM-F4. A Spigot missile struck the glacis at a steep angle and pummeled the men inside, but did only superficial damage to the slick-skin armor.

"Fire on opportunity," Tag commanded his gunner.

Before Wheels had the No Slack Too in its secondary position, Ham had made road kills out of the two lead BMPs. All around the tank, missiles and cannon fire from the attacking Havocs splintered the limbs and trunks of the forest. Half blinded by the smoke, Tag raked the trucks of infantry with a merciless stream of fire from his coax 7.62mm machine gun, leaving air defense to the voracious Phalanx and target practice to Ham Jefferson.

A chance round from the 37mm caused the nose turret on an Mi-28 to suddenly lose control, spraying fire wildly as it auto-rotated and struck one of its sister ships in both canopies, sending it in a drunken gyration down to a fiery death among the bunched vehicles in the convoy. Then the crippled Havoc opened along its belly like a locust shell, spilling its mechanical guts as it fell.

"All units, disengage," Tag said over the TAC frequency. "I say again, disengage. Individual evasive tactics. Report."

Out of the squelch and static on the TAC net, Tag could pick out only two responses, one in English and one in German, but could not identify the voices.

"Wheelman," Tag said to his driver, "do your stuff."

As the No Slack Too jerked among the trees, gathering speed, Tag's emotions were a confusion of conflicts. Six attack helicopters, three or four BMPs, and a whole slew of trucks and infantry ought, he knew, to be called a victory. But he also had at least one Bradley and one Jagd Kommando vehicle unaccounted for, not to mention (or even to think of) Giesla and Mathias Betcher. Subduing his emotions left him even more bitter: the convoy had been a ruse, a trap, and he had fallen for it. He hammered the hull of the No Slack Too in frustration, grateful for a crew who knew him and could ignore it and go on with the job at hand.

Tag let Wheels hotdog for a half hour, until they were on the crest of the Jura once again, then he called a halt, called up maps on the VDT, and called on all units to report.

Giesla, Betcher, and Jan all responded, as did an unfamiliar voice from Prentice's Bradley. There was nothing from N. Sain or from Heinrich Holz.

Tag set the No Slack Too on a course roughly due north, angrily hoping to cross paths with one of the Soviet units. He had no luck that day. Neither radar nor the audio amplifier picked up more than the scurry of wildlife.

Riding in the open turret hatch to let the air and sunlight and swift tacking of the tank absorb him, Tag saw a natural lean-to of creepers where two tall trees had blown across a third, and he ordered Wheels to park them there for five.

The crew dismounted, peed, mixed some instant rations, and shoved off again, making a shallow fish-hook bend around the expanse of fissures and coming up on the mineworks from the north. Tag got no radio response from the listening post of wounded, so he stopped the No Slack Too and sent Fruits ahead to scout.

Fifteen minutes later, Giesla's voice came over the TAC net, calling him home.

The scene inside the cavern was a calamity. The close air was acrid with ozone, the scorched smell of overheated engines, and just a whiff of cordite. A half-dozen men lay wounded on the floor, some moaning in pain. Bones, the medic, moved among them, administering morphine and first aid. The three commando cars all showed signs of having taken hits, but Prentice's Bradley was the worst.

A round or a rocket had sheared off the top of the Bradley's turret, and dozens of hard hits from machine-gun fire had pocked its hull like acne. Its freestanding machine gun was blown away, along with its floodlight, antenna array, and everything else on its armored skin, even to the painted insignia.

Tag could see at a glance that all the infantry were here, but there was no sign of the fourth gun buggy or of N. Sain's Bradley. Prentice, an oozing bandage tied clumsily around his head, met him as he scrambled from his hatch.

"How bad, Chuck?" Tag said.

"They got Weintaub and three of my men," Prentice said, "and six badly wounded." He jerked his head in the direction of the soldiers laid out on the floor of the cavern.

"What about Holz and N. Sain?"

Prentice shook his head. "I don't know for sure, Max. When we took our hit, Sain saved our butt, though. He took out the BMPs at our end of the column, then loaded all the troops in our track and covered us while we withdrew—or so Sergeant Dunn tells me. I was out for a while, and Dunn had to drive. Nobody saw him after that. I don't know anything about Rick."

Tag lay his hand on Prentice's back. "Can your track still fight?"

"The gun still shoots, but we've lost all our fire-direction systems."

"Okay. Go be with your men, Chuck, and get us some security out ASAP."

Prentice pulled his haggard face together. "Right," he said, and turned away.

Tag turned back to his tank and spoke to his driver, who

sat staring from his hatch. "Wheels, take it outside, back to yesterday's position. And I want all systems up. I have a hunch that these hills are gonna be lousy with bad guys."

"You got it, Cap'n," Wheels said. He kicked the turbines to life and spun toward the entrance.

Tag found Giesla leaning on the possibles box of her vehicle, a map spread before her. One fog lamp on the roll cage of the gun buggy dangled from its wires, and bullet holes had made sieves of the exhaust stacks. She looked up at him with eyes blurred by pent-up tears.

Before Tag could open his mouth, she said, "He's dead, Max."

Tag did not have to ask who. He reached out to her, but she stopped him with one hand.

"No, Max," she said, the tension straining in her voice. "Please. I will cry if you do, and I do not want to cry now."

"What happened?"

Giesla's shrug so reminded Tag of his friend, her brother, that a wave of grief washed over him.

"What is to tell?" she said, looking back at the map. "He was covering for us, Mathias and me. I saw him, Max. He was standing at the fifty caliber, firing at the Havocs, and his driver was still shooting the convoy. Then the missiles hit, and all I could see was one wheel from his vehicle that came flying from the smoke. That's all."

"Oh, sweet Jesus, Giesla. I'm sorry. I should have sniffed out the trap. I should have . . . "

"No, Max." She looked back at him. "You did what was right, and you saved the rest of us. You did not cause it."

The echo of his own words to her, when she had still blamed herself for the ambush in Africa that killed her husband, moved Tag. In that fleeting moment, the tough tanker drew strength from the woman on the edge of tears.

"What about the others?" he asked.

"Superficial damage only," she said, with a nod to the bullet-riddled gun buggy, "and Jan lost his radio. We can still fight."

"Any word from our buddies in the village?"

She shook her head. "I will try them now."

"Do that," he said, squeezing her arm. "I'm going to contact Command. And let's get these vehicles dispersed to the shafts."

Tag went out through the blackout drapes and crossed the barren ground to the trees, where the No Slack Too awaited. He encoded and sent a brief after-action report, ending it with a request for immediate response/instructions. Immediately meant a half hour to Command.

During that thirty minutes, Tag had time to reflect on their situation. His were not happy thoughts. Holz's death was a personal loss to Tag, but not the worst of their predicament. N. Sain and his Bradley would certainly be missed, if it came to another shootout, especially with Prentice's fire-direction systems knocked out. Worse still were the wounded. They needed serious medical attention, much more than Bones could provide under the best circumstances. Their existence was damn sure no secret to Ivan now, and it was just a matter of time and elimination before the Soviets would be back here looking for them. They had little room to run and no place to hide. And they still had a mission.

On the up side, they were still an effective fighting force, even if somewhat reduced. Fuel and ammunition were not yet a problem. And, as he watched Prentice's men slip from the mine shaft to take up their perimeter positions, Tag felt a tug of pride at how well everyone's morale was holding up. As long as they could do their jobs, answer the bell for every round, they had a fighting chance. The No Slack Too was essentially undamaged, with plenty of rounds in its magazine, and that alone was enough to give Tag a calm certainty about their chances.

The response from Command had, Tag thought, the earmarks of Satin Ass Menefee all over it. Couched in the telegraphic, impersonal style that passed for English among career-driven officers like the colonel, the message nevertheless contained hard intelligence that made it worth the wait.

Command was certain now that the nuclear devices were being brought up, but not in truck convoys. They were expected to be moved through the forest in tracked vehicles, under the protection of the antitank recon battalion, whose elements the partisans had been tracking. The message ended with a formal congratulations for work well done and a blanket order to interdict all movement through the Jura toward the front.

Fruits Tutti gave a low whistle as Tag put down the message. "Not askin' much, are they?" he said.

"We know more than we did, Fruits," Tag said. "And if you think about it, that may be a first coming from Queen Bee."

"How's Gies taking it about her brother, boss?" Ham asked, his voice soft with concern.

"You like her, don't you, Ham?" Tag said by way of reply.

"She's the freakin' Madonna," Fruits said emphatically.

"What he said," Ham added.

"Well, guys," Tag told them, "she's gonna be okay, but right now she's running on guts and nerves. The best thing we can do is our jobs. When all this is done, we'll have plenty to grieve for and plenty of time for it. But for now, don't say anything to her."

The men nodded their agreement. Tag took the computer printout of the message from Command and returned to the cavern.

Only Giesla, her vehicle, and the Jagd Kommando Horst were still there when Tag arrived. Giesla, her face pinched in concentration, stood with one foot on a tire, holding the radio handset to her ear. She motioned Tag to hurry.

"Max," she said, twisting the mouthpiece up over her forehead, "they have found N. Sain, or seen him, at least. But from what I am hearing, I think he is stalking one of the tank-killer units. It is all confusing, but they are close."

The radio console gave a tinny buzz and lit up to show an incoming message on the TAC frequency. Giesla reached in, opened the frequency, and flipped on the speaker.

" . . . aximilian, avatar of ambuscade, this is the disciple of death, coming to you with sacrificial offerings," N. Sain's oratorical voice boomed from the set.

Tag took the handset from Giesla and said into it, "This is Cap Max. Say again your last, Disciple."

"Pilgrims," N. Sain roared. "Appeasements to Kali, doubters of death. I will lay them at your feet in minutes."

"What do you have, Disciple."

There was a click and a hiss followed by a throbbing bass line and the familiar retro-soul lyrics, "Chain, chain, chain, chain of fools." Then the transmission went dead.

Tag ignored Giesla's questioning look.

"Bradley One, this is Butcher Boy, did you copy that last? Over."

"Roger, Butcher Boy," Prentice responded, "I copied. Over."

"Bradley One, I want everyone except necessary crews outside. Issue LAWs, and unlimber the Dragon. I think we have company coming."

"Roger, Butcher Boy."

Tag turned back to Giesla. "N. Sain is trying to lead them here. Get yourself a place to fight from, Gies."

She grabbed his arm as he turned to go. Tag faced her, and Giesla kissed him hard on the mouth. Horst could not have looked more shocked if it had been two men.

Giesla jerked her head back. "Yes, sir," she said, letting go of Tag and stepping into her vehicle.

Tag heard the first booming reports of cannon fire when he was still fifty meters from the No Slack Too and running hard, easily outdistancing the infantrymen with their unwieldy arm loads of LAWs and bandoliers of ammunition. Just as Tag reached the bushes that covered the pile of tailings where his tank was concealed, Giesla's gun buggy came blasting from the mouth of the mine, turned left into the woods, and disappeared.

Wheels Latta, his head sticking out of the open hatch, already had the turbines humming.

"What's the drill, Cap'n?" he asked, his grin wide and boyish as ever.

Tag hit his seat and bellowed through the crew compartment. "Fresh meat, you carnivores. N. Sain says he's bringing lambs to the slaughter."

"We heard," Ham Jefferson said. "That boy's got more soul than I ever expected."

"Load HE," Tag said to Fruits. "I'll shoot the Phalanx."

The loading carousel spun. Wheels double-cocked his coaxial 7.62mm machine gun.

Tag kept his hatch open to better judge the closing distance to the gunfire. He hoped N. Sain was as good as the lunatic thought he was. It was hope rewarded.

The 75mm burst from the rapid-fire cannon on N. Sain's Bradley signaled that the disciple of death had reached the east end of the barren mineworks. Tag dogged down his hatch and leaned into his scope. The Bradley broke into the clear, its gun firing at trail, as the machine juked and bounded through the litter of rocks and boulders. Tag still could not see the Bradley's pursuers when an ATGM *whoosh*ed from the tree line, flew high over the fleeing track, and struck the worked face of the mountain. The smoke and dust partially obscured N. Sain's Bradley. As it emerged in clear view again, Tag could also see the Communist tank-killer formation come charging out of the trees.

Tag was nervous. This ad hoc ambush had not been planned or rehearsed, and he prayed no one would get an itchy finger and shoot before the entire Soviet unit was in the open kill zone. N. Sain had made it past the abandoned crane, almost directly in front of the No Slack Too's position, when one of the fin-stabilized rounds from a 120mm smoothbore on one of the Communists' compact tanks struck the derrick and sent it crashing on top of the Bradley. The twisted steel boom knocked the Bradley sideways, then bounced to the ground. The turret twitched once or twice, and then sat immobile.

"Stand by," Tag said.

Suddenly the turret hatch on the motionless Bradley sprang back, and a white T-shirt tied to a pole waved from the opening.

The motherfucker is insane, Tag thought, but the gambit worked. The Soviet formation slowed, and one of the light tanks rolled ahead toward the Bradley.

The moment that the Communist tankers had to maneuver to clear the debris from the crane and take their bead off the Bradley, N. Sain's 75mm came alive, spouting white-phosphorous death at almost point-blank range.

"Shoot," Tag commanded, triggering the Phalanx as Ham brought the main gun around to take on the remaining armor.

Points of flame shot from three of the deserted-looking mine shafts as Prentice and the two Jagd Kommando vehicles unleashed a salvo broadside on the enemy formation. In the time it took for Ham to spatter the two remaining compact tanks, a fusillade of ordnance from the LAWs and the Dragon stand turned the BMPs into steel crematoria for their crews, as fuel and munitions inside the APCs roared like the heart of a Bessemer.

It was over in seconds. A total of four killer tanks and twice that many armored tracks lay in burning ruin.

Tag saw the danger in their victory almost at once and keyed the TAC frequency.

"All units, this is Butcher Boy. Clear out. Move upslope. I say again, move out upslope at once."

Prentice's Bradley broke through the facade of timbers and trash disguising its fighting position and ran across the death-studded expanse of stone. It picked up the infantry on the far side, then accelerated past Tag's position and out of sight into the woods.

"Wheels," Tag said, "give everybody another minute or two to clear the area, then get us out of here."

The Jagd Kommando gun vehicles bolted from the adit just behind the Bradley and were gone in an instant. Surveying the scene a final time, Tag realized that N. Sain had vanished.

"Go, Wheels," he said, and the XM-F4 reared as it spun through the heap of scree and crashed into the forest, heedless of any telltale sign it might leave. It was halfway to a point on the slope where it could find a level place to fight from when the air-alarm klaxon sounded.

Tag glanced at his radar screen and spoke to Ham over the intercom: "Fixed wing. Arm the War Clubs."

The two MiG-31s came in from the east and made their first pass at ten thousand feet, at the bottom of the wispy clouds. They wheeled in eschelon to the south, circling the woods that held the dispersed vehicles of Tag's raider command, then dropped to five thousand for a closer look, easily within the War Clubs' range.

"I've got a lock," Ham Jefferson reported.

"We'll take them both at once," Tag said. "On my command."

Wheels halted the No Slack Too, and the tank itself seemed to hold its breath.

"Shoot," Tag commanded.

"Shot," Ham replied, and on each side of the turret, one of the needle-nosed missiles sizzled from its clamshell shroud.

The pilot of the lead fighter picked up the signatures of the War Clubs in time to drop a flare and haul his jet into a banking climb, but it was too late. The missiles were too close. The first War Club detonated in the column of hot gas from the MiG's afterburners, five feet from its tail, pulverizing fins and stabilizers. The pilot and the systems officer both ejected, as the plane whipped into a pancake spin.

The second MiG never saw it coming. When his wingman rolled and radioed the alarm, the second pilot looked to his right. At the exact moment that he touched his controls to evade the incoming War Clubs, the missile struck the canard on the intake of his port engine, shearing off the wing and blasting the fuselage in two. The remaining wing and tail section tumbled in eccentric gyres and hammered into the woods just below the mineworks, its remaining fuel and alloy skin going off like flash powder.

"All clear," Tag said. He unlocked his hatch and threw it back, as did Wheels and Ham.

The gunner looked down from the turret at the scene of carnage below.

"My, my," he said, smacking his lips, "now that is what I call a pretty sight."

"Yeah, well I'm glad you like it," Fruits whined from inside, "'cause now we ain't got no home, Hambone."

"What'd you wanna do, Tutti Fruity," Wheels drawled, "plant you a little garden, maybe put up some curtains?"

"Aw, fuck you," Fruits parried.

"Actually, Wheelman," Tag said, looking at his driver across the glacis, "he's got a point. And remember, we've still got wounded."

"Boss," Ham barked, "something coming at our six."

Without being told, Wheels dropped back in his seat and spun the No Slack Too on one track. When it stopped, the muzzle of the 120mm cannon was staring face-to-face with the guerrilla leader Johann, who sat astride an ancient DKW motorcycle, with Giesla on the passenger pad on the rear fender.

Johann, his eyes wide, clamped on the brakes and brought the bike to a shuddering stop. Giesla got off and approached the tank.

"Woman," Tag said in mock severity, "don't come sneaking up on me like that."

"Johann thought we might need some help," she said.

"Oh?"

"Yes. He feared that N. Sain might cause us some trouble. Johann was the one who reported seeing him."

Tag shook his head in amazement. "Look, can he get us someplace where we can regroup and care for our wounded?"

"Better than that, I think," said Giesla. "Come, follow us."

She swung back on the motorcycle, and Johann nursed it up the hill.

Tag reassembled his unit a half kilometer away, but as they moved out behind Johann, there was no sign of N. Sain.

9

The column, moving slowly behind Johann's lead, had traveled less than a half klick when Tag heard the thick, unmistakable stutter of a Bradley's 75mm coming from somewhere behind them and higher up the mountain, no more than a few kilometers away. Tag's first emotion was anger, a frustrated fury that he had no control over his best Bradley crew, a crew that was endangering them all, though one he could ill afford to lose even as a free lance. But in the next instant, he was cool again, calculating all the possible options, all the possible consequences, while still damning N. Sain under his breath.

"Column halt," Tag ordered over the TAC net, and the formation of crawling vehicles jerked to a stop.

"Fruits," Tag said, unbuckling himself from his fighting seat, "get me an audio fix on the firing, direction, and distance."

"Roger, Captain Max," Tutti replied.

Tag came out of his hatch, slid over the glacis of the No Slack Too, and hurried to the head of the column. Johann was sitting on his idling motorcycle next to Giesla's gun buggie when Tag reached her.

"Gies," he said, "that's N. Sain back there. As long as he has contact, he's keeping Ivan in the area. You tell Johann that I don't want us anywhere near his town until we can move Ivan's interest a little farther from us. Now, look, don't argue with what I'm going to say. We've got wounded, and we've not got all our vehicles in fighting trim just now. You scatter these people in the woods here, and tell Johann to give you directions and get out. There would be hell to pay if he was caught with us."

"And what do you do?" she asked.

"I go back and get N. Sain to disengage, draw them off—something. The main thing is that we don't need to stir them up any more than we have, and I'm not going to take a chance on Ivan following us and creaming the village. This has got to be a clean break, if it's going to buy us any time at all."

Giesla looked squarely at him and nodded just perceptibly. "Perhaps you should at least take the other Bradley," she said.

"Too slow," said Tag. "This is a Ross Kettle Special, if you ask me. We're the only ones who know what we need to do, and we've got the only machine to do it with."

Giesla looked away from him and stared without focus through her windscreen. "I will set a perimeter," she said.

Tag loped off through the trees and stopped at Prentice's Bradley long enough to tell the lieutenant what was happening.

"Sorry about the wounded," Tag said, "but it's what we have to do right now. Bones," he said, turning to the medic, "can they hold out?"

"Nobody's critical, sir," Bones said, "and we got morphine, but don't be too long, okay?"

"You got it," Tag said. And he ran for his tank.

"Wheels," Tag said, clamping his CVC on his head, "Tutti get you a fix?"

"The fix is made, and the guns are laid," Latta replied as he ran a visual check of his instruments.

"How far?" Tag said.

"'Tween two and three klicks."

"Kick it," Tag ordered. "Fruits, shell rep."

"Ah, yeah, Cap. We got nine sabot, but plenty of HE and two more drums for de Phalanx, plus—what?—sixty percent still in de can I got on now."

"Roger that," Tag said. "Fill the breech with HE. Wheels, how long to get us there?"

Latta, intent on his electronic "window," spoke without looking up from it. "Maybe fifteen, maybe thirty minutes in this. I could put the top down and maybe pick up a little."

"Negative," Tag said. "Just hold it steady. I'll keep you locked on the audio fix, but they don't seem to be moving right now."

"You're the boss, boss," Wheels said absently, treadling his pedals and dipping the steering yoke.

Riding blind was always an eerie sensation for Tag, but especially when it was his job to navigate by sound. The audio-directional finder homed automatically, but at this distance in the woods, it could easily lose a target. Tag kept one hand on the manual control and one eye on the blipping screen that tracked the location of the sporadic cannon fire. It was a job that required less concentration than complete eye-hand reflex, a hypnotic task that deprived all other senses, allowing Tag's mind to gather a host of thoughts while never losing his single-minded awareness of the screen before him or the joystick in his hand.

Almost superstitiously, he thought of Giesla, as if his being able to think of her meant there could not be any immediate danger, thoughts of her having for him no breath of fear or peril. But they were not without concern. Her physical safety he could do nothing about, whatever his instinct, and he could accept this, accept her as a comrade. Worse was his fear of how she might eventually react to her brother Heinrich's death. War and the demands of the day would carry her, as they would him, for a while, pressing them forward in their ghastly duty, honing their sensibilities on the rough stone of survival. Tag wondered whether he would ever be able to look on a Montana sunset again and thrill in mindless awe of its beauty. Would he ever again want to linger over a line in a book just for its sound or sing unself-consciously? If he came through, as he fully intended, what would be left worth saving? Ross Kettle once wrote, in an article on command that appeared in a popular psychology journal, that the fundamental quality of command is compassion—not for one's enemies, but for one's army, its people, and the ideas they serve. Kettle went on to equate the interest in arts and literature among the general staff, which some civilians find peculiar, with this fundamental quality. The pulse of a people, Kettle contended, beat more strongly in history or music or literature than it did in political pronouncements or the voodoo of economics, and the officers who best understood this would best understand how to effectively lead their troops into that least compassionate, least human of endeavors. Would he, Tag mused, survive in that sort of human form? Or would he be so blunted, his edge so turned on what he has had to do, that all keen pleasures were denied him?

The image of the dulled sword could apply to all of them, he thought. Everyone in the raider unit was feeling the effects of fatigue, battle fatigue. That too, he knew, had helped insulate him and Giesla from their grief for Holz, a grief that even now was an abstraction to him, like thoughts of a place one has yet to reach. Better that he should keep his thoughts where he is now, and in that Tag found peace.

Taking stock of the No Slack Too and his crew, he had to admit that they were holding up probably better than anyone, his own megrims notwithstanding. What's more, they were, including right now, proving conclusively that with the XM-series tanks Ross Kettle's tank strategies would change the role of armor forever in the order of battle. Tag could not stop a lump of pride from swelling in his chest, pride in his men and the tank they had helped develop.

Speed and agility, Kettle had demanded, and Wheels Latta had shown them all what that could mean. He had raised the engineers' consciousness of what "handling characteristics" in a tank can mean to unthought-of levels. Not every driver could gauge the drift traction of a thirty-ton tank in a ninety-degree turn on fresh gravel, but Latta had shown it could be done. And he had been the one to convince R&D that an air-foil rear deck would keep treads on the tarmac at eighty. So far, that speed and agility had paid off, but with the man they had at the wheel, small wonder.

And Kettle had wanted superior firepower, especially for air defense, and Ham had first suggested the Phalanx system, even before the problems with the coaxially-mounted 75mm in the XM-F3. It took someone else to figure out replacing the navy Phalanx's 20mm with the No

Slack Too's 37mm, and so give it an antiarmor application as well, but Jefferson had the right idea. And no one in the field understood the unique ballistic qualities of the integral-propellant sabot better than Ham or had a finer touch on a trigger.

If none of the crew could take credit for the first-hit survivability of the monopolar carbide armor they called "slick skin," Tutti had had plenty to do with the No Slack Too's other technological edge, its electronics. The Beast With Two Brains, Fruits's omnibus operating program, had such adaptability and expansion capacity that it was virtually impossible for an enemy trying to design defenses to second-guess its evolution. And with the VLD to collate and synthesize satellite, LandNav, and direct-visual data, the intelligence capabilities of the XM-F4 were staggering.

But it was the men that counted. They would matter most to Tag anyway, but without them the No Slack Too was just so much metal and microchips.

Tag could distinguish separate sounds coming over the audio-directional receiver now, armored vehicles moving but not going anywhere, cannon reports. They were almost on them, and he sensed every man to be as sharp-set as he was.

"Pull up, Wheels," Tag said, releasing the dog on his hatch. He slipped off his CVC and hung it on the back of the seat before standing for a look outside.

By guess and the audio-directional finder, Tag calculated they were within a few hundred meters of the action, which seemed at one minute to be moving toward them, and at the next to be moving away. At that moment, it was coming their way. Tag dropped back in the hatch.

"Okay," he said to the crew, "it sounds like N. Sain is still in it; the firing is coming our way. They're close, gentlemen, and we're going in hot, so all eyes, you hear? Fruits, I'll take the Phalanx. Go, Wheels."

This piece of the mountain, for more than a kilometer, was a gentle slope dimpled with long, shallow depressions, where only scrub and briers grew. N. Sain was trapped in one of these, hemmed in by two of the 2S9-type toy tanks and three AT-configured BMPs. Another of the compact

tanks and two more BMPs were strewn in smoking ruin
farther down the open slope. From their positions on the
high side of the depression, they could not depress their
guns quite enough for a good shot at N. Sain as he juked
the length of his shallow trench and back again, unable
himself to fight effectively or to run. All the Soviets had
to do was wait, if they had the time and patience, wait for
N. Sain to make a break for it down the slope, through
their converging fields of fire.

Tag opened the TAC net and radioed to N. Sain, hoping
he had his ears on, "Disciple, Disciple, this is Avatar. We're
coming to take you home."

But as Wheels reared the No Slack Too out of the
forest shadows and into the clearing at the head of the
depression, one of the Soviet BMPs, its 73mm gun flanked
by pods of stubby ATGMs, was breaking around that end
to rush N. Sain's flank. The Soviet crew was good, reacting
aggressively to the unexpected presence of the No Slack
Too. The BMP locked one tread and slid into position
facing the careening XM-F4. It rocked once, righted, and
a pair of AT-4 Spigot missiles seared off the racks.

Tag registered the incoming contrails in his scope at the
same instant the No Slack Too flinched from the 120mm's
recoil. Before the tank could recover on its suspension, two
nearly simultaneous concussions drove it back, jolting the
men inside like a blind-side punch.

The Soviets in the BMP were luckier; they never saw
what hit them.

Before the Communist commander saw the two missiles
he had launched strike the fender and glacis of the No
Slack Too, before he saw the two black explosions or
registered the flame that leapt between them, the 120mm
high-explosive round that Ham had triggered tore through
the nose of the BMP and, striking the ammunition inside,
detonated with such a force that the backblast through the
entry wound flipped the gutted vehicle on its turret, its crew
flopping inside like seared meat dolls.

"Report," Tag gabbled, his head still ringing with the hits
by the ATGMs.

"Gunner," Ham responded.

"Loader," said Fruits.

"Present, sir," Wheels drawled through a split lip.

Tag was on his scope. "Hard left, Wheels," he ordered. "We need cover on the high ground."

The erstwhile moonshiner pitched the XM-F4 into an accelerating turn, narrowly evading a third Spigot missile fired from a second BMP that had come to its comrade's rescue—too late. The ATGM erupted in the forest, and the BMP that launched it reversed itself into the cover of the trees, just ahead of the gout of 37mm fire that Tag released to cover their exposed flank as they ran. Wheels jinked between two imperial larches, and they were back in the big timber. Tag navigated them in an arc that brought them four or five hundred meters farther down the length of the dimpled depression where N. Sain was still pinned down, then had Wheels swing them around and move as near the edge of the big timber as he could without giving up the shadows.

"That's good," Tag said, motioning to his driver as he spoke. "All systems up; I'm putting the top down."

Tag grabbed his binoculars, hauled himself up through the turret, and opened the main hatch, peering over it to all sides before standing, settling the eyepieces of the binoculars against his face, and slowly scanning the upper rim of the depression below.

There was a report to his left, and Tag turned and located one of the 2S9-type tanks, its cannon depressed to fire down on N. Sain's position. There was another vehicle—Tag couldn't make out what—perhaps two hundred meters closer to him than the 2S9, partially concealed by brush and small trees. A dull glint much farther to his right told him that the second BMP was where they had left it. Okay. He dropped back through the hatch, locked it down, and swung down into the commander's chair.

"Ham," he said through the CVC, "you have that one marked at ten o'clock?"

"Locked and cocked," Ham said, "but I got no shot from here."

"Okay," Tag said. "We've got another one partially concealed at about eleven-thirty, and our other buddy is back where we left him. Let's get us a good place to fight from, make two good shots, and whoever's left is dog meat. Wheels, I'm gonna stick my head out, so let's be quick about it."

"My fav'rite way to," Wheels said.

At Tag's directions, Latta maneuvered them along the verge of the big trees until there was a place where a gully choked with a mass of fallen and decayed timber opened a natural field of fire toward the Soviet positions.

"Okay, Wheels," Tag said to him, "ease her out."

"Don't think that looks a little shaky, Cap'n?" Latta said.

"We'll see," said Tag. "Do it."

Tutti, bat-blind at his position except for the Phalanx monitor, whined through the open intercom, "Oh, jeez, don't fuck with me this way."

The tangled raft of saw-log–size timber gave spongily beneath the XM-F4's weight, creaked, and began to settle when a round from the third BMP—the one Tag had not seen, the one that had broken from its position to intercept the No Slack Too in the woods—struck the compressing pile just beneath the left tread of the tank and detonated three feet below, shattering the solid trunks supporting Tag and his crew. Tutti saw it coming on the Phalanx screen, but had only enough time to squawk, "Movement, nine o'cl . . ." before the 73mm ripped underneath them and the No Slack Too tipped slowly up past forty-five degrees.

Reflexively, Tag cued the Phalanx, the only weapon system he could bring to bear from this crazy angle while fighting gravity and his seat harness.

The cupola of the Phalanx overrotated with the tilting of the tank. It recovered, snapped between two positions near the very top of its sphere of fire, stuttered once, and paused.

A second 73mm struck the edge of the No Slack Too's rear deck, just aft of the turret, doing no damage to the slick-skin armor but jolting the tank one crunching foot farther into the collapsing pile of drift timber.

Tag urged his driver, "Make it move, Wheels."

Latta wedged both throttles open full in reverse and lurched them backward a foot, then he nailed it full forward,

and amid a storm of mulch and wood chips, the No Slack
Too began to move steadily ahead, steadily and lethally
slow, still canted at its helpless angle.

The Phalanx's busy robotics whirred and spun, trying to
track the BMP as it closed on them from what the Phalanx
thought was above. With this vantage of attack and the
eclipsing trees, Tutti, usually blind to the outside from his
position, was the only crewman besides Tag who could
track the BMP. He keyed the heat-image overlay onto his
manual screen and said, "Cap, I got a lock."

"Shoot," Tag responded.

Fruits, his feet braced against the turret ring, let the image
in his scope cut a figure-eight, like a rifleman shooting
offhand, then triggered a syncopated burst from the bobbing
37mm.

The BMP, less than two hundred meters away, had just
exposed its nose and turret in a gap in the trees as it got set
to lay its gun for another shot when the stream of depleted
uranium slugs from the Phalanx swarmed over it, smashing
fist-size holes through the body armor and the crew inside
and pulverizing the cannon barrel, causing an explosion of
the round in its breech that ended all life inside the BMP.
It shuddered once and stopped suddenly, smoke beginning
to pour through the holes made by the Phalanx.

"Goddamn, Fruit Loops," Ham Jefferson said, "you
trying to get my job, son?"

"Keep us moving, Wheels," said Tag.

The XM-F4 was finding just enough traction on the
compressing, moss-slick drift to keep its momentum, but
not enough to gain any. And even if they didn't draw
any more fire, Tag could see that getting free also meant
debouching into the more open slope above the rim of
the depression, where the thin timber offered little cover
for a tank, and where at least two more pieces of Soviet
armor were awaiting, in addition to the other BMP that
he hoped was continuing to hold down the far end of the
line. He twisted his scope through its full range of motion,
anxiously trying to fix the positions of the 2S9 and the
partially concealed vehicle, but the angle and the lip of the
wash blocked his view.

Tag slapped the quick release on his seat harness, got on his knees in the chair, opened the latch on his commander's hatch, and threw it back, forcing himself up through the canted opening.

It was less dizzying in the open air, and the sharp smell of cordite cleared Tag's head of its few remaining cobwebs from the cannon shots they had absorbed. He still could not see back to his left over the edge of the wash, or to his right over the slanting deck of the No Slack Too. They were keeping their momentum, and in another fifty feet would clear the drift and be in the relatively open woods and thickets below. And Ivan would, by now, surely know that. He felt the bottom firming up and the XM-F4 beginning to right itself and gather fractional speed.

"Wheels, halt," Tag said through his CVC, and the driver brought them to a slow stop, feeling the tank rest as gingerly as if on egg shells. "Stand to," Tag told his crew, "I've got to go naked for thirty seconds."

Tag clambered out the hatch with his binoculars in hand and jumped well away from the tank onto the jackstraw mass of logs and vines, keeping his balance only by continuing to bound from log to log, until he reached the edge and threw himself into the bushes. He low crawled to the top of the wash, parted a stand of weeds, and turned his glasses on the flattening slope below.

Nothing. He could see no sign at first of either the 2S9 or the other vehicle. Had they had enough time to get back up here into the big trees, envelope him? No, surely not. There. Just a flicker of movement from the 2S9's 120mm multigun in the cover of a wooded swale gave it away. It had a dead-bead on the mouth of the wash where the No Slack Too would have to emerge. Okay, nothing to be done about that, Tag thought. He still had an approximate fix on the concealed vehicle, and could only guess and hope that it hadn't moved and was still focusing on keeping N. Sain bottled up in the depression. He scuttled backward out of the weeds and was down the bank, across the logs, and into his seat faster than it takes to tell.

"Okay," he said to his crew, "here's the skinny. Ham, we've still got one bogey at ten o'clock, but he's moved into a stand of trees, the only big one over there. And he's laying for us. The other one seems to be staying put. Wheels, I want you to give it all you can, whatever it takes to make that sucker miss. Got it? Gunner's choice. Sabot, Mr. Tutti. Let's go."

Wheels started them at a crawl, but by the time the No Slack Too had traveled its own length, gradually rising on the more solid footing, Wheels had pushed the turbines past idle and was gathering speed. Where the rack of drift fell away at the mouth of the wash, he popped both throttles, extended the suspension, and the momentum of the XM-F4 slung it into the open like a shot off a sling.

The tube-fired Songster missile from the Soviet killer tank had screamed from the muzzle the instant the glacis of the No Slack Too poked past the mouth of the wash, but the commander of the 2S9 had no reflexes to match the leaping burst of acceleration that the American tank put on. Leading it by a dozen feet, the Soviet's missile still passed a full one millimeter from the turret of the No Slack Too, above and behind it.

Ham's heat scope locked on the blossom of muzzle blast; the turret hummed in micro-movements; the target blips converged; and Ham pulled the string.

The 120mm buckled back in its dampers, the recoil slowing Wheels's turn.

"Shot," Ham reported, and Tag saw impact through his periscope, a flowering of flame and foliage below and to the left of the multigun tube, which he could see protruding from the shade of the copse. The explosion knocked it aside, and for a moment Tag thought it was only settling back. Then he saw the muzzle elevate.

"Target. Mark. Gunner's choice," he called to Ham.

"Confirmed," the gunner replied.

"Wheels, veer left," Tag ordered. "You're getting us between them."

"Bumps!" the driver shouted a split second before the No Slack Too was crashing madly through a series of smaller washes that cut into the benchland like the corrugations on a washboard.

A second Songster from the disabled 2S9 clipped the

steeply sloping leading edge of the glacis fender on the No Slack Too and swelled in a crash of black flak directly in Tag's line of sight.

"Fuck this," he cursed. "Right turn; full stop. Sabot. Gunner's choice."

Wheels spun the XM-F4 in the swirling cloud of smoke from the Songster; the turret hummed as the breech dropped shut; and Tag keyed the Phalanx to his optical sight before shattering the timber around the 2S9 with a fusillade from the Gatling-barreled gun. Wheels braked and locked the suspension in one motion. Ham fired.

The loader and driver of the 2S9 were already outside the disabled toy tank when the sabot penetrator punched through the glacis armor at the base of the turret. The explosion in the magazine knocked them both dead, fifty meters away, and separated the turret from the body of the killer tank, flipping it in the air like the lid off an exploding pressure cooker.

"Spa-lash," Tag said with satisfaction.

"Uh-huh," Ham Jefferson echoed. "That's more like it. Whatta we got, Cap, two more to go?"

"Two we know of, Hambone," Tag said. "Wheels, let's take that position. Give us some cover. We got to get closer."

Wheels tore through the light growth, riding down waves of saplings and tearing a path through the briers.

"Disciple, Disciple," Tag broadcasted over the TAC net, "this is Avatar. Come in Disciple. Over."

"Oh, Second Coming of the Revelation, how sweet thee sing," was the response. "We thought no human voice would wake us before we drowned."

"Roger, Disciple," Tag said, fighting back his irritation. "How many bogeys did you have here? Over."

"For you, the five, the pentagram."

"Roger. Listen, Disciple, there are two—I say again, two—remaining, but don't expose yourself. We've got it covered. You copy? Over."

But there was no response.

Tab cursed under his breath and refocused his attention on the leaning trees and walls of creeper that edged the upper rim of the depression where N. Sain was still dodging the Soviet guns. Squinting in concentration, Tag searched the area where the other vehicle had been partially hidden, but could see no sign of it or of its having moved.

"Heat blip," Ham announced as Wheels was cutting behind the copse of trees where the dismembered BMP lay in twisted bits.

"What's the fix?" Tag asked.

"Sorry," Ham said. "I lost it when we cut back. Might have been a false return."

"Not on my friggin' software," Fruits protested.

"Wheels," said Tag, "bring us back through this patch of trees, downhill from the BMP."

The No Slack Too eased past the broken bodies of the two Soviet tankers and came to a halt well back in the shadows at the edge of the trees. Partially obscured by its blanket of scrub and weeds, the two hundred or so meters between the grove and the dense cover where the other 2S9 was hiding was strewn with stumps and boulders that had washed down from above, not impassable but nothing to make real speed across. Tag stood in his hatch and surveyed the situation through his glasses. He knew the Soviet bogey was in there somewhere, but he couldn't risk a wild shot and give away their own position just in the hope of flushing him out.

Suddenly, in the middle of a thought, Tag's head snapped from the binoculars' eyepieces, as a series of cannon reports boomed like fulling hammers at the farther end of the depression and three balled, gray-white clouds of N. Sain's signature white-phosphorous rounds boiled out of the serried near horizon, followed by a single fourth and a tremendous secondary explosion that, even nearly a half klick away, shook the ground beneath the No Slack Too.

A single word—"Juggernaut!"—roared over the TAC net, and Tag could see how this one might just end.

"Wheels," he said, "forward. Get us clear of the trees and give us a big cone of fire. Fruits, load HE. And, Ham, on your toes; I think we're going to have a runner."

N. Sain, his troop compartment half full of extra ammunition, was less concerned about fire discipline than Tag would have liked. As the scar-bright Bradley inched along the strewment, hugging close to the trees and walls of creeper along the rim above where it had been trapped, N. Sain walked a steady barrage of WP along ahead of him.

Tag saw the movement and relayed it to Ham.

"I'm with you," the gunner said. "Oh, he be nervous now."

Unsure of the No Slack Too's location and unable to fire on N. Sain through the dense scrub, the commander of the 2S9-type tank had no choice. Ordering his gunner to shoot on the run at the advancing Bradley, he made a break for the big timber upslope from him.

"Here he comes," Tag said as the low, short-nosed body of the compact tank tore through the vines and charged clumsily up the gentle rise of the mountain, veering around boulders and logs in quick, evasive moves. A WP round from N. Sain went wide, momentarily clouding Ham's visuals. He fired on instruments.

The high-explosive round didn't carry the devastating punch against even light armor that the penetrator sabot could deliver, but the visual results were even more spectacular. Ham's shot struck midway in the track assembly, ripping off cogs, carriers, treads, and the entire length of the fender. The body of the beefed-up 2S9 crumpled like a kicked can as hissing chunks of ruined steel rained all around it. And the next moment it was all consumed in a white-phosphorous flash of blast-furnace heat and smoke.

"Disciple," Tag radioed, "this is Avatar. Stand down and hold your position." Then to Wheels he said, "Wheelman, get me over there to that lunatic, pronto."

Wheels cut back to the edge of the rim and made short work of the four hundred meters to N. Sain's Bradley.

Tag bailed out of his hatch and approached N. Sain's machine. It sat idling, smelling of white phosphorous and overheated engine. He slammed his fist down on the forward hatch.

"N. Sain," Tag bellowed, "get your cosmic ass out here."

The turret hatch banged open and N. Sain rose from it bare-chested, filthy, his eyes almost dewy.

"Captain Maximilian," N. Sain said contritely, shaking one hand as though something were stuck to it, "may your terror always go before you. This is my poor atonement, my burnt offering, my sacrifice to you in the name of Kali."

"Kali, my ass," said Tag. "Come down here."

N. Sain leapt from the turret to the ground, bounced once on his strong, bandy legs, and stood before Tag with a woebegone look on his face, the one hand still flipping nervously at his side.

"Oh, the sorrow; oh, the shame," N. Sain began.

"Oh, shut up," Tag said, "and listen to me, if you really are a true disciple. We've got people we have to move and wounded to care for. Dammit, N. Sain, we don't need to be drawing any attention. Do you understand? We need twenty-four hours to regroup and be ready for whatever is coming next. We do still have orders, though I doubt that means much to you, and I will not have you screwing them up or getting us all in the barrel the way you were."

The crestfallen N. Sain looked pleadingly at Tag, one eye losing its focus. "It's true; it's true," he said. "I am unfit, unworthy, unclean. Fallen from grace, out of the eternal loop. Krishna the Destroyer crush me! Leave me to wander lonely as a cloud, O Avatar, until I pick up the beat."

"Bullshit," said Tag. "I want you with us."

"Oh, no," N. Sain replied. "The gods are most harsh in their mercies. The Angel of the Apocalypse has shown its ill will by just barely refraining from my destruction, perhaps to spare her true believers, Mad Dog and Rabies. There is a wound in the natural order, and it's my cursed spite to put things right, affirm my oneness with death's dominion. You know." He essayed a boyish smile.

"Then you refuse to obey an order, an injunction from me?" Tag asked.

N. Sain shook his head. "I cannot accept. The moral force compels me to be a pilgrim."

Tag sensed the rooted intransigence behind N. Sain's dippy mannerisms and had an alternative at hand.

"Can you make that pilgrimage anywhere? Can you go where death needs you most?"

"That is my desire, my reason to be."

"Search south and west, my disciple," Tag said, experiencing that giddy feeling that always came with talking to

N. Sain. "Draw death to you"—and away from us, Tag thought—"and we will come for it when the time is right and the universe is in harmony."

"South and west, where the light dies in bloodred sheets, and our enemies strangle on their own nightmares, and where we again will meet, among the dead and dying, at last released from care. Your will is my way, O Avatar of Ambush."

A chill rippled between Tag's shoulder blades. "That's the ticket," he said to N. Sain. "Think on these things, meditate, purify yourselves." And take a bath, he thought.

N. Sain looked at him a minute, his face blissful, slack, then suddenly composed himself, eyes alight. "Rock 'n' roll," he said brightly and scampered up the nose of the Bradley and onto the turret as agile as a monkey. He faced Tag and threw him a two-fingered scout salute. "Come the revelation," he said, and dropped out of sight.

As the Bradley's motor revved, Tag turned away and walked back to the No Slack Too, where Wheels sat with his head through his hatch.

"Cap'n," he said to Tag, "you really unnerstan what you're talkin' about with that yo-yo?"

"No," said Tag, stepping up on the fender stirrup. He knelt and examined the impact damage from one of the ATGM hits they had taken. The Stealth polymer had been scorched off, and there was some shallow puddling, but it looked no worse than a bad paint job. Tag looked across at Wheels. "But, hell," he added, "just so long as he does."

Wheels shook his head. "What a joker."

"He is that," Tag agreed, "but at least in this game, we know when he does turn up, he turns up in our hand."

N. Sain's Bradley roared away toward the timber, and Tag and Wheels followed it with their eyes.

"Lord, I hope he knows that," the driver said.

"Both of us, Wheelman," Tag said. "Now let's get back to the flock."

"Flockward," Wheels replied, dropping the XM-F4 into gear.

Tag stopped them briefly at the east end of the depression, to inspect the configurations of the two BMPs, the first one

they had fought and the one N. Sain destroyed when he
broke the trap. Both were turret models, mounted with the
73mm cannon and antitank guided missiles, the AT-4s, in
addition to a pair of coaxial machine guns in the nose.
There was nothing new in any of this, Tag was thinking,
when the lifeless form of one of the Soviet crewmen that
lay slumped out of a turret caused him to do a double take,
flashing back to the two dead Communist tankers he had
seen in the copse of woods: they were all wearing bulky
nuclear/biological/chemical protective suits. Tag did
not know exactly what it meant, but no one wore those hot,
claustrophobic, synthetic skins for fun. He got back in the
No Slack Too and moved them out.

"Meat Grinder, Meat Grinder, this is Butcher Boy. We
are coming in. Out."

Tag heard a handset key twice in silent response, and he
felt an unanticipated relief. He had a trick, that sometimes
worked, of redirecting his excess adrenaline into high-
speed reverie, letting all that energy whip his imagination
into skeins of images that passed across his consciousness
without thought. It brought him a feeling of calm and
assurance, while never dulling his reactions. He seemed to
exist at once inside and outside himself, aware of everything
and attuned to its rhythm. But at this moment, that awareness included Giesla and his deepening, unbidden feeling
for her. The forces of war had, he knew, compressed their
relationship, condensed it to powerful proof devoid of all
small thoughts and emotions. But it was not unmixed.
Comradeship combined with desire, anxious lust with affection. That this feeling could survive—let alone grow—
in the face of massive and calculated slaughter gave Tag a
hope he took as an omen that all the best that's in us wouldn't
die with the survivors of this war. At another time, he would
have sung, off-key, out loud.

"Hey, whoda fuck's hummin'?" Fruits groused over the
open intercom.

"That's the sound of your master's voice," Tag said, "and
you better learn to love it."

"Sorry, Captain Max," the loader mumbled. "I thought
it's dat Baptist bootlegger."

"Fruit Loops," Wheels drawled amiably, "it is only Amazing Grace that I haven't sent you Farther Along already. You could do with a good dose of the old-time revival spirit, break you of playin' with yourself."

"Ah, up your paternoster," Fruits riposted. "I don't see you sleeping on your stomach."

"Gentlemen," Ham Jefferson said silkily, "gentlemen. That kind of talk is a sign of low IQ and breeding. Of course, we shouldn't expect any less from the untutored and ill bred, should we, boss?"

"Hell," Tag said, "I'm still trying to figure out what I did to get any of you. Must have been something in a past life. Maybe next time I'll get lucky and come back as a cockroach or something."

"You been talking to that N. Sain too much, Cap'n," Wheels said. "It weren't nothing like that. You volunteered, remember?"

"That's it," Tag said. "Sins of my youth."

Wheels and Tag kept their hatches open and made good time back to their rendezvous with the rest of the raiders. They identified themselves and passed inside the perimeter Giesla had deployed, stopping behind her vehicle. Tag got out and went to her. Giesla walked to the rear of her gun buggy and met him.

"Max," she said, "is everything all right?" There was a light of relief in her eyes as well.

"Yes," he said, squeezing her arm above the elbow, "as all right as it can be when N. Sain is involved."

"I do not like that man, Max," she said. "And I don't trust him."

"He's like having a bad dog, Gies: he only bites other people. But I think he's muzzled for the time being. And anything he does stir up will be away from us. It's a mission from God or the gods or something. Where's Johann? What's he got for us?"

"He's not far from here, with one of his people and a radio." She said to Jan, who was sitting in the passenger seat of the gun vehicle, "Call Johann in, Jan," then turned back to Tag.

"Max," she said in a lower voice, "I hope you do not

mind that I worried, because it was N. Sain out there."

"No," Tag said, recalling his own thoughts of Giesla, his rush of emotion, "I don't mind."

"It will not affect my duty," she said, adding a little starch to her voice.

"I believe it, Gies," said Tag. "You are an extraordinary woman, an extraordinary soldier. I worry too, sometimes."

"Is it wrong that I hold on to something just for myself, a good thing, and leave the bad until another time? Is it wrong that I lock sorrow away and want to be closer to . . . to that one selfish thing?"

"No," said Tag, "it's not. Things are bad enough without adding to them. Anyone who finds anything good in this should hold on to it. That's what I do." He looked her full in the face.

She touched him firmly on the jaw and let her hand drop. "So," she said, "what was your mad friend into out there?"

"A tank-killer unit. Four or five BMPs and a couple of those light tanks that look like 2S9s on steroids. They've got tube-launched Spandrels. Nasty buggers."

"Yes, we knew that. Was there anything else, Max, that might tell us something?"

"Yeah," he said, "but I don't know exactly what it means. The crewmen in that armor were all in NBC suits."

"Then they are part of the plan, aren't they? Not just patrols hunting us."

"I think they're hunting us, all right," said Tag, "*and* that they are part of the plan. We are the fly in Ivan's ointment right now. We're already dictating how he can do what he has planned. There aren't enough of us to stop him by main strength, but if we can just keep the pressure on, make Ivan fight our way, we can take him. We just have to recharge and find a safe place for the wounded. Where the hell is Johann, anyway?"

The sputter of the partisan's aged DKW answered Tag from the forest. Johann killed his engine and coasted the last twenty meters to where Tag and Giesla were standing.

Tag stood by attentively while Johann and Giesla spoke in German, the partisan gesturing toward the trees and

Giesla asking short questions, nodding, and listening. After a few minutes she turned to Tag and said, "We should be going now, Max. That antitank unit, it was not the only one. There is a lot of movement higher up the mountain, armored movement. But for now, Johann says there is nothing coming this way that might be a convoy."

"Okay," said Tag. "You and the other gun vehicles fall in behind Johann. I want to have a quick word with Prentice."

Tag found the lieutenant at his Bradley and told him to bring in the men from the perimeter.

"How are the wounded?" Tag asked him.

Prentice shrugged his bound shoulder. "No worse for the rest, I suppose. What are we into here, Max? Do you know?"

"You know about as much as I do, Chuck," Tag told him. "I do know that whatever Ivan is up to, it's real important to him. This damn mountain is lousy with AT patrols, and not just because of us, I think. Huh-uh. The Russians don't want anything left to chance. Still, we are making them nervous, aren't we?"

Prentice's cocky grin was the best thing Tag could have seen from him. Gone was the uncertainty that had bedeviled Prentice before the attack on the manor houses, and in its place there was emerging the sort of tough confidence that Tag associated with the best soldiers.

"Yeah," Prentice said. "And we'll make fools of them if they're not. What's the drill?"

"Stay tight with your men, Chuck. You guys have taken a real beating, and the ones that are left may start counting noses and get shaky. I don't know exactly where we're headed, but Johann says it'll be safe and have hot food. Anything else, you'll have to call out for."

"Let's get these men to the doctor," said Prentice as he mounted the turret of his APC.

10

A century ago, the place had been a breeding farm for the small, shaggy ponies that worked the Swabian mines, and had remained so until well after the Second World War, when it was converted first to a scout camp, then a breeding kennel, and finally to a veterinary hospital and research facility. It was on the main north-south route that ran past the village, across the Jura, and down to the Danube Valley, but its old barns and stables and silos offered the only structures for twenty kilometers around large enough to conceal something the size of a Bradley or the No Slack Too. It was also the only remaining medical facility, even if the doctor was a vet.

The veterinarian was a tall young man, with a thatch of straight hair and thick glasses and a stunted leg that had kept him a civilian. He wore a perpetual toothy grin and spoke very broken English with a smattering of Latin names for body parts, but he was able to communicate well enough with Bones to press the medic into service as a nurse. Together they extracted shrapnel, sutured cuts, and dressed burns on the wounded raiders.

Meanwhile, Tag and the others were under the care of a pair of thirteen-year-old twin girls who usually helped out at the clinic, but now, with earnest faces reflecting the gravity of the time, led the vehicles to various barns and stables and gave the raiders very specific instructions on how to conceal their vehicles. For the No Slack Too, they had Ham, Wheels, and Fruits forking shocks of loose straw over it inside the largest of the old barns.

Tag came into the barn with Giesla, having completed an inspection of the area and set standing orders for several contingencies.

The twins stood by, arms akimbo and faces set, while the men choked in the chaff and dust.

"Ah," Giesla said, "I see you have found who is in charge here."

Fruits Tutti turned away and spat politely. "Gies," he said, "these girls are gonna grow up to be just like you."

"Yeah," Ham added, "but you can tell 'em they don't have to be in such a hurry to grow up."

Wheels wiped his face on his sleeve. "Aw, hell, boys," he said, "this is light work. Just think: it coulda been in bales."

"That's right," Tag said, "or it could have come out of the kennels, been full of fleas."

"Small fuckin' favor," Fruits mumbled as he turned back to the chore.

Giesla spoke to the two girls in German, and they all three shared a laugh that drew glares from the sweaty tankers.

"Bye-bye," the twins said, heading for the door, "bye-bye."

"The good news," Tag said, "is showers and hot chow when you're through here."

"And what then, Cap'n?" Wheels asked, tossing another clump of straw on the rear deck of the XM-F4.

"Well, you know what we have to do, but right now's not the time to do it," Tag said. "We need some down-time, and we need some intel before we can do anything beside go crashing around in the woods and get ourselves shot at. If we're looking for just a few APCs infiltrating through the hills, instead of a road-bound convoy, we have to have something solid to work on."

"Understand, all of you," Giesla said, "our time frame is about forty-eight hours. We may not get any second chances, so we must be sure when we move."

Tag nodded. "That's right," he said. "Johann has people out right now, and they can do a hell of a lot better job than any of us. I think we'll be safe here for what little while we need to stay; Ivan's been here twice already. Tonight we'll get fresh satellite pictures and maybe some word from Command. After that, we'll see."

A young voice called Giesla's name, and they all turned to see one of the twins standing in the doors at the other end of the barn, holding a leather leash attached to a large, serious-looking Alsatian dog. She spoke to Giesla, who turned back to the men.

"Max," she said, "they have food ready now."

"Okay, you hayseeds," he said to his crew, "knock off. We'll finish here, and the girl will show you where you can clean up."

Fruits dropped his pitchfork with a load of straw still on the tines. "Hey, you're a prince, Captain, but, uh, could she do something with that dog."

Tag glanced back at the girl. "Looks like a nice dog to me, Fruits."

"Ah, shit," the wiry loader said, "the sonofabitch is big as I am."

Wheels said, "You afraid he's gonna bite you or rape ya?"

"No," Fruits said crossly, "I just don't like dogs, all right?"

"Out," Tag said.

Fruits lagged behind reluctantly, trying to keep Ham Jefferson between himself and the impassive shepherd.

"Don't worry," Giesla called after him, "I'm sure the girl will protect you, Fruits."

She turned to Tag, still smiling. "He is a funny man," she said.

"Damned if he isn't," Tag said. "Once in Honduras, our Sheridan got hit with an RPG, took a track off, started an engine fire, and that little monkey stood at the fifty caliber until he burned the barrel up, covering for the rest of us while we slipped around the flank of the ambush. There were rounds flying everywhere, and the Sheridan took two more RPGs before we could stop 'em. But Tutti never blinked, and when it was all done, the worst he had was powder burns on his hands. Afraid of dogs, and he's God's own altar boy."

"With a dirty face," Giesla said.

"Yeah," Tag agreed, "and a mind to match." He eyed her suggestively.

"Oh, no, Captain," she said, laying a hand on his chest. "First, the work."

He took the hand in both of his. "And be itching and covered with straw. 'Oh, no' is right. American ingenuity, not Teutonic duty, Lieutenant. That is an order."

He released her hand, and she slid it and her other around him, pressing her breasts lightly against his chest. He could feel them move beneath the fabric.

"Then I have no choice," she said. She brushed his lips with hers, her tongue darting against his teeth.

Tag tasted her salt and buried himself in a kiss as she sucked hungrily on his tongue, searched it with her own, pushed against it, then sucked again.

They clutched each other's bodies, tugging impatiently at the cloth of their jumpsuits.

Giesla slid her mouth away from the kiss, licked Tag's jaw, and whispered, "Come, over behind the tank."

They held each other by the waist, grinning wickedly, and hurried behind the heap of straw.

They stripped without saying a word, then sank together on the straw and tangled clothes. They kissed again, hard, then more gently, their tongues playing back and forth. Tag kissed the hollow of her throat, and Giesla gasped in anticipation. She felt his back and hips and chest, his hard thighs, his stiffening cock, as though wanting to memorize each part of him.

Tag ran his lips down her breasts in turn, taking the small, peaked nipples between his teeth before sucking greedily. She held the nape of his neck and pushed harder as his hand strayed up her thighs, passing gingerly over the still-tender wound on her thigh, to rest on the hot, engorged lips of her cunt. With her free hand, she pressed his more tightly down on her yearning clitoris and began working her hips against it. She shuddered once, then again, each time making a small noise that was not quite a syllable. After the second, she clamped his hand in place between her thighs and held him tightly in her arms.

Tag let her roll him to one side. She took his thick cock in both her hands and smiled at him like the "Mona Lisa," before dropping her head and taking him in her mouth. Giesla held his balls in one hand, while she moved the other up and down the shaft and rolled the head of his cock between her tongue and cheeks. She ran her tongue hard from the base of his balls up the bottom of his cock to the glans, then took all she could in her mouth, bobbing faster and faster, until Tag caught her head and made her stop.

"Careful," he said. "You're too good at that."

"Good," she said, smiling at him wetly. "I want to be good to you this way."

She dropped back on him, and he took her head in both his hands and let her go. It was an experience of complete abandon. When Tag came, it was catharsis, as though a lava of tension and anxiety were pouring out of him.

They lay like that awhile, then Giesla let his cock slide out of her mouth and fall slick and heavy against his thigh. Tag pulled her to him, lifting Giesla by her arms and settling her head on his chest.

"You needed that," she said playfully. "Admit you needed that."

"Mmmmm."

"Max?"

"Mmm?"

"Do you think we will ever have a bed?"

Tag's laugh jolted Giesla's head off his chest. She came down hard with her chin.

"Uh," Tag grunted. "Yes, then," he said. "Yes, just don't hurt me."

"Do you promise?"

"Yes," he said, hooking his arms beneath hers and drawing her to him. When their faces were almost touching, he said, "We will have a bed, and we will have nights and nights to euphemism in it."

"But first . . ." Giesla began.

"Yes?"

She boxed his ear with a wad of brittle straw. "But first, we have to work," she chirped, pronouncing it *verk*.

They threw straw at each other and dressed and finished covering the turret and main gun of the No Slack Too, competing for the largest forkful of the weightless straw.

Giesla showed Tag to a kennel between the barn and the main building of the clinic, where a dog-grooming area had been set up as a shower for the raiders. The three open, concrete stalls that faced the cages each had shower heads on hoses (with hot and cold water), soap and shampoo, and room enough for two.

Except for three Alsatians in the cages, the kennel was empty.

Tag and Giesla soaped and kissed and washed each other's hair. They tried to make love standing in the stall, but the slope to the drain made it treacherous, so they ended on the floor, first with her on top, then with him behind, and all along the three Alsatians sat with lolling tongues, watching from six feet away.

Dressed in fresh fatigues, Tag and Giesla met the tank crew between the kennel and the clinic, along a path screened by wild rosebushes. Wheels was picking his teeth with a rose stem that held one pursed bud. Seeing Tag and Giesla, he removed it from his mouth, snapped off the end, and held it out to Giesla.

"My compliments to the officer corps, Ma'am," he said gallantly.

Giesla hoped no one could see her blush beneath the glow of sex and hot shower on her cheeks. "Thank you, Sergeant," she said a little stiffly, then, to soften it, she slid the stem in Wheels's top buttonhole and kissed him on the cheek, adding, "But I am in uniform."

Two sixtyish women, working in a kitchen that was really no more than a galley for coffee and sandwiches in the rear of the clinic, had somehow whipped together a feast of *spatzle*, a carrot and pea casserole, mashed potatoes, preserved pears, ripe cheese, bread, and beer. At Giesla's insistence, the women sat and ate with them. Tag was grateful that they spoke no English: he was famished and wolfed down his food, oblivious of the conversation.

When Tag finally pushed himself away from a third helping of *spatzle*, Giesla was leaning on her elbows, watching him.

Tag burped and said, "Excuse me."

"I think," Giesla said, straightening in her chair, "that you needed that too."

Tag returned a satisfied smile. "I only wish," he said,

"that I had time to enjoy it. Where are the wounded? I want to see them before I head back."

"Most are back with the others, in the different buildings," Giesla replied. "Only three are still here."

"Okay, I'll look in on them at least. Anybody bad?"

"One broken leg—compound fracture, here." She touched her calf. "Two with flash burns; painful, but not so bad."

The veterinarian had set up a ward for the men in a basement storage room. Bones was still with them when Tag and Giesla came down.

"How are they doing, Bones?" Tag said.

"Well, Todd there"—he pointed to a man with a splinted leg and a fuzzy morphine smile on his face—"he wants to run the hundred meters, and Huey and Dewey here say they're gonna sue the tanning salon." One of the two men lying on their stomachs, exposing crusted blisters on their necks and backs, muttered, "Fuckin' A."

"Anything else we can do for them, Bones?" Tag asked.

"Not unless we can medevac them, sir," the medic said.

"Okay," Tag said. "You've done a hell of a job, Bones. Hell, you've done a great job."

"Hey, Captain," Bones said, smiling wryly, "I'm alive, ain't I. You don't do any better than that."

Giesla left Tag on the rose path to rejoin her commandos—now truly hers since Holz was dead—and Tag continued back to the barn.

Fruits, one eyebrow wrinkled in concentration, was drawing in the dirt floor of the barn when Tag returned.

"Writing a letter home?" Tag asked.

"Oh, hi, Captain Max," Fruits said distractedly. "No, I'm just thinking about how to fine-tune that Phalanx thermal radar, so's it'll like, you know, pick up on people."

"Tutti," Tag said, genuinely concerned, "don't you start fucking with that."

"I'm only *thinking* about it, for Christ's sake," Fruits protested.

"Right," Tag said. "Well, wake me up when you get it doped out."

And he joined Wheels and Ham in a nap on the hay,

stretching himself in the forked hollow where he and Giesla had lain.

In his dream, Tag was in a station wagon with a family he did not know—a young, good-looking couple, like people you expect to see on TV, with two tow-headed children and a handsome spaniel. Giesla was waving to him from the porch of a cuckoo-clock cottage as they drove into the deep woods, dark and forbidding as a forest out of the Brothers Grimm. Tag could not tear himself away from the rear glass of the station wagon, even when the cottage was out of sight. The farther they drove into the woods, the more his apprehension grew.

Then the car suddenly was in a glade, and the man and woman were outside spreading a picnic lunch, and the children and the dog were chasing one another through the trees, and there was no sound in the dream. Tag knew something was terribly wrong, and he yelled, yelled at them all to come back, but nothing came out.

And then there was a sound, the rising scream of incoming artillery. Tag ran one way, then another, then dashed for the children as the first rounds burst silently in the treetops, turning them to giant firebrands and filling the glade with shrapnel. But the children could not hear them. They ran away from Tag, thinking he was part of their game. He grabbed one, then another. He pulled them to the ground. He had a helmet in his hand. He dug, trying to make a hole to put the children in. Underneath the old leaves on the floor of the glade was a sheet of polished steel. More trees turned their canopies to flame. The dog ran past. The children fought to chase after it.

Tag started awake, suddenly disengaging the barking in the kennels from the dog in his dream.

"Easy, boss," Ham Jefferson said, laying a hand on Tag's shoulder. "It's just feeding time."

Tag shook his head clear. "What time is that?" he said, fumbling with the cover on his wristwatch.

"Coming up on nineteen hundred," the gunner said. "You been out for a while."

Tag stood and stretched. "Any word yet from Johann's people?" he asked.

"Nada," Ham replied.

Tag saw Wheels lounging nearby, reading from a paperback book. "Where's Fruits?" he said to Ham.

"Went to see if he could patch up any of the Bradley's systems."

Tag nodded approval. "Get him back, will you, Ham? And tell Giesla and Prentice I'll need them here too."

When the gunner returned with them, Tag had Fruits detach the mini-dish antenna and set it up outside. The satellite pictures showed little change in the Soviet positions, but the NATO armies of the southern sector were clearly massing for a push through the Jura.

Tag went ahead with an out-of-sequence transmission to Command, a brief burp providing sketchy details of their ambush of the tank-killer unit and admitting their lack of hard, current intelligence on Soviet movements in the immediate area.

Command's reply was more than Tag had hoped. It supplied him with the designations of the units thought to be bringing the nukes forward, complete with their last-known dispositions and estimated progress. It also confirmed Tag's suspicions about the Havoc with the unique missile rack that he had seen during the fight at the manor houses: the Soviets had been using the configuration to provide low-level, highly mobile launch stands for cruise missiles armed with conventional warheads in the northern sector, in the battle for the Low Countries.

Tag turned to Giesla. "Gies," he said, "have you had any contact from Johann's bunch?"

She shook her head. "Only radio checks," she said.

"Do we need more people in the field?" Prentice asked. "I still have eight or ten."

"No, Chuck," said Tag. "We only have the two Prick-Ms here, and with your track chewed up, we don't need to risk them. Fruits do you any good on the electronics?"

"We can move, shoot, and communicate," the lieutenant said, "just not very well."

"Okay," Tag said, "we're going to stay put for now and wait to hear from Johann. But let's get some security out as soon as it's dark, and have everybody ready to go on five minutes' word. Gies, I'd like you to stay here and monitor Johann's radios on the No Slack Too's set."

Prentice left to go set the perimeter, and Giesla settled inside the XM-F4 to man the radio, while Tag paced the length of the barn. He felt time drawing around them like a noose; he itched for action. But for now, he could only wait and pace.

When he had chewed a half bale of wheat straws and walked and thought for most of a mile, up and down the barn, Giesla broke Tag's funk with a shout from the turret of the No Slack Too.

"Max! Here, we've got something."

Tag had plowed through the straw and was on the rear deck of the No Slack Too before his crew were on their feet. He dropped inside the turret and crouched there, while Giesla asked a few questions in German over the radio and studied the map in her lap.

Giesla pushed the CVC off her head and looked up over her shoulder at Tag. "They found them, Max," she said. "One of Johann's men found a unit camped about ten kilometers from here that sounds like the one we want—BTRs with an escort of antitank BMPs."

"Come on," Tag said. "Let's get out of here and have a look."

He stood in the turret hatch, sent Fruits to bring Lieutenant Prentice, and told Wheels to take the radio, then climbed out and helped Giesla slide down the straw.

She spread the topo map on the packed-earth floor of the barn and smoothed out its acetate cover. By the time Prentice arrived, she had grease penciled in the approximate location of the Soviet contingent, and she and Tag were discussing likely routes it would take and places for ambush along them.

"Why not hit them now, tonight?" Prentice asked. His confidence and aggressiveness seemed to grow with the improvement in his separated shoulders: his left was tender but had almost a three-hundred degree range-of-motion, while his right was out of its sling, even if the upper arm was still taped to his chest.

"Bad idea, Chuck," Tag said. "Our scout didn't try to

get close enough to count the vehicles, so we don't know how many of what kinds there are. Judging from the map, they've got good defensive terrain, and you know they're not being casual, not after the way we stirred things up. No, we're better off to leave Johann's man out there to let us know when they move out, in what direction. They'll be a lot more vulnerable on the move, and we can fight from someplace we choose, not their turf."

Prentice smacked his left palm against his right fist, grimacing at the pain it caused his shoulder, then did it again.

"Damn," he said. "I want those bastards, Max."

"I want them too," Giesla said, "but it is what we must do. If we were to hit them and scatter them at night, they could all escape. We are too few to surround them."

"Come on, Chuck," Tag said, gesturing to the map, "let's get down to planning a surprise party for Ivan."

It was an hour's work to sort out the several most likely routes the Communists could take, and another hour to establish interdiction points, estimate travel times, and work up rough action plans for the various strike locations. The demands of the job helped settle all of them.

At 2200, they called it quits, and Prentice and Giesla went back to their units to brief them. Tag fussed with some personal gear and twice made sure the turbine intakes were free of straw, before he at last turned the watch over to Ham and tried to sleep.

11

At 0430, Tag was pitching in a fitful half sleep when word came in from Johann's man that the Soviets were stirring.

Tag ordered the raiders to assemble in the barn. Within ten minutes, it was alive with men and machines anxious for a fight. The men got fresh coffee and instant rations and gave their weapons a final once-over. The crew of the No Slack Too pulled the straw off the tank. There was a lot of coming and going between the barn and the latrine in the kennel.

When the partisan next made contact, Giesla's face deepened into a frown, and she spoke in rapid German over the radio. At one point she turned to Tag and said, "They are splitting up," then turned her concentration again to the transmission, scribbling notes and dotted lines on the acetate-covered map.

Tag stood by in apprehension, feeling angry, frustrated, and increasingly concerned about their ability to scotch the Communist movement. His mind worked frantically, searching for possibilities.

Giesla snapped the handset of her radio back in its cradle and swung her legs out of the vehicle, spreading the map on her lap.

"Here it is, Max," she said. "The Russians have split into at least four columns, but maybe more. These routes— here, here, here, and here"—she pointed to the lines she had drawn on the map—"are all going to be used, it appears."

"Do we split up?" Prentice asked.

163

"No," Tag said at once. "We can still get an angle on them. We've got to concentrate our firepower, Chuck. We don't need to get tied up in a firefight."

He looked at the map a moment longer, then went on: "We can take the first element here, where they have to cross the road above the village, then we can quarter across the ridge, maybe take the others from behind, if we miss intercepting them. But it's got to be hit and run, run, run."

"Let's do it," Prentice said, and he turned and walked rapidly to his track.

Tag gave Giesla a thumbs-up and hustled back to the No Slack Too. In the darkest part of morning, the half hour before dawn, the raiders rolled out of the clinic grounds, running fast on the paved road toward the first interdiction point.

It was still dark when they reached it, and the No Slack Too's audio-directional amplifier could detect the growl of the Soviet light armor from somewhere in the forest, but could give no accurate distance through the baffles of the trees. Tag laid his ambush in a horseshoe, with gun buggies and infantry equipped with LAWs on the long arms of the U, and the Bradley and the No Slack Too closing the two-hundred-meter arc between them. Wheels had no more than dropped the turbines to an idle when Sergeant Dunn reported the first BMPs entering the kill zone.

There were five of them—one at point and two on each flank—surrounding the four lumbering, eight-wheeled BRMs. Tag locked the Phalanx on the first of the transports and laid the main gun on the lead BMP. His heart hammered as the sky began to gray. He held their fire until the column was within fifty meters of their position, then gave the command over the TAC net and the intercom at once: "Shoot!"

Every vehicle in the Communist column was hit in the first withering salvo from the raiders, instantly transforming it from a fighting unit into a disarray of burning and disabled wrecks. Bursts from the Phalanx and another volley from the 106s finished off the cripples, who had the chance for no more than a few wild shots before their guns were silenced in a chaos of fire, explosions, and buckling armor plate.

The Soviet crewmen who survived the vicious onslaught and pulled themselves from their blazing APCs were cut down by small-arms and machine-gun fire.

"Mount up, mount up," Tag bawled over the radio. "Point Bravo. Move it."

As the foot troops poured back into the Bradley, Tag thought: *And so much for the element of surprise*.

Even in the rising light and with the gun buggies scouting their route, the passage through the woods was no sprint. More than by the Bradley, they were slowed by the unfamiliarity of the terrain and the need to move at oblique angles to the natural courses of water and wildlife, crashing through brambles and detouring around thickets of saplings too thick to ride down.

Near the crest of the ridge, Jan, in the lead vehicle, radioed that he had another Soviet unit in sight, moving away from them.

With no time to organize an ambush, Tag urged the No Slack Too and the Jagd Kommandos forward, hoping the Bradley could bring up the infantry in time to put the LAWs into play, but determined not to let the nuclear couriers pass unchallenged.

As soon as the XM-F4 came into view along the crest, Jan unleashed his recoilless rifles on the fly, causing more surprise and confusion than real damage among the Soviet vehicles. Two of the trailing BMPs peeled off to fight a rearguard action, and Ham caught one of them with an HE round from the 120mm that sent the APC's turret whirling off the body trailing crescents of smoke and sparks, like some monstrous St. Catherine's Wheel. Giesla's vehicle shot past, its perforated exhaust stacks splitting the air, and was into the rear of the Russian formation before anyone knew what was happening, charging the BRMs and their cargos of atomic annihilation.

Through his scope, Tag saw two of the wheeled vehicles erupt in flame—one of them that Giesla could not have hit—and he was fighting the No Slack Too into the fray when the air-alarm klaxon bawled inside the tank.

Coming in at treetop level, the pair of Mi-24D Hinds were literally on top of the raiders before any of them were aware of the hulking ships. But under the canopy of the forest, the raiders were hard to distinguish, and the Hinds made their first pass without firing a shot. Once they had a bearing on the fight, one of them swung to hover over the Communist formation, firing blindly into the trees with its 30mm cannon, while the second circled wide, nose down, searching for targets.

Tag threw the automatic air-defense toggle on the Phalanx console and turned his own 7.62 coax machine gun on the fleeing BRMs, aiming for the tires, while Ham and Fruits continued a steady pounding barrage of HE from the main gun, and Wheels held them steady in the teeth of the blizzard of fire from the machine guns and 73mm cannons on the BMPs. Tag was aware that the Phalanx stuttered only once before it ceased fire, and he saw the Hind hovering above them belch fire from its engine cowl and veer crazily downslope into the trees. He had time to wonder what had become of the other helicopter, but no chance to see the combustion of its alloy skin when the 75mm white-phosphorous round drilled its armored belly.

Then Prentice's Bradley was in the fight, doing what it could with a visually sighted cannon and its remaining coax machine gun. Wispy contrails of LAW rockets cross-hatched the scene of battle, and through it all, Tag saw a BMP protecting two of the eight-wheeled armored cars as they made a break from the fight, zigging through the trees and offering no clear shot.

"Wheels," he shouted to his driver, "don't lose those three."

"Got 'em," Wheels replied, opening the throttles and pitching the No Slack Too headlong into the screaming matrix of lead and steel, in a beeline for the escapees.

An AT-4 Spigot fired from the BMP struck the clamshell edge of the turret on the XM-F4, leaving a peen in the slick-skin armor as it crushed the air and rocked the XM-F4 on its air-torsion suspension.

"Shoot," said Tag.

Ham called his shot and released a 120mm HE round, the integral propellant dragging flames six feet out the tube. Its impact collapsed the forward plates of the BMP, imploding them with a concussion that its crew did not live long enough to feel.

"Fruits, shoot the Phalanx," Tag said, drawing a bead with his coax on the nearest armored car. He shredded three of its honeycomb tires before the BRM went down on its axle and heeled against a tree.

Fruits led the other BRM on manual and when he thumbed the Phalanx's trigger, the stream of depleted uranium slugs sliced like a router through the crew compartment and laid open the flaming motor block. The machine went up in a fierce, hissing explosion. Tutti spun the cupola and whipped a stream of fire down the length of the BRM that Tag had disabled, the 37mm filling it with the howling fragmentation of its own hull.

"Freeze it, Wheels," said Tag. "I'm gonna put the window down."

He opened his hatch a crack, listened, then put his head out. *Scattered small arms.* The heavy firing was finished.

"Wheels," Tag called down the hatch, "the kill zone. Go."

Tag rode with his head out the hatch, and when they turned back into the wind, he could smell the chemical stench of smoldering white phosphorous: *N. Sain.*

Prentice's Bradley sat in the middle of the ruins of the Soviet formation, surrounded by the burning remnants of the light Communist armor like a victorious Custer—except for the white twists of smoke rising from the Bradley's front drive cogs. Sure as hell, N. Sain's Bradley was parked not far away, flanked by two of the gun buggies. Giesla's was not one of them.

Prentice had moved his men away from the disabled APC and set them with their LAWs at the ready in defensive positions around the vehicles.

The No Slack Too sped through the smoking scar on the forest where the battle had been and swung to a stop in front of N. Sain's track. The contrite lunatic was leaning out the turret hatch, bare-chested, wearing his CVC, and wringing his hands.

"I strayed; I know I strayed," Tag heard N. Sain say,

once the XM-F4's turbines wound down. "I passed from grace, and only you—O Avatar of Ambush—*only* you know where the action is. Please, we hadn't made a convert all day till now. And this . . . this is too fucking much. Berserker nirvana, man."

N. Sain flashed a smile of polished reason.

"Are you on the bus or off the bus?"

"On the bus, the magic bus," N. Sain scatted.

"Further," said Tag.

"Whoever strives upward," N. Sain intoned, "him can we save."

Off to his right, Tag heard the approaching rap of the third gun buggy—Giesla's—and he said to N. Sain, "Never question Kali. You're on the bus."

Prentice hurried up to the No Slack Too, and Tag said, "Get your people into N. Sain's track, Chuck—no questions.

"Jan," he shouted to the Jagd Kommando, "take point. Steer us for position Charlie Two."

Jan threw him a wave and peeled away, passing Giesla as he shifted into second gear. She braked her gun buggy to a stop between the Bradley and the No Slack Too. Horst sat in the seat beside her, his uniform riddled with bloodstains, rolling his head in pain.

"Bones, up," Tag yelled, and the medic broke from the group of men filing into the Bradley and dashed to the wounded commando. Tag leapt to the ground and helped Giesla and Bones ease Horst out of his seat. Bones peeled back the blood-soaked jumpsuit and cut away the arm, exposing a dozen shrapnel perforations oozing from Horst's shoulder and upper chest.

Bones doused the wounds with water and began sprinkling them with antibiotic powder. "No chest suckers," he said, unrolling a battle dressing and pressing it to the commando's chest. "Let's get him in the Bradley; I can finish up in there."

As they passed Horst inside the track, Giesla turned to Prentice and said, "Chuck, I need a loader, anyone who can put shells in a one-oh-six."

Prentice called out Sergeant White, who grinned as he

mounted the gun buggy and said to Giesla, "Lieutenant, I just want you to know that this ain't my MOS."

Giesla looked back over her shoulder as she spun the vehicle in reverse. "Cross training," she said. "It is good for your career."

The raiders sped away from the smoking wreckage of the battle.

"All systems up," Tag ordered. "Fruits, shell status."

"Down to five HE, Captain," Tutti replied, "but we got plenty of sabot. Looks like fifty percent on the Phalanx."

Wheels pushed the XM-F4 hard, its suspension fully extended to absorb the bumps and flying leaps, as the freckle-faced moonshine runner found straight courses where there were none in the forest, across washes and gullies and over spills of rock, keeping pace with the quick, nimble gun buggies.

Tag pulled his head in to avoid the lashing branches and checked the LandNav's VDT to confirm their position. He looked at his wristwatch: 0725. He thought they just might make it.

Jan led them a few hundred meters past position Charlie Two, then hooked back wide left to cover the flank. Tag halted the No Slack Too and strained against the earpiece in his CVC, trying to pick something up on the audio-directional receiver. The other two Jagd Kommando vehicles fanned out, and the Bradley growled to within earshot, and still he heard no enemy movement.

"Meat Grinder One," he transmitted, "this is Butcher Boy. We have no movement; I say again, no movement. Any signs of tracks? Over."

"Negative, Butcher Boy," came Giesla's reply. "We are early."

"Roger, Meat Grinder. Can you get us a local report? Over."

"Wait, Butcher Boy."

N. Sain took a position some hundred meters to the left of the No Slack Too, and Tag watched as Prentice dispersed his men to either side of the APC. *They are getting good,* he thought. His pride in the transmogrified ordnance clerks was made bitter by the time he felt slipping away.

He heard the distinctive nattering of Giesla's bullet-riddled exhaust, and in seconds she was sliding her gun buggy beside him.

"Max," she called, "we have lost them."

"Lost them?!"

"There is one of Johann's men I cannot raise, but none of the others have anything to report."

"Who's the one?" Tag asked. "Where was he before?"

"Call-sign Alpha," Giesla said. "The one who made the first contact. He was supposed to be following one of the elements."

"Shit," said Tag.

"Max," Giesla said, "I want to send Mathias to scout; we do not all need to be burning fuel for nothing."

Tag thought a moment, then said, "Okay. Have him work up from this saddle and across our projected routes through position Delta, then circle back toward position Bravo and see if he crosses their trail."

Giesla revved her engine and reached for the gearshift.

"Giesla," Tag shouted over the engine, "tell him the rest of us are going to follow the crest southwest.

"Wheels," Tag said as Giesla slewed her gun buggy in a tight spin, "whip it over to the Bradley."

The No Slack Too rose on its air shocks as it accelerated, like a cheetah extending itself for a kill. Wheels moved the thirty tons of cutting-edge technology through the trees as deftly as a big cat. And when he braked to a stop behind N. Sain's Bradley, the XM-F4 settled on its suspension in an idling crouch.

N. Sain stood in the Bradley's turret, his face unnaturally dour.

"I'm a Jonah," he lamented, and he beat his bare chest with his fist.

Irritated, Tag jabbered, "They're hiding in the fog of their fear of you, O True Believer," then to Prentice: "Mount up, Chuck. We've lost contact; gotta move."

"Mount up," Prentice called to his men, then said to Tag, "What's the drill, Max?"

"Betcher's out making a loop, looking for tracks. There's one of the graybeards still out, but I think Ivan has gotten past the rest of them. All we can do is make a run and hope we end up ahead of the pack."

"Between here and the line?" Prentice asked.

Tag nodded, and the lieutenant turned away.

"Chuck," Tag called to him, "you've done a hell of a job with these guys."

"Thanks," Prentice said grimly, without looking back.

Tag turned his eyes again on the forlorn N. Sain. "Best of the bad, we need you now; I need you now. Come as fast as you can. My apprentice will show you the way."

"Pity the fools," N. Sain said solemnly. "They know not the bad karma of my disappointment." He dropped inside the turret.

The No Slack Too churned the loam floor of the forest as it raced to rejoin the two Jagd Kommando vehicles. Together, they formed a flying wedge, with the No Slack Too at the apex, and turned squarely up the slope of the ridge. Wheels worked his controls like a manic organist playing the stops of his instrument, wiping bark off the trees as the XM-F4 cut among the towering trunks.

When the raiders made the summit of the mountain ridge, they turned back southwest toward the Soviet line, tearing in column along the trace of an old trail at eighty kph. Tag looked at his watch again: 0837. At 0838, the air-alarm klaxon shattered the relative quiet of the crew compartment in the No Slack Too.

Tag alerted the Jagd Kommandos, who peeled off to either side of the trace, then he keyed his optical scope to the radar's azimuth and angle. A leafy picket of treetops flashed across his field of vision, then through a gap in the woods he saw them: two strings of Mi-28 Havocs, each with a long, ugly tube slung beneath its belly, moving up the Danube Valley at an elevation just below that of the ridge, using it to shield themselves from radar. At three thousand meters distance, they were pushing the envelope of the Phalanx, and Tag knew he could not afford to miss.

Knowing, too, that the Havocs' radar looked forward and down, he halted the No Slack Too in a bare clearing along the old trail and called the War Clubs up.

There were eight of the needle-nosed missiles remaining

in the scalloped shrouds on either side of the turret. Two by two, Tag ordered Ham to release them. The sizzling ignition of the rocket motors made a sound like rushing water inside the tank.

One of the War Clubs, confused by the impact of another, went wide; two struck the same Havoc; and the other five burst the flying weapons platforms in black smudges of flack. Suddenly the sky above the valley was filled with fragments of falling helicopters, hot comets of fuselage and motor parts. The four Mi-28s that survived the missile barrage banked heavily, struggling for altitude. The pair that wheeled back toward the ridge passed within range of the 37mm Phalanx, but they did not pass out of it. The first burst from the chain gun found the fuel cells in the cruise-type missile beneath one Havoc's belly, turning it to a fiery incubus that gnawed through the Mi-28's armor. The helicopter bucked like a thing in pain, side-slipped, and lost the air beneath its five-blade rotor. As the Havoc fell, the second ship shuddered from the solid stream of fire from the Phalanx that crushed metal and flesh with its impact, locking the blades. The second Havoc fell like a sack of salt.

Somewhere down the valley, below Tag's radar horizon, the two surviving Russian choppers pushed on.

As Wheels brought the No Slack Too back onto the trace, Giesla's command car came racing out of the woods. Tag came out of his hatch as she stopped.

"Max," she said, leaning out and gripping the roll cage, "Mathias found them. They have just passed below the village, and he said they are on a route for the mineworks."

Tag made a quick calculation of angle, time, and distance to the mine. The cagey bastards were expecting them to have cleared out of there.

"We can make it," he said. "Follow me."

He fed Wheels the coordinates, then radioed N. Sain to turn back for the "catacombs." He got no answer.

The No Slack Too's mad rush down the mountain was a hair-raising experience, even for tankers accustomed to Wheels Latta's daredevil skill. But it was the Tarheel's penchant for launching the XM-F4 airborne over dips and low shoulders of stone that landed them—literally—in the lap of a Communist tank-killer patrol well before they reached the mine.

A thick stand of elderberry bushes screened the ten-foot drop beyond the salient that Wheels tried to leap. He and Tag, peering over the rims of their open hatches, both experienced a moment of heart-stopping shock as the bushes flattened and the nose of the XM-F4 sailed into space. But they were never so shocked as the commander of the toy tank that they landed on.

The Soviet recon leader was standing in the flimsy turret when he heard the whine of turbines and whipped his head from side to side, trying to locate the sound. And then the sound was all over him and the sky blotted out, and the 60,000-pound No Slack Too slammed down like a sledge on a snuff can, compressing the light armor into jaws of death for the men inside and shearing the commander in two on the rim of the hatch.

The impact broke the fall of the No Slack Too. Rattled by the jolt, Wheels still kept the turbines spinning, and the XM-F4 half lurched off its accidental victim, plowing one track skirt in the dirt and hanging in precarious balance for a second before it dropped to both treads.

Ham found his sights as the No Slack Too settled, a second of the tank killers filling the grid. He and the Communist gunner fired almost at once. The fin-stabilized rocket from the 120mm Soviet smoothbore sang past the cupola of the Phalanx; Ham's round penetrated the toy tank's glacis before the sabot could separate from the core. It traveled the length of the tank and exploded on contact with the engine. The ensuing back-blast vaporized the clothes and skin of the men in the crew compartment and licked out the gaping hole in the puckered glacis.

Behind the burning tank, out of Tag's sight along the face of rock the Communist column had been following, two more explosions rolled, sending geysers of fire and smoke up from the two tanks hit by Jan and Giesla.

"Move us, Wheels," said Tag, and the driver jockeyed for position between the hulk of Communist armor and the low bluff.

"Oh, creeping Jesus," Fruits Tutti whined, "is this any way to fight a friggin' war?"

"Don't worry, Fruits," Ham Jefferson said, "We learning."

The No Slack Too followed the bluff past the other two destroyed tank killers and picked up the Jagd Kommandos as they maneuvered themselves down to the benchland.

"Butcher Boy, this is Meat Grinder." Giesla's voice was emotionless. "Status, Butcher Boy."

"Strack," Tag rasped. "Follow me."

"What the hell was that, boss?" Ham asked.

"*That*," Tag told him, "was four assholes we don't have to worry about anymore. Probably flank security, Hambone."

"And, hey, cracker," Ham said to Wheels, "you finished showing off?"

"Aw, sorry, fellas," Latta drawled. "But it sure broke the monotony, didn't it?"

He slammed the XM-F4 through a series of jinks and barreled down the mountain.

"Butcher Boy, this is Meat Grinder One." Giesla's voice came through in a series of gulps as her vehicle jolted through the woods. "Meat Grinder Three"—Mathias Betcher's designation—"reports tanks, BMPs, and BRMs all moving into the tree line below—I say again, below—the mine. Over."

"Roger, One. Stay with me."

As Wheels cut among the trees, tacking toward the mine area, Tag reviewed the surrounding terrain in his mind until he had a plan—a desperate plan.

12

Past the end of the mining area, where the mountain regained its normal slope, the stretch of creeper-hidden fissures left a navigable passage less than two hundred meters across. With enough firepower on the Soviet column's right flank, Tag hoped he could turn it, force it into the fissures or at least into the tight gap, where a single XM-F4 could command the bottleneck.

He sent Giesla and Jan on to circle the crevassed rock and link up with Betcher on the far side, while he picked himself a place to fight. Despite the heavy forest, he found a position that commanded three natural alleys through the woods, each of them covering a part of the zone between the cracks in the mountain and the worked face of the mine.

Tag pulled himself up through the turret and stood in the hatch, surveying the lay of the land. The high bench above the mine face loomed disturbingly on his right, and to the left the wooded mountain rolled away as evenly as a tilted cobbler top. Three hundred meters to the front, second growth and scrub blocked the waste of tailings from his view. The low, dark profile of the No Slack Too was almost invisible in the midmorning shadows of the forest. The leaf-heavy treetops rustled in the cool breeze; birds called; the air smelled of moss.

The first sound Tag heard from the Soviet column was the grating crash of a heavy machine on rocks, followed by a low, undifferentiated growl of engines. He dropped back through the turret and down to his seat.

"Be sharp, now," he told his crew. "Ham, just stay on your

alleys; I'll cover the difference with the Phalanx. Wheels, I
hope you remember your way around down there, because we
are probably going to get 'em scattered."

"I feel like I was born in that brier patch, Cap'n," said
Wheels.

The sounds Tag had heard were from the three toy-tank
killers securing the left flank of the Soviet column, as
they reconned the remains of battle littering the abandoned
mineworks. A total of six more held the other flank and
point, all of them in support of the dozen antitank BMPs
and nine BRMs making up the body of the convoy, which
crawled through the woods in a staggered double column.

The Russian commander of the unit was secure in the
superiority of his numbers against whatever spongers had
been wreaking so much carnage in the area. His tank killers
had been drilled in counterambush procedures, and he was
determined to make the raiders pay if they were foolish
enough to attack him. So when the scything volleys of 106mm
recoilless rifle fire from the Jagd Kommando's L-shaped ambush cut through the right-front of his formation, the Russian
commander had no thought of turning from it.

Three BMPs rushed up in support, laying down deadly
suppressing fire from their 73mm rapid-fire cannons and
20mm chain guns, forcing the Kommandos out of their
positions. A toy tank from reserve and one from point
shifted to replace the two taken out by the 106s, slowing
the Communist advance, but not stopping it.

Giesla regrouped her Jagd Kommandos long enough for
Jan to obliterate one of the prowling BMPs and for her and
Betcher to rake the Soviet flank again.

The Soviet armor was heavy enough that the hot, jagged
fragmentation of the recoilless rifle rounds exploding among
the trees was less than a distraction, and the Kommandos had
no time to wait for a clear shot, for they were already on the
move again, attempting to outwit the BMPs and make their
way back to the front of the column, in another attempt to
turn it.

Running headlong, on instinct and adrenaline, Giesla led
the gun buggies within a hundred meters of the questing So-

viet BMPs. She glanced them through the trees, moving away, and increased the pressure on her gas pedal. Beside her, Sergeant White gripped the padded handle on the dash, ready to face a battalion of tanks, if only this ride would be over.

Giesla found a place to fight and spun her vehicle into the notch between two black larches. White had the tubes reloaded only seconds before the first toy tank appeared, then another and another, and everywhere there seemed to be the rattle of tracks from the BMPs.

"Get in," Giesla said to him. "There will be no second shots."

With a silent prayer on her lips, Giesla triggered her guns.

The moment her first two rounds struck the compact killer tank, stopping it in a shuddering ball of fire, she expected Betcher and Jan would follow and that the Soviets would return their fire. But she was not prepared for the body of ordnance that sprang from the floor of the forest. LAWs flew from their tubes, shredding tracks and punching through the body armor of the BMPs, mangling the men inside with shrapnel. The cyclone of back-blasts from the other Jagd Kommando 106s was punctuated with the throbbing report of a 75mm cannon.

Giesla released her second pair of tubes. An HE round from one of the compact killer tanks burst high on the bole of one of the larches, splintering the trunk and sending the branchy top crashing down on Giesla and White in the gun buggy below.

From the first truncated reports of the Jagd Kommando's guns and the volume of return fire he heard rise from the Soviets, Tag knew something was wrong. Each time he heard one of the recoilless rifles speak, his hope tightened another notch. He was blind to the action from this position, but he could not risk giving it up on a hunch—not yet, at least. He put his head up through the commander's hatch and conned the forest with his binoculars, preparing himself for what he knew would be a reckless gamble and throwing the No Slack Too into the teeth of the Communist formation.

That was when he heard the tide of ambush turn. Even at this distance and with the muffling woods between, Tag could pick out the impacts of LAW rockets and the cadence of a Bradley's 75mm. He heard explosions and the slap of shooting flames. This had to be it—this or nothing at all.

It was all more than the Soviet commander had counted on, but especially the skill and daring of the men who had crawled—or *burrowed*—through the leaves on the forest floor to within thirty meters of his armor before unleashing their light antitank weapons. Infantry equipped with those could be disastrous for armor in wooded terrain. He ordered a turn to the left, while concentrating enough firepower on the right to cover the maneuver. That was why only two of the toy tanks led the formation that veered toward the fissures and the gap Tag was covering with his XM-F4.

Trying to avoid exposure in the waste of rock fronting the worked face of the mountain, the Soviet tank killers probed the crazy-quilt of crevasses and eventually worked their way into one of Tag's fields of fire.

"Targets," Ham said, pressing closer to his sight and centering the first tank in the grid.

"Confirmed," Tag responded, relief welling in his voice. "Shoot."

The Phalanx and the 120mm blasted away at once, turning the leafy alley into a corridor of death. Ham's tank absorbed the penetrator core of the sabot like an amoeba, only to rupture on its other side from the searing heat of its own exploding ammunition. Tag's target turned the initial burst from the Phalanx with its thick turret armor, but the second found the seam between the turret and the body. The depleted uranium slugs disintegrated the turret cog and ate their way through the tank's forward plates, creating thousands of ricochets that flayed the Communist tankers inside.

A BMP flashed past the burning tanks, firing its 73mm as it ran, trying to cover for a BRM that wallowed behind. Tag sighted the Phalanx visually to cover the second of his fields of fire, but led the BMP a fraction too much, and managed to shoot away only eight inches of its nose before the Soviet driver could reverse and lose himself in the timber.

* * *

The steady exchange of fire from the far flank as the raiders began to advance behind the heroics of Prentice's infantry and the white-phosphorous fury of N. Sain's maniacal intent, together with the confusion of vehicles trying to find ways across the fissures, was rapidly turning the Russian commander's aggressive confidence to palpitating fear. He was losing armor at every turn and running out of real estate. If he could get even three of the BRMs through, he would not have to die for a failure, but the only direction where he wasn't taking fire or being blocked by the terrain was back into the wasteland of the mineworks, where the gutted victims of the raiders' previous ambush lay as blackened memento mori.

The Russian commander ordered his beleaguered flank to break contact and regroup for a concerted assault to the left, determined to break through into open forest and, at the least, give his unit the chance to scatter and present more targets than the raiders could engage.

Tag's ambush was beginning to take shape.

The Soviets abandoned the engagement with the raiders on the flank so suddenly that Prentice thought his men had silenced all the guns themselves, until Dunn reported the movement. He moved out toward N. Sain's Bradley, calling in his troops. Betcher roared up in his gun vehicle.

"Lieutenant Ruther," he said to Prentice, "where is she?"

They found Giesla and Sergeant White pinned in their seats by the spiky branches of the larch, bloodied and unable to move. Betcher's loader scrambled over the gun buggy, trailing cable from his own vehicle's winch, and passed a loop around the large end of the treetop. Betcher eased the winch back, allowing Giesla and White to free their arms and fight off the branches before he jerked the splintered evergreen back and away from the car. Aside from bruises that they wouldn't feel until tomorrow and enough ugly cuts for a razor fight, White and Giesla were okay. Most of the impact of the tree had been taken by the right-hand bank of recoilless rifle tubes, which were now crushed together in the middle, splayed as a threadbare broom.

"Go, go," Giesla shouted as she backed her vehicle free and licked blood from a cut on her lip. "Upslope, around the crevasses."

Tag had heard the firing cease and guessed what the Russian commander was up to.

"Ham, Wheels," he said, "get ready for showtime."

Fruits Tutti fidgeted with the loading carousel. "You know, Ham," he said to the gunner, "this is the bad part about ambushes."

"What do you mean the *bad* part?" Ham said. "This is the best."

"Yeah," Fruits said, "that's what I mean: the good part always comes first."

"Targets," said Tag.

"Mark," Ham called.

"Take 'em as they come, Hambone," Tag said, laying the barrels of the Phalanx down the axis of their third field of fire.

Flames gushed from the weapons of the No Slack Too as Ham and Tag opened up with their heavy guns on the swarm of Soviet armor that came rushing through the wooded gap firing wildly, not certain of the position of the XM-F4. The tanks, BMPs, and eight-wheeled armored cars flashing through the openings in the forest were like tricky targets in a shooting gallery for the No Slack Too—except that they were shooting back. The contrails of two Spigot missiles crossed ten feet in front of the No Slack Too and passed inches from its turret; a series of hits from a 73mm blackened the impervious slick-skin armor; and Tag knew it was time to dance.

With the simple command, "Go," he threw the snarling, low-slung tank forward. The XM-F4 rose as it ran, appearing to the Soviet gunners to leap from the bushes and shadows. The HEAT round fired from one of the tanks coming up from the engagement on the flank could find no flat surface where it could puddle and burn on the art-deco contours of the No Slack Too, and it expended itself in a blast-furnace gush of white heat above the American tank's rear deck.

Ham returned the fire, clobbering the killer tank with a

sabot. Wheels cut behind the piece of dead armor like a dribbler coming off a pick, while Tag raked every quadrant with streams of 37mm slugs, but it was like swatting hornets.

The wild assault did panic some of the Soviet vehicles, and a pair of BRMs and their escorting BMPs broke off, only to find themselves throwing tracks and breaking axles among the rents in the rock face of the mountain. One of the BRMs was able to back off and rejoin the scattering of vehicles that were fighting their way through the No Slack Too's onslaught, but the others were duck soup for the enveloping Jagd Kommandos, who were only now moving into positions to command the breaks and the cone of dispersal from Tag's lonely gap.

Thorns of fire crowned the No Slack Too as countless Soviet rounds deflected off the armor and exploded on the tough carbide skin. Blinded by the smoke, Tag and his men fought on instruments and instincts. In the course of five minutes of battle, they had crippled or destroyed eight of the enemy—although the eighth was costly.

Reversing his field in a cat-quick bootlegger's turnaround, Wheels spun the No Slack Too out of a cloud of cordite and broadside into one of the BMPs that were closing in on the XM-F4. Without momentum, the tank jolted hard, its turbines lugging toward a stall. Wheels revved them in neutral, dropped the transmission back in gear, and hammered into the Communist APC, rooting under its track skirt and flipping the mangled remains on its roof.

As Wheels jerked free amid the screaming complaint of buckled plate and scraping steel, a well-placed round from a 73mm caromed off the track skirt and clipped the treads, its blast separating two of the track links and immobilizing the XM-F4.

Tag nailed the BMP that fired it, angrily pounding the dead box of steel with 37mm fire longer than was necessary—almost two full seconds.

And then his targets were vanishing, being swallowed in the trees and shadows of the forest, and the guns of the No Slack Too fell silent.

"Meat Grinder One, this is Butcher Boy," Tag transmitted over the TAC frequency. "We are hit. Lost contact with targets; they're coming your way now. Over."

"Roger, Butcher Boy." Giesla's voice came through against a background of shell fire. "We have a rat race. Out."

Tag threw back his hatch, and he could hear the ragged reports of cannon and machine-gun fire, each more distant than the last.

"Target," Ham called, kicking the turret into motion.

"Check fire!" Tag bellowed as he tracked the 120mm with his eyes and, in a glance through the smoke, recognized the profile of the Bradley.

N. Sain took up a position protecting Tag's busted tread, and Prentice and his men poured from the back, fanning out around the tracked vehicles. N. Sain's Bradley looked as though it had been sandblasted with ball bearings and broken glass. It had lost one flange on its gun mantle, and the running lamps and one antenna mast had been shot away. The karmic killer had never looked jollier than when he popped through the turret and said to Tag, "I am delivered; I can fly."

"Zoom," Tag said, making an airplane with his hand. "Fly the disco idolaters to hell. We'll be here when you get back."

"The rock; death's Polaris." N. Sain struck his chest with his fist and disappeared inside the hatch. The Bradley tore off toward the sound of the guns.

"Come on, Wheels," Tag said. "Let's see if we can fix it. Ham, you and Fruits stay at the guns. We may have strays out here yet."

Except for two shattered links, the damaged track was still intact, despite being slung from under the skirts by the drive wheels. Wheels said he couldn't fix it, but could tell somebody else how, since all he knew how to do was drive and boss a gang. Tag said he'd have to be shown, and they both went to work.

With the help of two large privates from Prentice's dwindling platoon, the tankers spent until the heat of the afternoon jockeying track into position, coaxing it through the alignment wheels while in motion, having to redo it over and over, before the heavy work began of hauling a ton of track through skirted fenders, manually, then driving out the bent link-pins and, finally, wrestling on the replacements.

Wheels stepped back, wiped his face with his sleeve, and kicked the track. "Whatta you think, Cap'n Max?" he said. "Want to take her for a little spin?"

"Yeah," Tag said, frustration still creeping through his fatigue, "but just to a better place to wait. I think up there, above the mine face."

It was a crowd, but Prentice, Bones, three wounded, and ten effectives climbed piggyback on the No Slack Too and rode it up the slope to a knoll on the benchland above the mine, where they took up positions, tended the injured, and wolfed down double rations of dehydrated meals.

The shadows lengthened. The dying crackle of smoldering Soviet armor sounded like insects. Occasionally something burst from the heat or a small-arms round cooked off, silencing the birds. For a while Tag thought he was hearing the distant concussion of cannons, but then he saw the mare's tail clouds leading the high thunderheads and could not be sure. He left the No Slack Too to tour the perimeter and found Prentice at one of the OPs.

"Still no word from them?" Prentice asked.

Tag shook his head. *"Nada."*

"So, what do we do?"

"They'll make it," Tag said. "So for now, we wait."

Prentice looked out into the forest. "And what about our next move, Max? I've got wounded, and we're running out of everything, even luck, it looks like."

This appealed to Tag's perverse humor and cheered him up. "Chuckles," he said, "we're not even supposed to be *alive*. Now how much luckier than that do you get?"

"Still. . . . " Prentice began.

"Hell, Chuck," said Tag, "I don't know. I really don't. I know we've got wounded, and we've had to leave our dead or bury them with dogs. But the rest of us are going to do whatever we have to do. I'll talk to Command tonight, my friend, but I have a bad feeling about things. Something a lot bigger than we are is about to happen, and believe me, I don't want any more of it than you do."

"The nukes?" Prentice said.

Tag nodded and paced away.

The gathering thunderheads had already darkened the sky,

and Tag could smell rain on the rising wind when the radio at last broke his anxiety.

"Butcher Boy, this is Meat Grinder One. Approaching your position. Over."

Tag fumbled with the mouthpiece on his CVC, bent into it, and answered: "This is Butcher Boy. All clear, One. From our last, come right and up."

"Roger. Out."

The wind was coming hard when the Jagd Kommandos arrived, turning the leaves to show their silvered bellies and dragging dark skeins of cloud across the sky. The gun buggies wound up the slope in column, and as they drew nearer, Tag could see the broken suspensions, the gouged tires, and the bent spray of recoilless rifle tubes on Giesla's lead machine. She stopped them by the No Slack Too, and Tag met her as she stepped to the ground. Her eyes were empty and wild in the bramble of scratches and dried blood on her face.

Tag said, "Thank God."

"There were too many of them, just too many of them," Giesla said, her voice rising childishly. "And we couldn't get to them, Max. We couldn't get to them all."

"Maybe it will be enough, Gies. We hurt them, ruined them. I think it will be enough," Tag lied. "N. Sain—did he find you?"

"And lost us again, when we fell back," Giesla said. She shook her head. "A remarkable man."

"Anyone else hit?"

She looked at him, and her eyes regained their focus. She cocked her head, passed one hand over her face, and said, "Only scratched."

They gripped each other by the wrist as the first heavy drops of rain rattled on the leaves.

"Let's get in the dry," Tag said.

"Yes," Giesla agreed. "I think the rooms downstairs are vacant."

With the wounded and the infantry aboard, the No Slack Too led the remnants of the raider command back down and into the mine cavern, not quite beating the first sheets of driving rain that lashed down out of the north. But being back in the cavern was like returning to the womb after the battles these soldiers had fought that day: cold stone was a comfort.

No one had entered the cavern since the raiders last fought from it. The towed stands of antitank missiles were still there, along with a few crates of rations, some odd pieces of gear, empty ammo boxes, and the two demijohns of white wine. Giesla organized a mess around one alcohol stove and two cook pots, while Prentice made sure the men had dry uniforms or blankets. Tag had his crew break up ammo boxes and build a fire.

The storm wrecked any attempts to lock on a satellite or make contact with Command, so Tag brought the antennae in and shut down the radio for the night.

In a half hour, with thunder bashing the sky and lightning flickering eerily in the mine shaft, the raiders were in a circle around their fire, drinking coffee and eating freeze-dried stew, while the wet uniforms that hung on the vehicles steamed.

When everyone had finished eating, Tag pulled out one of the demijohns, peeled off the lead foil over the neck, and worked the cork out with his teeth. He hefted the jug and walked among the men, filling their canteen cups—two for Mathias Betcher.

"I'd said," Tag explained as he poured, "that we wouldn't be drinking any of this until we had something to celebrate. Well, we do." He looked now at Prentice's troops, battle-tempered commandos who less than a month ago had been drivers and ordnance clerks. "I don't know whether any of you realize what you have done, the odds you faced, and what you overcame just to be here, alive.

"We can't win the war alone," he went on, taking in every-one. "We can only do our all, give our all. It's few who really can, but I'm drinking to those who have: to all of you and all our fallen comrades."

They drank.

Then Betcher toasted Tag, Giesla toasted Sergeant White, who raised his cup to Prentice . . . and so it would have gone and gone, but Tag called it a one-jug party. It was just enough wine to help the men wind down through their adrenaline and fatigue and into sleep.

Tag awoke once in the night, panic gripping his chest, until he realized it was only that the rain had stopped, and a steady wind now blew across the mouth of the mine shaft, making a soft moan.

He had come up into the shallows of sleep, where dreams become a part of the world, and the things of the world invade dreams, like an alarm clock intercalated into a dream of church chimes, when the madness of the National Anthem that played as he saluted the dream flag made him fight against it. He continued to fight even after he was awake, because in the dark of 0445 inside a cave, he could not recognize the warped chords of Jimi Hendrix's "Star-Spangled Banner" as coming from anywhere but a bad dream: *N. Sain.*

Others who had been less tangled in their sleep were already up and moving toward the shaft. Someone turned up a gas lantern, and Tag saw Giesla and Ham Jefferson running in stride across the cavern. He whipped back his sleeping bag and dashed after them barefoot.

He caught them in the darkness of the shaft and together they staggered to a spot in the moonlight at its mouth. N. Sain's scoured track glinted dully in the rubble waste, seeming to shimmer with the slurring of the notes that keened through the open hatches. N. Sain was on the turret, standing, stark naked, as though posing for a crucifixion.

N. Sain dropped his arms as Tag ran forward, and the music stopped, leaving a ringing in the air.

"You goddamn lunatic," Tag screamed. "What the hell is this about."

"Here comes the sun," N. Sain said, pointing to the southwest, "turned back on its course."

Tag scrambled onto the back of the track and looked. He could see a glow that suddenly brightened intensely somewhere beyond the horizon of the hills, then another, and another, and then the first cat's paw of shock wave passed, as though the air were lightly gelled and shaken.

"A new day," N. Sain shrieked.

"Max," Giesla said, looking up at him, "is it?"

"Yes," Tag said simply.

It was the nuclear dawn.